Lost in You

By: Angeline Larson

Published: ALH Books 2025
Cover Design: Angeline Larson 2025

ISBN: 979-8-9916346-8-7 (paperback)
979-8-9916346-9-4 (hardcover)

To my many passing ships.
Specifically, the one that inspired this story.

Note to the Reader

This is one book from a connected series. The books do not have to be read in a particular order, and the reader does not have to read the other books to understand the events in each book.

However, please understand that not every book will visit each connected scene in detail if that scene was a focal point in another book. Each book is told form a different perspective, and the scenes have different levels of impact on the characters. That is why some scenes may seem like they are being overlooked or shortened. This was done intentionally.

Please be advised that each book may contain subjects that are of an emotional nature, include foul language, have descriptions of sexual contact, discuss substance abuse, and make references to or include descriptions of harmful acts. These books are recommended for mature audiences.

Each character is their own person, with their own perspective, and these books act as a telling of the interconnections that these characters have throughout their lives. These are flawed characters, with issues that may or may not be resolved. These are stories about life and the people who do their best to navigate it.

This particular book is Derek's and Addy's story and begins later than some other books. The companion novels to this story are Back to You and Finding You, but it is not necessary for you to read those books to enjoy this story.

PS. No offense is meant by the pop-culture references. Enjoy the ride.

And now,

Lost in You.

"Ships that pass in the night, and speak each other in passing, only a signal shown,

and a distant voice in the darkness;

So on the ocean of life, we pass and speak one another, only a look and a voice,

then darkness again and a silence."

Henry Wadsworth Longfellow

A chance encounter becomes a once in a lifetime moment.

Addy has known the pain of loss but the promise of embarking on a new adventure, a new life, has her finally looking forward instead of back.

Derek carries his grief with him every day, but a captivating stranger just may hold the key to his forgiveness.

What begins as a chance encounter could be the defining moment in both Addy's and Derek's lives.

Fate brings them together, but circumstance tears them apart. Old wounds seep into the promise of tomorrow and the only thing standing in their way is time. They both struggle to keep from getting lost so they can find their way back to one another, but the past haunts them both.

Two hearts, longing for the other, but torn apart.

Did they miss their chance?

1   **The Meet**

Cursing, as he dodges through the crowd of fellow sky travelers, Derek picks up his pace. He has exactly three minutes to make it to his gate before he misses his flight. He couldn't miss this flight. His mother was counting on him to be there. It didn't matter that he had absolutely no desire to return to the house that he ran away from nearly four years ago. He couldn't run fast enough back then, and he was having the same problem today.

Stupid Vegas traffic.

Derek glances at his watch. Two minutes left. He is going to make it even if he has to sprout wings and fly there himself. It isn't his mother's fault that the man she had married was a drunken fool. It isn't her fault that that same man was now lying on his death bed, and she just couldn't help but be there for him. She had a kind heart, after all. Nope. Not his mother's fault at all.

One more minute remaining and the gate was now in view. Derek grins.

He is gonna make it.

As he is coming up to the gate, ticket in hand, he watches as the attendant at his gate picks up the talking gadget thing and speaks into it. Her voice rings out across the airport speakers.

"Attention passengers for flight 2257 for Milwaukee, Wisconsin. There has been an unexpected mechanical complication with the airplane and flight 2257 has been cancelled. Please come to the desk and we will provide you with an alternative flight. On behalf of the airline we apologize for this inconvenience and will provide any assistance you require to ensure you reach your final destination.

Thank you for your understanding." The attendant puts the speaker thing down and turns her attention to the person standing at her desk.

Derek is standing there, staring at her blankly. He blinks.

"May I help you sir?" she asks brightly. Derek just keeps staring. He's clutching his boarding pass, and it starts to crinkle in his grasp.

"Sir?" the woman asks again, the smile still upon her face. Except this time her eyes betray a hint of concern.

Derek watches as her hand starts to reach for something out of his line of sight. Probably a panic button like they have at banks for the crazed robbers. Shaking his head, Derek clears his throat and speaks.

"I'm supposed to be on this flight," he says and gestures to the screen behind her, flashing the word *cancelled* next to 2257.

"Yes. You must be Mr. Richards. We have been waiting for you, sir. I do apologize for the cancellation. Unfortunately, the next flight is already full. The next available flight we have going to Milwaukee leaves tomorrow morning at 8:15. I can place you on that flight and the airline would like to offer you some complimentary sky miles for your next date of travel. We do hope you will continue to choose us for your travel needs," the attendant says, her fingers tapping away at the keyboard in front of her.

Derek hears everything she says but all he can focus on is how his mother had been crying when she called him. He told her he would be there tonight and now he has to call her and say he wouldn't be there until tomorrow afternoon. With the flight time, drive time, and the time difference he would arrive home after noon.

Why did he have to choose now to go on his celebratory graduation trip to Vegas? It wasn't like he had even graduated with some illustrious degree. The only reason he had a job lined up was because his buddy's father ran a company in Colorado and had hired Derek at the recommendation of his son. He hadn't intended to do

2

anything with computer programming but there weren't many options for an Applied Science graduate. Colleges really need to provide better education when it comes to picking your major. No one mentioned to Derek during his four years at college that an Applied Science degree was equivalent to toilet paper – only useful if you have to take a shit.

"Sir?" the attendant says as she hands Derek his new boarding pass. He takes it from her, nods his thanks and leaves the desk without saying another word.

Defeated, he walks back the way he had come. Without a destination in mind, he just sort of wanders for a bit. It was seven at night and he was supposed to be holed up in some casino with his college pals, putting back the drinks and winning at blackjack.

Okay, so he probably wouldn't have won any money, but he would have at least had a good time while losing his money. Instead, he was wandering aimlessly through the airport trying to figure out how he was going to tell his distraught mother that he wasn't going to be there for her until after noon tomorrow.

Sure, his siblings were there but she also wanted him there too. She said his father didn't have much time left and it was important to her that they all be there. Derek hated disappointing his mother. She had been disappointed her entire adult life and deserved better.

While Derek tried to work out what he was going to say he came face to face with one of those multi-screened boards that displayed all the incoming and outgoing flights. Right there on screen ten was his flight.

2257 – Milwaukee, WI – Cancelled

Cancelled was displayed in bold letters, emphasizing the flight's current status. The words stared back at him, mocking him. Derek couldn't help but wonder if some poor schmuck would go up to the desk thinking all was right with the flight and attempt to board, only to be disappointed with the news that the flight had been cancelled?

Wait. Some poor schmuck had, and he was now staring at this screen hating the word cancelled.

While Derek continues to stare at the offending word another sky passenger walks up to the board and begins searching for her flight. She soon locates the information she needs and promptly lets out a series of curses that would make any soldier blush. Turning on her heels she digs her cell phone out of her purse and drags her wheeled luggage behind her. Angrily, she searches through her contacts until she finds the one she needs. She presses call and puts the phone to ear, waiting for the familiar voice to ring out. When she hears it, she starts to talk rapidly but stops once she realizes she has gotten the voicemail. Frustrated, she taps her foot as she waits for the beep.

"Jules, it's Addy. Pick up your phone. Wait…this is voicemail, you can't hear me. Ughh…why did the world ever turn to cell phones? Instant gratification has made us all impatient. My flight has been cancelled, Jules. I'm really freaking out here. What if I don't make it to my interview? What if they decide they won't hire me because if I can't even manage to be on time for my own interview then I can't possibly manage a department? Why am I even going to this interview? I hate retail. Oh, I remember. I'm going because you convinced me moving to Arizona would be a great idea. This is all your fault, Jules, remember that when I miss my interview and return home with my tail between my legs. Okay. Gotta go. Love you, bye," Addy says in a rush and clicks the phone off.

She puts the phone away, turns around and is about to walk off when she notices the man that had been looking at the screen when she walked up was still looking at the screen. She tilts her head to the side slightly in question and takes a step towards him. Turning her gaze to the screen she tries to identify what has him so perplexed. Everything on the screen was working properly so she doesn't have a clue what is keeping him. She wonders if he is having trouble seeing. Maybe he lost his glasses or something.

"Excuse me, Sir, is there something I can help you find?" she asks.

He doesn't acknowledge her, and she thinks, wow, nearly blind and deaf. It must be terrifying trying to get through an airport that was this busy without your sight and hearing. Taking another step closer to him she reaches out and quickly taps his shoulder. He turns and she takes a step back to accommodate for the shifting position.

Derek stares at the woman standing next to him. She is smiling at him and waiting for him to say something, but he is still reeling from the events of the last few hours. He just stands there and blinks at her. It isn't until she starts to move her fingers and hands in a rapid motion of disjointed gestures that he feels compelled to speak.

"What are you doing?" he asks, and she jumps back in surprise.

"Oh. You can speak," she says and smiles wider, revealing a mouth full of perfect teeth. Each tooth, perfectly aligned and straight.

"Of course I can speak. Why did you think I couldn't?" Derek asks, his brows narrowing in consternation.

"I thought you were deaf, so I was using sign language to talk to you. Did you need help finding your flight?" Addy points at the screens and Derek follows her pointed finger to stare at the offending screen once again.

"No. I found it," he says, defeated. "It's right there, mocking me." He turns back to the lady, and she smiles slightly at him.

"Okay then. Well, have a nice night," Addy says and begins to turn to walk off.

As she is turning, Derek is suddenly struck with a sense of déjà vu so strong he has to take a step back. Something about this woman is strikingly familiar. Her hair is pulled back into a lose ponytail and the copper highlights in her hair shines when the light catches them just right. She has the body of an athlete, trim and toned, but not muscular. She's wearing a wispy top with thin sleeves and it provides him the opportunity to see the small crevice leading into her shirt. His gaze travels down quickly and examines the rest of her body. She's definitely attractive. He tries to place her, but he is unable to recall where he has seen her before.

"Wait! Do I...do we know each other?" he calls to her as she starts to walk off.

Addy turns back to him and studies his face. He did seem very familiar to her but nothing in her sparks a memory and she shakes her head slowly.

"I don't think so. Maybe we just both have the kind of faces that seem familiar. Enjoy your flight," she says, still smiling.

He's cute in an awe shucks kind of way. She has no doubt that when someone tells him he is attractive his response is probably just that – *awe shucks*. He has hair the color of umber that appears to be a bit on the unruly side, in the stage between haircuts. It's long enough to run your fingers through it, but not long enough to tie back. He's tanned, so she figures he enjoys outdoor activities. His hips are narrow, and she can tell by the way he carries himself that he is no stranger to the gym.

"That's not gonna happen. It was cancelled," Derek shrugs and puts his hands in his pockets.

Awe shucks, Addy thinks and smiles slightly at her joke.

"Really? Mine was too. Were you searching for your replacement flight?" she asks and takes a step closer to him.

"No. I'm stuck here until tomorrow morning. Next available flight isn't until 8:15 a.m."

"Me too! My flight leaves a little earlier than yours, but I'm stuck here too. They offered to send me to a hotel for the night but

I'm already nervous and do not want to risk missing another flight," Addy laughs and shifts her weight.

"Because of the interview?" Derek asks and Addy gives him a narrowed look of suspicion.

"How do you know about my interview?"

"I sort of heard you on the phone. Not deaf, remember? I think everyone within ear shot heard you," Derek grins and she laughs again. He really liked her laugh.

"Yeah, I tend to forget that my voice carries when I'm excited. I'm Addison," she says and extends her hand for a formal greeting.

"I'm Derek," he replies and takes her hand in his for the customary shake. There is definitely a spark of recognition again.

"Are you sure we haven't met before Addison? I can't help but feel like we've crossed paths before," Derek says as the same strange sense of déjà vu overcomes him.

"I don't think so, Derek. It was nice to meet you though. I hope everything goes smoothly for your next flight," she says, and once again starts to walk away.

"Wait!" Derek stops her again.

"Yes?" she smiles sweetly at him, amusement in her eyes.

"Sorry. I don't mean to keep you, but it seems we are both stranded for the night. It's almost eight and I haven't eaten yet. Would you like to join me? We may be stuck here but no one said we had to spend the time alone."

Derek realizes he was probably coming across as some strange, creepy guy in an airport. He isn't sure why he keeps stopping her from walking off. It is this feeling he can't shake, and he wants to explore it further. Plus, he really doesn't want to spend the next 12 hours alone in this bustling airport. He can hear the bells from the airport slot machines sounding and they just keep reminding him how he isn't even supposed to be there right now. He needs a distraction, and this gorgeous brunette is a welcome one.

"Well, Derek, I don't normally spend the night with random strangers I meet in airports but since we are both going through the same struggle, I suppose I can make an exception. But just this once. Don't expect me to do this again if we meet at the next airport. I'm a lady of values," Addy says and comes back to Derek's side.

Grinning, Derek chuckles and bends to pick up the duffle bag he had dropped at his feet earlier. He is glad this trip had been spur of the moment and he had packed light. If he had to mess with luggage during this ordeal he probably would have been fuming.

"What should we do?" Derek asks Addy.

"I saw a restaurant around that corner. I'm sure they will serve us hobos," she replies.

"Lead the way," Derek gestures and Addy begins walking.

Derek is not at all ashamed to admit that he checks her ass out as he follows behind her. Like the rest of her body, it is a sight to appreciate. For a minute he starts to think a cancelled flight may not be such a bad thing after all.

2 *The Greet*

Addy and Derek secure two seats at the end of the bar. For approaching the late evening hours, the restaurant is still quite full. After they get comfortable and receive their drinks from the bartender, Derek holds up his scotch on the rocks and offers Addy a toast. She matches his gesture with her pint glass.

"Here's to cancelled flights and perfect strangers," Derek says.

"Here, here," Addy states and they clink their glasses. They each take a drink.

"So, Derek, where were you headed?" Addy asks as she flips through the small food menu the bar offers.

"Back home," Derek replies and chuckles at Addy's narrowed gaze. "What?"

"You are such a man. Answering but providing absolutely no details. Why do men do that?" Addy asks, returning her gaze to the menu.

"I don't know. We just met. You might be some crazy stalker for all I know. Maybe I didn't want to give you the opportunity to follow me," Derek jokes.

Addy laughs, which pleases Derek because her laugh is probably the greatest laugh he has ever heard. It isn't boisterous, but it isn't low either, she laughs at the perfect pitch and volume.

"Okay. I can understand your theory. In the spirit of our mutual safety let's agree to remain perfect strangers. No details that could reveal our identities will be shared."

"Agreed," he smirks at the silliness of her rule.

"Okay, so you were heading back home. What for?" Addy asks. She turns on her stool, so she is facing him. Once she turns, she is able to see his smile drop and his brow furrow. Instantly, she becomes concerned and reaches her hand out to touch his shoulder.

"Hey, sorry. I didn't mean to upset you," Addy says as she rubs his shoulder.

"You didn't. Will you give me a minute? I need to make a phone call," Derek says.

"Sure. Take all the time you need," Addy replies and removes her hand from his shoulder.

He apologizes and leaves his stool and goes to the opposite end of the restaurant and away from the noise of the bar slots. Addy sips her beer and tries to keep her focus on the various television screens displaying a variety of sporting events, but her gaze keeps returning to Derek. He's standing in the dark, cell phone clutched to his ear, and he is clearly distraught. She wonders what has him so rattled.

Derek shuffles his feet as he waits for his sister to pick up her phone. If only his mother had a cell phone, this would be so much easier. Unfortunately, his mother never really picked up on the whole technology boom and she rejects everything computerized. She still relies on a landline. Instead of just calling her directly he has to call one of his siblings so they can give his mother the phone. Of his two siblings his sister is by far the better option.

"Derek? Aren't you supposed to be on a plane?" His sister answers the phone. She never says hello when he calls. She always greets him by saying his name.

"Yes, Mary I know. My flight was cancelled. Is Ma there?" he asks.

Just give the phone to Ma, he thinks.

"Cancelled? Derek, please don't do this. Ma really wants you here," Mary says, not believing for a minute that he is telling the truth. He doesn't blame her. There is no love lost between him and his father and if he was Mary, he wouldn't believe him either.

"I'm not doing anything, Mary. The next flight is not until eight tomorrow morning. I'm sitting in the airport right now, I swear. Where's Mom?" he tries again.

"She's right here," Mary says and then her voice lowers. "It doesn't look good Derek. Any minute now," she whispers into the phone.

Derek is about to respond when he hears voices in the background.

"Who's that? What's going on?" he asks Mary. He can't understand what the voices are saying but there is shuffling.

"It's Drew. He wants me to give him the phone," Mary says.

"Don't you da,"-

"Derek?" Drew's voice comes through the speaker.

Crap!

"Yes, Drew?" Derek waits for the lecture that is bound to follow.

"What is going on? Why aren't you on the plane? I can't believe you are doing this to Ma. You know she wants us all here. This is just like you. I don't,"-

"Drew! My flight was cancelled. I'm not doing anything to Mother. Now give her the phone," Derek says angrily. The last thing he wanted to listen to right now was another of his brother's high-handed lectures. Drew was famous for them, and Derek was famous for being on the receiving end of them.

"Yeah, sure. It's time to stop playing around Derek and grow up," Drew, his older and obviously more responsible, brother says. It's the same song and dance Drew has been spewing for years.

"Yeah, I know. Be a real boy and all that. Just give her the phone," he says with every bit of frustration he was feeling at having his brother lecture him.

There is some more shuffling as the phone is handed over to Carol Richards, the wonderful woman he calls mother.

"Derek? Sweetheart? Is that you?" Carol calls into the phone. She is speaking louder than she needs to but Derek smiles. She has always thought she needed to speak loudly into cell phones because she thinks they are just like walkie-talkies. The louder the better.

"Yeah, Ma, it's me. My flight was cancelled but I'll be on the next one out, I promise. I should be there tomorrow around two in the afternoon. I'm sorry, Ma. I really did try," Derek says and wishes, yet again, that his stupid flight hadn't been cancelled.

"I know, Baby. Don't you worry about us. We are fine and your father is still with us. I'll tell him you are trying to get here as fast as you can. I'm sorry your trip was cut short," his mother says, and he cringes. She was the one going through a hard time and she is apologizing to him.

"No, Ma. It's okay. I love you," he says.

"I love you too, Baby. Be careful and we'll see you tomorrow."

"Bye, Ma," Derek says and listens as his mother asks his sister how to turn the phone off. There is more shuffling followed by his brother saying *hit end* and his mother asking where that is. He laughs silently until the phone disconnects and all he is left with is silence. He's running through all the disappointments his mother has experienced when he sees Addison, the girl sitting at the bar, staring at him with a concerned look.

Sighing, he returns to the bar and to Addison. Time to make the most of the situation and get to know this pretty girl a little better, he thinks.

"Everything alright?" she asks as he takes his seat. He finishes the rest of his drink and gestures to the bartender for another one before answering her.

"No. I hate disappointing my mother," he says and looks at her.

"I understand. I've spent my whole life trying to make my parents proud. I hate disappointing them too," she says.

"I don't give two shits about disappointing my father, but my mother, she's different."

"Oh. Why is she different?" Addy asks, intrigued.

"Because she's the one that took care of us and was there for us. All my life my father has been disappointing her and the last thing I ever want to do is be like him. She deserves better," he answers. The bartender brings his fresh drink, and he thanks him.

"Did you order some food?" Derek asks Addy.

"Yes. Just a burger and fries. I wasn't sure what you wanted so I just ordered two. Hope that is alright with you," she says.

"I'm a vegetarian."

"What? Oh my gosh. I'm so sorry. Stupid. I shouldn't have ordered for you," Addy says and starts waving her hand for the bartender so she can stop the order. As she's frantically waving, Derek starts laughing hysterically. Addy stops waving at the bartender to give Derek a confused look.

"What?" she asks.

"I'm just kidding. I eat meat. A burger is perfect," he says, a sheepish grin on his lips.

"You're an asshole," she declares, but she's grinning when she says it.

The bartender comes over and an embarrassed Addy orders a second beer in an attempt to recover.

"Yeah. My brother would agree with you."

"Sounds like your brother and I would get along," Addy says and finishes her beer so she can exchange glasses with the bartender.

"I'm sure you would. He's a nice guy. The perfect, stable family

13

man type of guy. He never doubts himself and has all the answers," Derek says and rolls his eyes. It's clear he doesn't actually believe what he is saying, and his statements have undertones of resentment.

"Hmm. No one has *all* the answers," Addy says, curious about the brotherly relationship dynamics.

"Tell him that. He seems to think he walks on water, and he makes damn sure everyone else knows it."

"Sounds like you don't like him very much?"

"What?" Derek's head quickly swivels to her. "He's my brother. I'd die for him." He stares her in the eyes and speaks with utter seriousness.

"I'm sure you would, but there's a part of you that doesn't like him very much," Addy stands by her observation.

Derek mulls it over for a bit before responding.

"I just wish he wasn't so damn pretentious. I don't understand him at all. Growing up we used to equally hate our father. We would say we would never be like him and then Drew turns around and makes all the same decisions. He joined the Army, just like Dad. He married young, just like Dad. He drove his wife away, just like Dad. He became a cop, just like dear ole Dad. The guy is basically a carbon copy of our father, and he acts like I'm the sell out," Derek says and turns the tumbler in his hands.

"My sister, well, she's really my cousin but we grew up together, so it feels like we are actually sisters, is an accomplished classical musician and ballerina. We used to take lessons together, but I never could master the violin and my pirouette has never been described as graceful. I used to think I had to be just as perfect at things as she was because if I wasn't our parents would notice, and they would realize I wasn't worthy of being their daughter. I spent so many years competing with her and trying to be just as good, if not better than her. One day, my father came to me and told me that Julie had

14

always been their daughter, but that they chose me and that was something Julie could never claim. I remember telling him they didn't have a choice but to take me in and he told me that everyone has a choice. He said I could choose to spend my life competing with Julie or I could spend my life trying to be happy. The choice is yours, he said."

Derek waited for her to continue but she didn't. She slowly took a sip of beer and once she placed the pint back down, he asked, "What happened?"

Addy smiles and turns her heads towards him.

"My pirouette is still shit and I haven't picked up a violin in ten years," she smiles and this time Derek was the one laughing.

3 The Game

Addy puts her half-eaten burger down and picks up her beer. After she swallows a healthy portion of it, and places the pint back on the bar, a very unattractive belch rings out. She covers her mouth, mortified, and glances at Derek out of the corner of her eye.

"Sorry," she says apologetically.

"Everyone has gas. I read somewhere that if we don't release it, we could spontaneously combust," Derek dips a fry into his ketchup and mustard concoction and throws it into his mouth.

"You should probably stop getting your science tips from Archie comics," Addy says, waving the bartender over again for another beer.

"Hey, don't knock the comics. They got me through college," Derek teases.

"Yeah? Which college did you go to?"

"Nope. No details, remember?" He says, shaking his head at her.

"Right. Okay, is telling me what you studied too personal to discuss?" Addy asks, half joking.

"Not at all. I am a proud graduate of a Bachelor's degree in Applied Sciences." Derek puffs out his chest when he says this. He fists his hands and puts them on his hips in a half superman pose. Addy stares at him with narrow eyes.

"And what are planning to do with that?" she asks.

"Not a fucking clue," Derek says bluntly and drops the superman pose.

Addy chuckles and thanks the bartender for her beer.

"Would you like another drink?" the bartender asks Derek.

He shakes his head and places his empty tumbler on the edge of the bar.

"No, thanks. I've reached my limit. I'll just take water," he answers.

"Your limit? Two?" Addy asks, curious.

"Actually, three."

"Why three?" She is really curious now.

"Well, when I was a kid, I noticed my father was normal after one drink. After the second drink he would burp a lot, but he didn't act any differently. And after the third drink his eyes would kind of shift and he didn't really like us kids around making too much noise. But it was after the fourth drink that his alter personality would appear and the only one who would ever go near him was our mother. Usually, it was to hand him another drink. I guess I've just gotten into the habit of stopping at three," Derek explains and promptly gulps down the water the bartender places before him.

"Wow. That wasn't the answer I was expecting. Sorry you had to experience that growing up," Addy replies, sympathy in her voice.

Derek brushes it aside because it didn't matter anymore.

"What about you? Any parental shame in your youth?" Derek asks, shifting in his seat so he could face her.

"I don't think so. My parents died in a car accident when I was seven. I don't really remember much about them and the things I do remember are all good things, or things that have been told to me."

"Shit. I'm sorry," Derek says, apologizing for bringing up a painful memory. Foot, meet mouth, he thinks.

"Oh, don't apologize. My story doesn't have a sad ending. My aunt and uncle adopted me, and they are the best. My cousin Julie is also amazing. I really lucked out I suppose," Addy smiles. She meant every word she said. The event that shattered her life at seven was more than a distant memory, so far removed from her life that the only reality she had ever known was her current one.

"You are amazing," Derek blurts. Immediately, he straightens in his seat, embarrassed by his sudden exclamation.

"Really?" Addy asks, surprised, and a little bit flattered.

"Yeah. I mean, most people wouldn't be able to let go of the shit hand they were dealt with. But you are always smiling. Even when you were talking about the accident you were smiling. How do you stay so happy?"

"Valium."

She said it so quickly and with complete seriousness that Derek just stares at her, baffled. It made sense. The only way someone could be this happy is if they were medicated. Derek starts to nod in understanding. When he hears Addy start to chuckle, he realizes that she had been kidding.

"See, still smiling," he says, grinning at her.

"I just couldn't help it. I don't know if I'm always happy. I just decided a long time ago that I spent enough time being sad and now I make the decision every day to just be happy. So, I am."

"It's that simple?" He asks the questions, doubting her life philosophy completely. There was no way life could be boiled down to such a simple mindset.

Addy tilts her head, thinking. "Hmm. Most days it is. Some days it's a struggle," she says, and her eyes cast over with a fleeting sadness.

"What was that about?" Derek asks her.

"Geez, Derek. You haven't even bought me dinner yet and you want to know all my dark secrets? I'm a lady," she jokes and quickly lifts her pint glass to her lips. There were just some things she never talked about.

"Fair enough. I'll pay for this meal, but don't feel obligated to share your secrets with me. Although, now would be the perfect opportunity to unload anything that is weighing you down. I'm a stranger and after the next ten hours we will never see each other again. I'm the perfect person to reveal all your secrets to," Derek says as he rummages through his wallet for the money to pay the bill. He throws enough down to cover the bill and a generous tip.

"You make a valid point. However, I think if we are going to turn this into a revelation of our secrets, we should up the stakes a bit."

Derek raises an eyebrow at her and waits for her to continue.

"If one of us divulges a secret then the other must also reveal one. And we have to swear that we will only tell the truth, no lies. We are allowed one dodge only but if we use the dodge then the one asking the question gets to choose a task the dodger must complete. We will take turns revealing secrets. Deal?" Addy asks and holds her hand out to Derek. She smiles at him, her gaze challenging him to accept.

He grins, folds his hand in hers and says, "Deal."

4 The Secrets

The game starts out innocently enough. They leave the bar where they ate their dinner and find their way to an all-night coffee shop in the airport. After they each receive their caffeinated beverage and choose a booth in the back, so they wouldn't disturb any of the other travelers, Addy asks the first question.

"What did you want to be when you grew up?" She swivels the coffee stick around in her drink.

"Well, if you ask my brother, I still haven't grown up so…" Derek trails off.

Addy takes note of the hurt in his voice but decides not to bring that up. Family drama was not one of her specialties and she did not want to bring down the mood.

"When you were a little kid. What did you want to be?" Addy asks again, undeterred.

Sighing, Derek leans back in the booth, drapes an arm over the back and settles in to answer.

"When I was really little and didn't quite know my father was a drunk, I wanted to be a cop like him. I used to dress up as one every Halloween until I was ten. I would tell everyone I was gonna be a cop like my dad someday. Well, that quickly faded away when he started drinking more. After that I didn't really have a clue what I wanted to be. I just knew I didn't want to be him," Derek finishes. He sees the sad expression on Addy's face and bursts out laughing.

"It really isn't as sad as it sounds," he says.

"Yes, it is. It is a really sad answer. But what's sadder is that you don't realize how sad it really is," Addy continues to stare at him, sympathy in her eyes.

"Whatever. What about you? What did you want to be?" he asks, dismissing her sympathy and shifting the topic to her. Recognizing his desire to move on Addy smiles and gives her answer.

"A ballerina."

"What? You said you were horrible at it?"

"Oh, I was. Didn't change the fact that I desperately wanted to be a ballerina. I loved the costumes, and I thought all the men were so beautiful dancing with their partners. I just loved going to the ballet and I wanted so badly to be in one of them," Addy confesses.

"So why did you quit?"

"Because I really was terrible at it. I spent years taking lessons and could never manage the basics. After a while I began to hate the ballet because I wasn't getting any better at it. I decided that I would much rather sit on the sidelines, watching something I loved, than participating in something I was starting to hate. Every now and then there is a little pang of regret, but I know I made the right choice. Your turn."

Derek isn't as convinced as she is that she has moved on from her childhood dream, but in the spirit of the game, he moves on to a new topic.

"Most embarrassing moment," he says.

"Wow. I'm not sure I can choose. There have been so many of them," Addy laughs.

"Well, tell me all of them."

"Oh no. I couldn't possibly. We would be here all night and never get through them all. I guess if I had to choose one it would be the day my sister's boyfriend caught me dancing in my underwear and singing a Spice Girls song."

"Oh, no. You can't just say that and not give the backstory. Come on, tell me all of it," Derek grins at her pursed lips.

"Fine. I had just got home from volleyball practice and was going to take a bath. I had done really well on a test and wanted to celebrate. I thought I was the only one home, so I cranked up the Spice Girls, took off my uniform and walked into the hallway to go to the bathroom. Well, my sister had come home before me and her boyfriend was there. He was coming out of her room to go to the bathroom at the same time as I was coming out of my room. The Girls were blaring, and I was grooving along and didn't notice him until I started to take off my bra. I turned, saw him standing there and I screamed. I flung my arms across my chest to keep my bra in place and ran the rest of the way to the bathroom," Addy finishes her cheeks blushing.

Derek laughs the entire time she tells her story. She throws her coffee stick at him, and he tries to deflect it. It bounces off his arm and onto the table, little droplets of coffee sprinkling on the surface.

"Stop laughing at me." She isn't at all convincing however, because she is laughing too.

"What song were you singing?"

"If you wanna be my lover," Addy says softly, and Derek just laughs harder.

As his laughter dies down, he realizes that he is a bit jealous of her sister's old boyfriend. She probably looked stunning naked.

"Okay, okay. What is your most embarrassing moment?" Addy asks as Derek gets his laughter under control.

"Some friends of mine dared me to jump into a lake naked one night. Well, they took my clothes with them while my dumbass went into the lake. I came out and they were gone. I had to walk home with my hands covering my junk. My brother hasn't let me live this down, ever," Derek shares.

"Boys are weird," Addy says and shakes her head. The coincidence of both of their story's involving nudity is not lost on her and she uses her coffee cup to hide her grin. She wouldn't mind seeing a grown-up Derek, naked, running through the streets.

"Yeah. We kind of are. Your turn now." Pushing all thoughts of a naked Addy out of his mind Derek shifts in his seat and leans his elbows on the table.

"Biggest failure," Addy chooses.

"Hmm. Besides not being there for my mom tonight, I'd have to say having to take Econ twice."

"Really? That's your biggest failure?". She doesn't believe him for a moment. Besides, it was a lame response.

"Yeah. So?"

"It sucks. You mean to tell me in all your life you have no greater failure then having to take a college course twice?" Addy stares at Derek in disbelief.

"Yeah. I guess I don't fail at things," he shrugs and she scoffs at him.

"Then you aren't really living. Failure is how we mark our success. A life without failure is a life seldom lived," she declares.

"Says the great philosopher Addison?"

"You mock but just wait. There will come a day when you look around at your life and realize that you aren't really living. Mark my words," Addy promises.

"Okay. Well, that day isn't here yet and you still haven't revealed your greatest failure," Derek points out.

"Not forgiving my ex for hurting me," she answers quickly.

"What? How is that a failure? Maybe he doesn't deserve your forgiveness."

"It isn't about what he deserves. It's about my own peace of mind. I want to forgive him but for some reason I've held on to the anger and that is my greatest failure," Addy explains.

"You are unlike anyone I have ever met before," Derek states without thinking. Once again, he is surprised by how quickly he blurts his thoughts out. Addison has him baffled and enthralled.

"I'm glad. If I was like everyone else than I think I wouldn't be nearly as interesting. Your turn," she smiles.

"Ever been in love?" Derek doesn't know why he chose this question. Of all the questions he could have asked he had to go straight for the big one. In fact, it was a question he really didn't want to answer himself, but now that he had asked it, he would have to. Unless he took the dodge.

"Of course I have," she answers quickly.

"The ex?" he asks and her smile drops slightly.

"Yes. And maybe one other time."

"Maybe?" he asks, curious.

"Well, I think it could have been love if we had been different people and in a different time."

"What? That doesn't even make any sense."

"Well," Addy chuckles, "it's my secret and it doesn't have to make sense to you."

"Fair enough," Derek admits.

"And you?"

Derek pauses and draws in a breath before answering.

"Yes."

Addy notices his reaction and decides there is more to this answer then a simple yes. He is clearly affected by his own question, and she wonders what must have happened to affect him so. That was a *yes* heavy with emotion.

24

"Will you tell me about her? Is it a her? I don't want to assume anything," Addy says in a rush.

"It's a her," Derek chuckles.

"Ok. Will you tell me about her?"

"I'm not sure I really want to."

"It was that bad?"

"I don't know if I'd call it bad. There wasn't any fighting or drama between the two of us," he explains.

"Then why did it end?"

"She chose somebody else," he responds simply.

"Ahh. Love triangle?" Addy asks, laughing at her joke. She quickly stops laughing when she sees the expression on Derek's face. "Oh," she says quietly.

"She just didn't love me. I never stood a chance," Derek says somberly. Realizing the stillness that has seeped in, Derek stands and picks up his empty coffee cup.

"Want to check out the magazine store?"

"Yes. I could definitely browse through some reading material," Addy says, stands and threads her arm through Derek's. He looks down at her, smiles, and the two of them walk towards another area of the airport.

5   *The Dark*

"I never understood why the photos in magazines are always air brushed. The women are all gorgeous. And I don't care what Cosmo says. No woman has a thigh gap this big," Addy says and turns the magazine she's holding over to Derek for his appraisal.

Derek turns his head and glances at a picture of some actress he vaguely recalls seeing in some B rated movie. Personally, he preferred his woman to have less of a thigh gap than what is in the picture. He could also point out that the bones protruding from the woman's collarbone isn't exactly appealing either, but he wasn't about to share his thoughts on a woman's body to another woman. His mother didn't raise a fool.

"You should protest," he says to Addy before turning back to his Men's Fitness magazine.

"I will. After I ace this interview, I am going to become an activist for women in magazines everywhere," Addy says and flips to the next page.

"How would they know you were speaking for them?" Derek is once again enthralled with Addy's passion for all things.

"Hmm. Maybe I'll start a website. *Women for TG.*"

"TG?"

"Thigh Gaps."

Derek laughs and tucks his magazine under his arm as they move on through the aisles. Addy suddenly jerks to the left and he watches her go for the candy. She picks up a Snickers and a Resees and holds them up.

"If you had to pick one which would it be?" she asks.

Derek walks up to her. He stares at the two candy bars like he's contemplating which sugary treat he would prefer. He leans forward, like he is going to choose, then he reaches around her. He shifts his gaze to hers, maintains her eye contact while he invades her space and chooses an item behind her. Withdrawing slowly, he shows her a small bag of cashews and she drops the candy to her side.

"That wasn't the game," she says, and he grins.

When he had leaned forward and was inches from her she couldn't help but hold her breath. The closeness gave her an opportunity to take in his musk and visions of throwing herself at him played through her mind. And then he showed her the cashews, effectively breaking the spell he has over her.

"I don't eat sugar," he replies.

"Bullshit you don't eat sugar. You put ketchup on your fries! Do you know how much sugar is in ketchup?" Addy stares at him like he is an alien from another planet. Doesn't eat sugar? Who is this man?

"True. But I did cut it with mustard. Okay. I don't eat candy and do my very best to avoid most other types of sugar. Better?"

"No. What kind of person doesn't eat candy? Are you even human?"

"Yes. I just don't really like sweet food. Besides, it really messes with my run time," Derek says and walks over to the drink cooler.

Addy follows close behind him, the Resees and Snickers still firmly in each hand.

"Ugghh, that explains it," she says with disgust.

"What does that mean?" Derek asks as he pulls open the cooler to get a bottle of water.

"You're a runner. You are all freaks. You never gain weight, think running is fun and spend more on a pair of shoes then I spend on my entire wardrobe," Addy says as she takes a cola out of the cooler.

Derek looks at all of her selections and raises his eyebrow at her.

"Don't be hating on my diet choices. I don't have any body shame issues and love every inch of this body designed by candy," she says and turns on her heels to emphasize her point.

Derek watches her walk away. He notices the way she sways her hips and he keeps his eyes on her rounded bottom as she takes her items to the register. If that body was provided by candy, then he just might be a convert.

"You are a very beautiful woman, Addison," he says as he comes up behind her.

"I know that," she replies. The lady ringing up their items gives Addy a side glance but doesn't comment.

Derek just laughs. This was one entertaining woman he had met.

"So, what do we do now? We still have about seven more hours before your flight," Derek says as they leave the small shopping center.

"I saw some massage chairs in another wing. Want to pay for a chair massage?" Addy asks.

"Lead the way," Derek says, and he follows Addy down the corridor. The airport continues to become more deserted as the hours pass into the night. Some of the lights in sections of the airport have dimmed. Derek imagines this is done in an attempt to save some money on lighting during the off hours of the airport. The chairs that Addy brings them to are in one of the dimmed sections.

"Spooky," Addy says as they sit in the chairs.

"Are you afraid of the dark?" Derek teases.

"Not the dark. Just the things that are in the dark," Addy answers as she puts her money in and makes her selections. Her chair starts to hum and vibrate. Closing her eyes, she sits back and enjoys the subtle movements smoothing out the tightness in her muscles. Soon, she hears the chair beside her hum to life. The two of them sit in silence for a minute while the chairs work their magic.

"Do you miss her?"

Derek opens his eyes and glances at Addy. She still has her eyes closed and a peaceful expression on her face. He would doubt she had spoken if he hadn't caught the slight tick at the corner of her mouth.

"I don't know. It's been a few years. I have a girlfriend now," Derek answers and watches Addy for her reaction. The tick at the corner of her mouth makes a reappearance but she keeps her eyes closed.

"I miss him sometimes. Actually, I think I miss the me I was back then more than I miss him. Does that make any sense?" She finally opens her eyes and turns her head to stare at him. Both their heads are now turned towards each other as they recline back in the chairs.

"Yes. I know I was a better person back when I was dating her. I wish I had that back."

"Why do you think you were a better person back then than now?" Addy looks into his eyes.

"I wasn't jaded back then. I actually believed in love."

"And now you don't?"

"No."

"I think this answer is sadder than your costume story," Addy says, and Derek sees the sympathy return to her eyes again.

He blinks and turns away from her. The conversation turned to heavier things than he was ready to discuss.

"You don't love your current girlfriend?" Apparently Addison was not bothered by the conversation because she kept on with the questions.

"No." He says it so coldly that Addy sits up and shivers.

"Do you think you might ever love her?"

Derek turns to her, expressionless. "No."

The chairs hum to a stop as Derek and Addy look into each other's eyes. One is searching for light, and the other is determined to remain in the dark. Two contradictory paths converge and the people embarking on those paths stand up and walk further down a dimly lit corridor.

6 *The Walkway*

"This is pointless," Derek says to Addy. He is walking down the up moving walkway and she is walking up the down moving walkway. Neither of them is actually going anywhere and they've been doing this for the past twenty minutes. When Addy had suggested they go walking he hadn't pictured this.

"Exactly my point. Has the American populace gotten so lazy that we can't even walk the normal way? We've eliminated stairs and replaced them with escalators and elevators. And now, we've replaced walking with moving floors. We have pizza delivery and fast food. Everything can be accessed at the touch of a button on our smart phones. We never have to leave our own living rooms anymore because Amazon can just have everything we need or want sent directly to our door in less than twenty-four hours," Addy finishes, throwing her arms up in frustration. The gesture throws her balance off and she has to quickly grasp the railing. Walking down the opposite path and making a wild gesture on the downfall of American Society is not as easy as it looks.

Derek smirks as she rights herself and is grateful she didn't fall.

"What does us walking the opposite direction on a moving walkway have to do with all that you mentioned?"

"It's all pointless."

"I'm still not following you. What's pointless?" Derek's eyebrows lower in confusion.

"Life! We've taken the joy out of everything. E-books have replaced the feel of a page between our fingertips. The joy of going to the store on Sunday with your family to pick out your next

Sunday dress is gone forever. Food from scratch – gone! Talking to your friends in person – gone! Walking down the sidewalk all on your own and without any aide from a mechanical walkway – gone!" Addy's voice rises with each *gone* until she is practically shouting on the last one.

"Okay. So, what I'm hearing you say is you miss simpler times?"

"Simpler?" Addy's gaze immediately falls upon Derek, and he is a bit taken back by the expression on her face.

"Yes. Less complicated?" He asks it as a question because she appears to be angered by the term.

"Was it really simpler? I think the times we are living in now are *simpler*. Everything is just too easy. No one works for anything any-more. The appreciation is gone because everything has just become so simple to do. I miss the journey one experiences by making a pizza from scratch, going to the local general store with your parents and picking out a toy, holding a book in my hands and smelling the ink on the pages, walking down a walkway with my own two legs and without assistance from a series of levers and pulleys." Addy glances down at the walkway, frowning.

Derek follows her gaze and looks down at the ridges on the moving walkway. The black surface really is devoid of any warmth. It is an emotionless floor and staring at it soon makes him feel just as sad as Addy looks. He quickly lifts his head and finds Addy staring at him now. She smiles.

"You think I'm crazy, huh?"

"Actually, I don't. I've never really looked at a moving walkway as the cause of the downfall of American Society before. I just assumed it was to help keep the flow of traffic moving in an efficient manner but hearing you describe all the things you miss I think I'm starting to come around to your side of things. You know, all those things you described are still available. No one says you can't make a pizza from scratch or buy a book in print," Derek reminds her.

"Oh no. I can't cook. And the e-books are just so much more economical," Addy says, shaking her head, her eyes wide the entire time.

Derek tilts his head and busts out laughing.

"Now I think you're crazy," he says. Addy narrows her eyes at him and waits for him to finish laughing.

"Okay. Confession time," Addy says. Derek waits for her to continue. "Remember, no judging."

"No judging. I promise," Derek says.

"Pinkie swear?" Addy holds up her pinkie to him while they both continue to walk in opposite directions but never advancing. Derek, amused, lifts his pinkie and joins it with Addy's.

"You have just agreed to one of the most sacred secret sharing rituals in the world. This means if you ever share this with another soul a bolt of lightning will come down from the heavens and smite you," Addy says, looking very seriously at Derek, who is grinning the whole time.

"Well, if I am ever so callous to share this secret then the smiting will be warranted."

"Damn straight. Okay, here goes," Addy takes a deep breath and says the rest in a quick rush, "I was a super fan of the all-male group Hanson. I don't know what it was about those long-haired boys that just called to me, but I couldn't get enough of them."

Derek is silent and just stares at her. Addy waits but his continued silence begins to make her uncomfortable and she throws her hands up in frustration once again. This time she keeps her balance.

"You said you wouldn't judge me!" she accuses.

"Oh. I'm not. How can I judge what is clearly a cry for help? I'm sure we can find a psychiatrist somewhere in this airport. They can help you through this delusion," Derek says and reaches out to politely pat her hand like she is some wayward child, lost in her delusions.

Addy pulls her hand out from beneath his and glares at him. Derek starts to chuckle, and she sticks her tongue out at him.

"What was it about them? Their sweet baby faces or the catchy lyrics in *MMMBop*?" Derek asks between chuckles.

"Ah ha! See you can't judge me because you only know that one song, don't you? Well, the Hanson boys had so much more to offer than just that one pop song that everyone can't get out of their heads once they hear it."

"Okay," Derek responds, placating her.

"Their song *I Will Come to You* changed my life. It touched my soul. Haven't you ever experienced something that just reached right down to the depths of your soul and grabbed a hold?" Addy looks at Derek with a sparkle of hope. Surely, he has encountered something in his life that just totally flipped his world upside down.

"No."

And with that single word Addy feels a deep sadness for this man she has only known for a few hours. To go through life and not be able to identify a single moment in which your life was forever altered because your soul was touched in a way that couldn't possibly be described was the very definition of sadness. Addy could name many moments in her life when her soul was forever marked by an experience or a person.

"I think it's my turn," Derek says, drawing Addy out of her trance. She shakes her head to clear it and smiles at him.

"Okay. Make it a good one," she says.

"I used to follow my ex around campus during my senior year. She was officially dating that guy, the one that came between us, and he was always with her. I never saw her without him. I found out

34

after she broke things off with me, he had been in rehab for an addiction to pain pills and alcohol. I used to tell myself I followed her around because I was making sure she was safe but that wasn't the real reason," Derek says, avoiding Addy's eyes.

"What was the real reason?" This time Derek looks Addy straight in her eyes.

"I wanted to be there to swoop in when he hurt her again. I wanted her back. I still loved her even though I knew she didn't love me. She had never actually loved me, but I had been happy with her and I wanted that back, even if it was a lie. Pathetic, huh?"

"Not at all. It takes time to get over a love like that. Sometimes we never actually do get over it. I think, in some way, we always carry those we have loved with us in some form or another. That love may shift over the passing years, but it is always there. Just because a relationship ends that doesn't mean our connection to that person disappears. I know there will always be a part of me that loves my ex, despite the way it ended. I just hope that someday I will be able to look at that love with fondness instead of anger and regret," Addy says. She completely understood the feelings Derek had for a past love. Letting go was never an easy thing to do.

"It's your turn," Derek says.

"Why are you going home?"

Derek grimaces. Technically it was her turn to confess something, to reveal a secret, but he could tell by the expression on her face that she wasn't going to let this go. He knew she would ask it again the next time around. She really did know how to ask the hard questions.

"My father is dying. Actually, that isn't why I'm going home. I'm going home because my mother asked me to because my father is dying. If she hadn't asked, I wouldn't be going," Derek admits.

Addy isn't sure how to respond so she says nothing. They

continue to go nowhere on the walkways, both staring straight ahead. Addy remembers the story he told about his childhood and the condition his father was in. She knows that they don't have a good relationship, but she can also see the pained expression on Derek's face, so she says the only thing she can think of.

"I'd give anything to have just one more day with my parents."

She says it so quietly that Derek isn't entirely sure he heard it, but he did. He quickly glances at her.

"They weren't like my father," he replies.

"Maybe not but I have so many regrets. It's the regrets that keep us from moving on. Don't spend your life full of regret," Addy says warmly and suddenly stops walking.

Derek watches while she slowly drifts away from him as the moving walkway takes her away. He stops walking too and drifts even further from her.

Derek knows why she said what she did, but he also knows that some whispered words in a silent airport can't bridge the gap that has grown over the years between him and his father. There are just some wounds that can't be healed with gentle words of wisdom. Sometimes there is a love that one wishes they could cast out of their memory. For Derek, that love belongs to a young boy in a police officer costume, sitting on the stoop, waiting for his father to wake up from his drunken stupor to take him trick-or-treating. The long-ago dreams of a lost boy.

7 — *The Last Hour*

Addy bites her lip in concentration and looks intently at the object before her. She has never been any good at competitive sports, but she is determined to win this time. She holds her breath and lets the quarter soar through the air. It hits the side of the cup and looks like it's about to fall in but at the last minute it tips towards the outside and falls to the carpeted floor. She sighs in frustration and glares at Derek as he jumps up and down in victory.

"Nobody likes a sore winner," she says and walks to the cup. She begins picking up the quarters on the carpet. The majority of the misses were hers. They were playing best two out of three. Then it became five out of seven. They were now on seventeen out of twenty. The score was: Addy – seven, Derek – fifteen.

"I think it's time you called it. You just aren't going to catch up. I've got this in the bag," he says and does a mock throw of a basketball towards the cup.

"We are using quarters, not basketballs. Stop showing off your skills," Addy says as she walks back towards him. She hands him his quarters and gets herself set for the next round.

"Aww, don't worry, Babe, you'll do better this time," Derek teases.

"Don't call me Babe," Addy warns. She fixes her sight and lets her quarter fly. It lands directly in the cup and makes a plink sound as it bounces on the bottom. She turns towards Derek, a smug expression upon her face.

"Okay, okay. Everyone gets lucky at some point," he says and lines up his shot. His goes wide and misses the cup entirely. He hears Addy snicker behind him and he turns his head towards her.

"Now who is being unsportsmanly?"

"Is that even a word?" Addy asks as she takes the place Derek just vacated.

"It is today, *Babe*," Derek leans forward and speaks the last word in her ear. She drops her arms to her side and glares at him.

"Do you kiss your girlfriend with that mouth?" she asks and squares up her shot again.

"Actually, yeah, I do. And she likes it."

"Doubtful."

Derek laughs and stands back as he watches Addy take her next shot. After the walkway they got another coffee and when they were finished, he suggested they play a friendly game of toss the quarter. He had made it up on the spot, but Addy had been thrilled to do something sporty. He had just laughed and now they were set up near their gates and tossing quarters at an empty coffee cup. They didn't have much time left before she had to go to her gate. The airport had more people in it and their little game was starting to become interrupted by the passerby's.

"Hole in one!" Addy declares as her shot goes in the cup.

"Wrong sport," Derek replies.

"Don't be hating on my mad skills," Addy says and does a horrible impression of a moon walk as she steps out of the way.

Derek laughs and is once again struck by a feeling of recognition. He couldn't place it, but he really thought he had known Addison from somewhere. She held him to the *no details* rule of their little airport encounter and refused to give him specifics. He found her infuriating and fascinating at the same time. If he was being honest, he didn't want this, whatever it was, to end.

He was setting up his shot when he heard a voice come over the intercom system. Addy turns her head, trying to listen to the voice and he sees the recognition in her eyes before she speaks.

"They're announcing my flight. Boarding will begin in ten minutes," she says. Derek nods and tosses the quarter to the cup without looking at it. It lands squarely in the cup and Addy frowns.

"I hate you," she says and crosses her arms across her chest.

Derek laughs as he goes to collect the quarters and the empty cup. He tries to hand Addy her quarters and she shakes her head.

"Keep them. You still have two more hours, and you didn't sleep. You might need some more coffee or snacks to keep you awake," she says and places her hand on his, closing his fingers over the quarters to form a fist.

Derek looks down at her hand on his and feels the same tension he felt when she touched him over the night. "Do you feel that?" he blurts out.

"Feel what?" she asks and removes her hand from his to reach down for the handle on her suitcase.

"Nothing. Sorry. I'll walk you to your gate," Derek says and puts the quarters in his pocket. They both begin walking towards Addy's gate in silence.

Addy had pretended she didn't know what he was talking about, but she had felt the same thing. There was something familiar about his touch, but she had feigned ignorance because there was no point in addressing it. She was heading to Arizona, and he was going to Wisconsin. They were strangers who had happened to cross paths at an airport in Nevada. There was no logical reason to address the feelings that were coursing through her right now. It didn't matter that her entire being was screaming at her not to leave this man.

Derek wanted nothing more than to reach out and touch her again, but he held back. They didn't really know each other and in the next ten minutes she would board her plane, and they would just be two people that had a random encounter in an airport one night. Even as he thought it, he knew it wasn't true. This was more than just some random encounter. He had told this girl things he had never told anyone else. There was something special about the last ten hours.

They reached her gate and they both looked somberly at the line forming.

"This is ridiculous. We are being ridiculous, right?" Addy asks Derek while she looks at the line of people.

"What do you mean?" Derek asks and looks at her. She meets his gaze and straightens the strap of her purse.

"I don't want to get on that plane."

"I don't want you to get on that plane."

"I have to get on that plane," Addy says and tears her gaze from his.

"The interview," Derek says and lowers his gaze too.

"Yes. And your family needs you there," Addy reminds him. He nods, accepting the reality of both their situations.

"So, what happens now?" Derek asks. He's not sure why he asks. He knows exactly what is going to happen. She is going to get on her plane. He is going to get on his and they will go on living their lives as if they never had this chance encounter.

"I'm not sure. Do we exchange phone numbers?" Addy asks.

"Do you want to?" Derek asks, hope in his voice.

"Should we?" And just like that Derek's hopes are dashed. Addy notices his defeated look and quickly explains. "I mean, this could forever be a moment we both cherish. We had an amazing connection with a stranger, and we could always look back on this fondly. Nothing about this has been tainted and it could forever remain a perfect memory. Or we risk corrupting it by exchanging phone numbers."

Derek thinks about what she says and even though he wants to tell her that is complete crap, he doesn't. She may have a point.

"Okay, so we walk away and keep the memory as it is," Derek says and takes a step back. Her flight has begun boarding and there are people all around them maneuvering to get through the line.

"It was a pleasure getting to know you," Derek says and holds out his hand to her. She stares at it for a little bit before slapping it away.

"What is wrong with you? You are supposed to tell me I'm being stupid," Addy declares and reaches into her purse. She withdraws a pen and a receipt from the coffee they had purchased a few hours ago.

"But I thought you wanted to preserve the memory or something?" Derek asks, confused.

"We aren't bronze statues. Take this," Addy says and thrusts the paper at him after she is finished writing on it.

"Okay. What is it?" he asks.

"It's my email address. Nobody said the game had to end just because we are leaving the airport," Addy explains.

"The game?" Derek asks.

"Yes. It's your turn and I expect a good secret so don't send me anything until you have a really good one," Addy says and glances over her shoulder. The line only has a few people in it now. "I have to go," she says.

Derek looks in the direction of the gate entrance and nods.

"Don't forget," she says and turns towards her gate. He waits until she is finished handing over her ticket to the attendant before he calls out to her.

"Addison!"

She turns towards him, smiling.

"This right here. This was a moment," he says and grins back at her.

Addy's smile widens and she nods her head because she knows exactly what he is saying. Their meeting touched his soul, and it also touched hers.

Derek watches as she walks through the gate and disappears behind the doors when the attendant closes them. He looks down at the piece of paper in his hand and laughs out loud when he reads her email address: *siezethemoment69@gmail.com.*

She's amazing.

8   *The Reunion*

Derek stands with the other airline passengers, waiting for their rides to come pick them up. He had told his sister when his flight would arrive, and she had told him their father was still holding on. According to their mother it was because he was waiting for Derek. This was not a theory that Derek agreed with. If anything, the old man was hanging around just so he could spend more time torturing his ex-wife.

As more people got into cars Derek checked his watch again and impatiently looked down the road for his sister's car. She was thirty minutes late and he was growing concerned. He had already tried to call her, but she hadn't answered. This wasn't unusual. If she was driving, she wouldn't answer the phone because it violated her safety rules. She believed strongly in setting the perfect example for her young kids. It didn't matter that they were seven-year-old twins and had years to go before they actually got behind the wheel of a car. She often said they were sponges and it would be a cold day in hell if she was the bad example they followed.

While he's internally laughing at his sister's outlook on child rearing, Derek sees a dark SUV driving down the road and he cringes.

Please let it be Mary. Please let it be Mary, he thinks over and over until the SUV comes to a complete stop before him.

His shoulders sag when he sees his brother, Drew, come out of the driver's side door. His older brother is the typical muscle clad police officer; the one that takes his profession way to seriously. Everything to him is a potential criminal offense and everyone is most likely a criminal. He's often made Derek feel like a member of the criminal element a time or two. It doesn't help that he is taller, bigger and older than Derek.

"Where's Mary?" Derek asks when Drew comes to the passenger side and takes the duffel bag from him.

"Hello to you too, brother," Drew says and walks to the back of the SUV to deposit the bag. Derek closes his eyes and tilts his head back. He looks up at the sky and sends up a silent plea for patience.

"Hi, Drew," he says once his brother has closed the back door.

In response, Drew just grunts and goes around to the driver's door. Derek counts to three before he gets into the passenger side. Just another fun filled family adventure.

A few minutes pass and the SUV remains stationary. Derek turns to Drew and raises his eyebrows in question. Drew motions with his head towards the seatbelt and Derek lets out an exasperated sigh before reaching back for his seat belt.

"I'd get the ticket. Not you," Derek says as he clicks the belt into place.

"It isn't about the ticket. It's a safety issue," Drew says, turns his signal on and glances out his window for oncoming traffic. Seeing none, he enters the thru lane and heads towards the direction of the highway. There is nearly a two-hour drive ahead of them and they may not have two hours. Time is not on their side today.

"So, why didn't Mary come to pick me up?" Derek asks as he looks out his own window. He notices Drew turn towards him slightly, but his safety conscious brother quickly brings his head back forward and towards the road.

"She didn't want to leave Ma and her kids," Drew answers.

"How are the twins?"

"They're fine. They don't understand what's happening so they think we are just visiting a sick man. They know he's their grandfather, but it hasn't sunk in yet that he's dying. It's a good thing," Drew says and merges on to the highway. Derek notices how he used the signal in the proper amount of time.

"And Connor?" Derek asks, inquiring about Drew's own son. He notices the slight wince his brother makes at the mention of his son.

"Tammy doesn't think the hospital and the situation is one he should be in," Drew answers flatly.

Derek can tell his brother is upset by his ex-wife's choice. She has primary custody of their son, and she is always placing some new stipulation on the time Drew is able to spend with his son. Derek doesn't blame her. Drew did put her through hell, and she has every right to be concerned about her son spending time with a man who probably likes the drink a bit too much.

"And Ma?" Derek asks, shifting to a topic that is neutral for them both.

"You know, Ma. She's being strong for everyone but she's hurting. He doesn't look good, and it bothers her. He keeps telling her to stop fussing but, well, it's Ma." Drew says and shrugs. Derek nods because he knows how their mother is when it comes to taking care of her family.

They both fall silent and the sounds of highway traffic seep in. The two brothers haven't been close since childhood and their reunions are often marked by long stretches of silence. Derek settles into his seat, leans his head back and prepares to get some sleep. He slept a little bit on the flight, but he still hasn't recovered from being up for over twenty-four hours. Flashes of his time with Addy in the airport invade his thoughts and he slowly drifts to sleep.

Nearly two hours later Derek is jerked awake from Drew shaking him.

"I'm up, I'm up," he says and pushes his brother's hands off of him.

"You still snore like a banshee," Drew says and exits the vehicle.

Derek takes a play from Addy's book, and he sticks his tongue out at the closing door. He would never do it to his brother's face, but the small retaliation feels good.

Stepping out of the vehicle he stretches his arms and legs. Five hours of travel time stuck in places that are too small for him have taken their toll on his body. He hears cracking from many bones as he stretches. Drew comes to his side, asks if he's finished primping and then starts walking towards the hospital entrance. Derek glares at his brother's back for the primping comment, but he soon follows behind him.

Derek has never really liked being in a hospital. He spent enough time in them as a child waiting for his parents. His father would often get injured from falling or running into something during his drunken benders. A time or two he had been asked questions by hospital staff because they thought his mother was somehow hurting his father. He laughs at the memory now because the whole thing was absolutely absurd, but he was terrified as a child. He feared they would take his mother away and he would be left with alter-ego Dad.

Drew takes Derek to the elevators, pushes a button and they step off on the fourth floor. Derek sees the sign on the wall, *Palliative Care.* Derek knows this is the ward they send the patients to that are dying, the ones that have no other options available to them. If there was any doubt about that all one would have to do is inhale through their nose. From the moment he stepped off the elevator his nostrils had been assaulted with the smell of death. It wasn't a pleasant smell. He didn't blame Tammy for keeping Connor away from this.

"His skin is beyond yellow, and he looks almost skeletal. I'm telling you this so you don't freak out in front of Ma," Drew says as he comes to stop before room three. The ward is eerily quiet and the only sound that is heard is the beeping from machines and the soft

46

steps of the nurses as they move around.

Derek nods but his focus is on the stillness of the nurses. He has never seen people move so quickly and soundlessly.

"Derek, pay attention," Drew says and snaps his fingers in front of his brother's face. Derek scowls at him and slaps his hand away.

"I am. Yellow, skeleton, got it," he says and goes to open the door. He steps through and sees his sister sitting in a chair on the far wall. She smiles at him but doesn't come to greet him. It isn't until he gets closer that he sees the tears in her eyes. He tilts his head, questioning her silently, and a sob escapes her lips.

"Derek?" Carol Richards says.

Derek turns and sees his mother sitting beside the hospital bed, her hand clutching a yellowed and thinly skinned set of bones. Tears are falling from her eyes as well and her eyes are blood shot. Her other hand clutches a tissue. Derek smiles at her but she does not return the smile. She brings the tissue in her other hand to her mouth and starts to shake from the sobs. Derek is immediately angered because he has no doubt the tears are due to his father. His mother only ever cried because of his father. He starts to say something to the man in the bed for making his mother cry, but Drew's reaction stops him.

Drew rushes to their mother and wraps his arms around her. She releases the hand she was holding and wraps her arms around Drew and buries her face in the folds of his clothes. It is then that Derek really looks at the figure in the bed. He doesn't recognize this man. This man is past the point of skeletal and his skin is a sallow yellow. His eyes are closed but the sockets are sunken. While he's staring at this stranger Derek notices there is no beeping in this room. The only sound is the sobs coming from his sister and mother. Quickly, he glances at the monitors and sees they are all turned off.

He thinks, *Why would the nurses do that?*

Taking a few steps closer to the man in the bed it suddenly dawns on him why the machines are off. This man, this stranger, his father, is dead.

9   *The Interview*

Nervously, Addy straightens her skirt and taps her foot. Thankfully, the floor is carpeted, and the receptionist can't hear the taps of Addy's foot as it meets the carpet. She doesn't know why she is so nervous. She isn't even entirely sure she wants this job, so why is this getting to her so much? Maybe it's because she had to rush here from the airport and wasn't able to complete her customary ritual when embarking on a major event.

Julie has told her that her ritual is a sign of obsessive compulsiveness but she likens it more to a ball player refusing to change his socks during the playoffs. Everyone has something they equate to a ritual, or luck. Hers just happens to be her *pre-game* bath, dance, and singing. And, of course, the lists. Sometimes she enjoys it so mufch that she repeats the process at the conclusion of the event too. Addy had told Derek about one time she had celebrated after acing a test and found herself naked in a hallway, standing before her sister's high school boyfriend. It didn't matter that the ritual had been invaded by her sister's boyfriend that time, she still completed it. The ritual helps her relax and her body was currently going through ritual withdrawal. If she had to wait any longer, she would seriously blow a gasket.

"Ms. Katz? Mr. Lieberdauer will see you now," the receptionist says from behind her desk and gestures to the door on her right. Addy nods, thanks the older woman and walks to the door. Taking a deep breath, she opens the door and steps in.

The office is floor to ceiling windows and the sun is blinding as she enters. She intended to close the door gently behind her, but she releases the door handle to block the sun and the door closes firmly behind her, making an unpleasant noise at it quickly closes. Addy jumps and nervously looks for Mr. Lieberdauer, her interviewer.

"Sorry about the light. I've put in several requests for curtains, but I think Janice is still upset with me for forgetting her birthday," a very male voice says to her left.

Addy, turns and sees a large desk strewn with papers and a man standing behind it. She is taken back by how young the man is. She was expecting a grey-haired executive, but this man appeared to be no more than a few years older than her. He comes out from behind the desk and reaches his hand out to her.

"You must be Ms. Katz. I'm John. I mean, Mr. Lieberdauer. I just can't seem to get used to that," he says and smiles at Addy.

Addy smiles back, takes his hand and gives it a firm shake. She had been practicing her handshake with her father for this very day. She was confident that John…Mr. Lieberdauer…would be impressed by her handshake.

Unfortunately, she doesn't pull out of the greeting and continues to shake his hand while she tries to recover from her shock of seeing a very young, very attractive executive before her. He has fair features with business hair that was almost golden, trimmed just perfectly. His sky-blue eyes sparkle back at her as he glances down at their still joined hands. Embarrassed, she quickly withdraws.

"Sorry," she apologizes, mortified by her mental brain freeze.

"Perfectly fine. Let's sit over here, the sun isn't as devastating in this corner," Mr. Lieberdauer says and gestures to a small sitting area that has a sofa and an armchair.

Addy follows him, clutching her small briefcase in front of her. He sits on the armchair and she sits on the sofa. It is a firm sofa, and not at all comfortable. Awkwardly, she tries to adjust her position to give the impression she is relaxed but she imagines she appears to be a squirming bag of nerves.

"I have to say I was very impressed with your resume," Mr. Lieberdauer says as he sits back and opens a file, she hadn't noticed he held. He shifts through some papers.

"Really?" Addy asks, the shock ringing out. She immediately turns red and Mr. Lieberdauer chuckles softly.

"Yes. I know you haven't had much work experience in this field, but your internship supervisor was very impressed with you. She wrote a glowing recommendation, and your volunteer work has given you a background that would benefit the team you would be joining," he says, puts the file down beside him and crosses his legs.

Addy starts to speak but the office door suddenly opens and the receptionist enters carrying a tray of drinks. She comes to the sitting area and sets the tray down on the small center table.

"Thank you, Janice. Have I told you how stunning you look in that outfit today," Mr. Lieberdauer says as he leans forward to take a steaming cup of coffee from the tray.

Addy is stunned by his remark. She looks at the receptionist, expecting an unfavorable response. She is surprised when the older woman clucks her tongue and shakes her finger at her boss.

"Flattery won't make up for what you did, mister," she says, turns away and leaves the office.

Addy is staring at the closed door in disbelief. Mr. Lieberdauer is laughing behind his coffee cup.

"I got her a gift card to a home and bath store three days after her birthday. She hasn't forgiven me for it," he says.

"Oh. Well, maybe a bottle of whiskey would have been better," Addy responds before thinking.

Mr. Lieberdauer makes a choking sound and Addy watches as he coughs down the coffee he had been drinking. She winces because she is sure he is going to tell her to get out of his office. To her surprise he smiles at her, blue eyes sparkling the whole time.

Why did he have to be cute?

"I like you. You've got spunk," he says.

"My father says the same thing. It usually isn't a compliment, though," Addy replies, averting his gaze to hide her blush.

"Well, in this case, it is. Let me just cut to the chase Ms. Katz. The job is yours if you want it," Mr. Liebedauer says and leans forward to take a wafer off the tray. He dips it in his coffee before taking a bite.

"Really?" Addys asks, shock in her voice once again. She is met with more laughter.

"Yes, really. There will be a stipend for relocation costs since you are coming from out of state. I can recommend a realtor if you need one. We also have a wonderful benefit package and retirement plan. Janice can get you all that information. When would be the earliest you could start?"

"But you didn't ask me any questions?" Addy blurts out and immediately wants to take it back. Who gets offered a job and then questions that offer? She really must be crazy.

"Would it make you feel better if I did?" Mr. Lieberdauer asks.

"I'm not sure. Maybe," Addy answers, her eyebrows drawn in confusion. Nothing about this interview is typical and she is beyond confused.

"Do you prefer vanilla wafers or scones?"

"What?" Addy stares at the man before her, wondering if maybe he is crazy.

"Ms. Katz, I don't have any questions for you because I've already done my research. I've checked you out," he says. Addy narrows her brows even further and Mr. Lieberdauer sits forward, shaking his head wildly.

"That isn't what I meant. I mean, it is, but it came out all wrong. What I meant is that I've called all your references, contacted your university and spoke to every director of all the programs you volunteered at. Your reputation speaks for you, and I want you on our team."

Addy rubs her hands on her knees and looks around the room. This room, this man, this interview, this whole day is not at all how she pictured things. A voice is telling her something is off, but she can't quite figure it out. She blames her inability to complete her morning ritual for her uneasiness and pushes the doubt aside.

"Well, Mr. Lieberdauer, I guess you've got yourself a teammate," she says and stands. She puts her hand out and waits for him. He stands, chuckles and takes her hand in his.

"Please call me John. I will never get used to Mr. Lieberdauer," he says. She gives his hand a firm shake, thanks him and starts to walk towards the door.

"Uh, Ms. Katz," he says behind her. Addy turns. "Your briefcase," he says and points to her forgotten briefcase sitting beside the sofa.

"Right. That is mine," she says and walks back to the sofa. It only holds a couple of papers, some of which did not pertain to the interview she didn't have, but she wanted to look important, so she brought it along.

"Before you leave, please see Janice so she can get you started on the paperwork."

"Yes. I will do that," Addy says and begins walking backwards toward the door.

"And Ms. Katz, welcome to the team," John says and smiles at her. Addy thanks him and exits the office.

Once she is safely out of the office she leans against the closed door behind her and lets out the breath she was holding. Her new boss is not at all what she had been expecting, and she can't believe she just accepted a job that she still isn't sure she wants.

What just happened in that room?

Addy knows exactly what happened. She took one look at her young, attractive boss and forgot she was an independent woman with ambition. Why couldn't he have been a grey-haired, married grandpa? She had been prepared for senior executive to be a little further up in the age department. The shock of staring into the eyes of someone just a few years older than her was jarring. This was all Julie's fault. She told Addy to take this interview and now Addy had a job, but she had absolutely no clue what the job really was.

A throat clearing draws her attention and Addy turns to the receptionist who was unhappy with the birthday present she had received. Janice gives her a knowing look as she examines her and Addy swallows nervously. When the older woman starts to smirk, Addy hugs her briefcase closer to her chest.

"Not fair, Janice. You could have warned me," Addy scolds the amused receptionist.

"Honey, I get my entertainment however I can. And something tells me, your presence here is going to be plenty entertaining," Janice laughs, then turns back to her computer and begins typing away on the keys.

Addy narrows her brows and starts to leave the reception area. The sound of snapping figures has her drawing up short and turning back. Janice is holding up a blue folder and is waving it. Addy goes back and gently takes the folder. Her name is scrawled across the center and below her name are the words *Hiring Packet.* Feeling the pressure of the major life decision she just made, Addy goes to a chair and slouches down, taking a moment before she opens the blue folder and gets lost in the sea of paperback.

She is going to have a retirement plan. She is now officially an adult, and she is terrified.

10 ***The Funeral***

Many think that goodbyes are the hardest part of life. So much emphasis is placed on a life when it ends. Mourners gather to pay homage to the extinguished life; they embrace with tear filled eyes and share memories of the lost soul. They gather to say their final goodbye and honor the moments in which their lives were touched by the extinguished soul.

So many goodbyes for a man that had long since faded out of this world.

Derek looks around his sister's living room at all the faces of the people that came to pay their respect to Gary Richards: police officer, veteran, husband, father, alcoholic. So many faces filled with goodbye; except for one. Derek held on to the coffee mug in his hand and silently watched as the mourners came up to his mother and sister sitting on the couch. The people would reach out and take hold of his mother's hand and offer their deepest condolences.

Didn't they know his parents had been divorced?

This entire display was quickly getting on his nerves. Goodbyes weren't the hardest part of life. Not at all. The hardest part was pretending to give a shit about the goodbye. Derek had left his father and everything that came with him in the past long ago. He had said his goodbyes when he was still a child. He didn't see the point in this whole charade of grief and remorse. Gary Richards had died at the bottom of a bottle many years ago. The person they were mourning today was nothing but a ghost, a figment of what they had all imagined Gary Richards had become. Beneath all the bluster was still a man that had ignored his children, neglected his wife and

56

chose whiskey over his family. Gary Richards didn't deserve to be mourned.

"Try not to look so pissed off. Ma doesn't need to witness your childish antics today," Drew says from behind Derek.

Derek groans and turns his head to see his brother standing behind him and to the left, further in the foyer than Derek dares go. He is hovering in the space between the living room and the kitchen for a reason. Those in the kitchen are busy with purpose, preparing snacks and beverages for the visitors. While in contrast, those in the living room are teary eyed and somber, definitely not his scene.

"Always a pleasure to see your smiling face, brother," Derek says and holds up his coffee mug in a mock salute. Whoever made the coffee did a terrible job but the sludge was helping get through this farce.

"Cut the shit. Ma has enough going on right now. She doesn't need to deal with your issues too," Drew says, a scowl on his face.

"How's Tammy doing?" Derek asks because he knows it will only piss his brother off further. Sure enough, Drew's face constricts in anger, and he makes a growl sound in the back of his throat.

"Stop being juvenile and greet the guests," Drew barks and starts to join their mother and sister in the living room.

"But I can't help it Gepetto. I'm not a real boy yet," Derek mocks and before Drew can walk back to him, he turns into the kitchen, walks out the back door and into the backyard.

Thankfully, the yard is empty, and he goes to the swing set and begins to swing on the double sided wooden bench that is some makeshift swing for kids. He has to sit in the middle and not on the ends because it would tip back but he manages to get a good swing going.

Amongst the stillness of the backyard and viewing the silent figures moving on the other side of the patio door Derek's thoughts once again drift to Addison and the airport. He wishes he was back there now instead of surrounded by all these people he doesn't even know, pretending to mourn the death of a man he also didn't know, or want to know. His siblings were acting like they had lost some great father, but they hadn't. They hadn't lost anything this week because it had been lost many years before and he just doesn't understand why they were all acting like this was the worst possible scenario.

Lost in thoughts of times long past and of Addy in the airport, Derek doesn't notice the figures walking in the house until they have both paused before the kitchen windows. He can tell they have stopped by the sink and were getting some water. Derek watches as the man hands a glass of water to the woman. She smiles, most likely saying thank you and brings the glass to her lips.

Derek remembers those lips. He had kissed those lips. He had whispered *"I love you"*, against those lips. Those lips had uttered the words that had torn his heart out two years ago.

And the man – that man had taken everything that Derek had cared about. Here they both were, standing in his sister's kitchen, drinking out of his sister's glasses after his father's funeral! This guy was the worst kind of asshole. Who shows up at the house of your girlfriend's ex's sister on the day of said ex's father's funeral?

What the hell were they doing here?

Derek quickly pushes off the makeshift swing and stomps towards the patio doors. This was his father's after funeral mourning gathering and he wasn't about to let this jackass taint this too. It doesn't dawn on Derek that he had just been thinking of how pointless this gathering was a few moments earlier. The only thing he can think about right now was that the very person he equated to the destruction of his happiness was standing in his sister's kitchen with the girl that should have ended up with him.

The sliding patio door makes a banging sound as it connects

with the wall when Derek opens it. He doesn't bother closing it behind him because in about five seconds he plans on throwing someone out that same door. He approaches the couple at the sink and he sees the moment recognition comes across Kelly's face. Her eyes widen and she puts her water glass down on the counter. She puts her hand on Brad's shoulder and whispers to him. Whatever she says causes Brad to turn around. Derek smirks because Brad just gives him better access and when Derek reaches them, he pulls back his fist and punches Brad right in the face.

Something he had longed to do for years.

Kelly lets loose a soft cry as Brad goes down and she tries to catch him. Derek isn't sure how Brad manages it but he catches himself on the counter and quickly stands back up. The onlookers all stop what they were doing and are now watching the display before them.

Let them look, Derek thinks. They were all full of shit anyway for pretending to be sad for a worthless ghost of a man.

"You have exactly ten seconds to tell me what you are doing here?" Derek says to Brad as he tries to tell Kelly he is alright.

"We came to pay our respect," Brad answers, rubbing his jaw. He isn't bleeding but Derek knows there will be a bruise there in the morning.

Good.

"Respect? How the hell do you even know where my sister lives?" Derek is torn between keeping his eyes on the asshole, or trying to find his sister. He stays where he is, glaring at Brad *fucking* Klauzek.

"I didn't know she was your sister. I didn't know this was your family," Brad says.

He has finally righted himself and is standing next to Kelly. She has her arm around him, but she keeps looking at Derek with the most pathetic look of empathy and it sickens him to see her looking at him like that. It bothers Derek but he continues to ignore her. Looking at her would bring back memories he would rather avoid.

"If you didn't know this was my family then why are you here?"

"I knew Gary in rehab. He contacted me when he got sick and we've been in touch ever since," Brad says each word carefully. It is clear Derek is still not over his initial anger at seeing him and he doesn't want to make him even more upset.

"And I guess this means you're here to support him," Derek says, finally bringing his attention to Kelly. She nods but says nothing. For some reason this makes Derek laugh. It is during his disjointed laughter that his brother enters the kitchen, clearly fuming.

"Derek, what the hell! You punched one of our guests!" Drew comes up behind him and grabs Derek by the shoulder and turns him around. Derek allows his body to be turned but he keeps his head and eyes on Brad and Kelly. Their very presence offends him, and it is like the last two years have slipped away and once again they are back on the college campus, flaunting their relationship in front of him.

"It's okay, Drew. He was just leaving," Derek answers, his eyes on Brad the entire time.

"Hello Drew," Brad says and Derek's whole world just tumbles as he turns to look at his brother, accusations of betrayal in every hardened breath.

"Hell, Brad. I'm sorry about my brother. Are you alright?" Drew says and reaches forward to shake Brad's hand.

Derek watches as their hands meet and they begin talking with an ease that betrays their familiarity. Betrayal up on betrayal builds inside him and with every word spoken Derek feels the cuts of a thousand knives in his back.

His own brother. How could he do this?

"I'm fine. It's my fault, really. Derek and I have a bit of a past," Brad shrugs.

Derek glares at him angrily. *Understatement of the century, prick.*

"Still. At our father's funeral service, Derek? What is wrong with you?" Drew asks, bringing the focus back to Derek.

"I was thinking that my ex-girlfriend just showed up with her new boyfriend, the guy she left me for, and neither of them should be here. I was thinking that they showed up to rub their happiness in my face. I was thinking I hadn't punched him in a while and I knew it would feel good, so I did it," Derek releases every pent up frustration he had, not showing mercy to any of them.

"When will you realize that it isn't all about you? Do you need me to get him out of here?" Drew says to Brad and once again Derek laughs at the absurdity of this. His brother should be asking Derek if he wants Brad out of here, but nope, in typical Drew fashion he takes the side of the other person.

So much for brotherly love.

"No. It's fine. I was actually hoping Derek would go outside and talk to me for a bit," Brad says.

"You're kidding me?" Derek responds in disbelief. Brad must still be on drugs if he thinks he's going to spend another minute with him.

"Please, Derek. It's important," Kelly says. She's looking at Derek like he is some lost puppy she wants to rescue. It is all very insulting, and Derek just wishes she would disappear from his life again.

Derek folds his arms over his chest, and he looks briefly at Kelly before nodding his head in agreement. If this was the only way to get rid of them then he would talk to them, but he isn't about to promise to not punch Brad again. He steps aside and lets Kelly and Brad pass. They go out the patio door and into the backyard. As he's about to follow them Drew reaches an arm out and grabs his shoulder once again.

"Don't do anything stupid. He was important to Dad and Ma is expecting them to come back into the living room. He better not come back with any more marks on him," Drew warns.

Derek jerks his shoulder out of his brother's grasp and narrows his eyes at him in contempt.

"Your concern for me is touching," Derek seethes and walks into the backyard. He closes the door behind him but doesn't move to get closer to Kelly and Brad. They are standing next to each other, their shoulders touching. It is a stance that displays their closeness, and it makes Derek sick to his stomach.

"I'm sorry for blindsiding you. That wasn't our intention. I made a promise to Gary, and I never knew he was your father," Brad begins.

"Would it have made a difference if you had known?" Derek glances at Kelly when he asks this.

Brad understands exactly what Derek is asking. He wants to know if Brad would have walked away from Kelly forever if he had known Derek was Gary's son. No matter how much affection Brad had for Gary it wouldn't have kept him from Kelly, and he tells Derek the truth.

"No. It wouldn't have mattered," Brad admits as he takes Kelly's hand in is. He doesn't do it to upset Derek, but to bring himself the courage he needs to continue. Kelly squeezes his hand and smiles at him encouragingly.

"Uggh. Just say what you came here to say and get the hell off my sister's property," Derek growls.

"I met your father in rehab. He was in my group therapy. He, um, got in contact with me once his condition worsened. I think he felt he had to make sure I was alright before he died. Well, he made me promise that if he hadn't reconciled with his children that I would contact them. Your brother and sister have been in contact with him for months," Brad pauses to remove something from his back pocket.

Derek is just floored. He had no idea his siblings had been speaking to their father again. He knew his mother had but not once had Mary or Drew told him they had been on speaking terms with their father. He keeps his face expressionless because he doesn't want to give Brad the satisfaction of knowing he has more knowledge about his family than he does

"I think I reminded your father of you in some way. When you refused to talk to him, he began writing down everything he wanted to tell you. He said he didn't want to give it to your mother or siblings because he didn't want them reading it. He asked me to give it to you. I haven't read it. It's still sealed," Brad says and reaches out. In his hands is a leather-bound journal, sealed with wax.

Derek glances at it questioningly. This does not look like anything his father would have made. He doesn't reach out for the journal and Brad slowly drops his hand to his side. He looks over at Kelly and she drops his other hand to take the journal from him. She walks over to Derek and stops before him, the journal held in both her hands.

"I know this is probably very confusing and I'm sorry it had to be us to bring this to you. We've hurt you and nothing will ever change that. Your father hurt you and he wanted you to know how sorry he was. These words may not change anything, but they may help you understand him and maybe this journal will help you heal. Don't take it for your father, Derek. Take it for you," Kelly says and reaches one hand out. She takes hold of Derek's, turns it palm up and places the book in his hand.

Her hand lingers on his for a moment too long and Derek breaks his gaze from Brad to stare down at her. She is still as beautiful as the last time he saw her. He is suddenly struck with a desire to run his hands through her luminescent hair, just like he used to do when they made love.

"I think it would be best if you both go," Derek says to her, softly, achingly. He longs for that which he can no longer have, had not had for two years.

Kelly nods, holds her hand out for Brad and they begin to walk back through the patio doors.

"I'm sorry, Derek. Your father was a good man, and he loved you," Brad says as he passes Derek.

"Don't," Derek warns him.

Brad nods, says nothing more, and he and Kelly go back into the house, closing the patio door behind them, shutting out the world inside the house of mourning.

Derek remains standing on the concrete slab with the small leather book in his hand. He looks down at it once but tears his gaze away from it like it will blind him. He doesn't want this. He doesn't want to be here. Closing his eyes he pretends he is back in the airport on that moving walkway. The memory is pleasing at first, but then it shifts to the moment when Addison started to drift away from him, and he suddenly feels panic.

Opening his eyes, Derek sprints out the fenced gate and begins running down the street. He doesn't know where he is going. All he knows is that he is suffocating, and he needs to get as far away from this house and those people as he can. The book is still clutched in his hand as he tears down the street, the blazing sun beating down on him.

The Meltdown

Email

To: seizethemoment69@gmail.com

From: derekgrichards109@yahoo.com

December 23rd 2007 12:04 a.m.

Subject: Hello Perfect Stranger

Addison,

I hope you remember who this is by my oh so clever email address, or the not-so-subtle subject line. If neither of those give you an indication of who this email is from than allow me to refresh your memory.

Remember that guy you met at the airport nearly five months ago? The one that was going to let you just walk away without a second thought? Well, that guy is me. You're probably asking yourself why has this guy just popped back up and waited five months to send me an email? I'm sure you thought by now that I had forgotten about you. Well, Addison, I never forgot about you. I just lost the receipt you wrote your email address on. I probably should have disclosed that I am famous for losing things.

I had wanted to write you many times, but I could never recall your email address. I know. Your email address is very memorable and what does that say about me since I clearly forgot it. In fact, I didn't remember it until a friend of mine at work got on my case for being "boring". I told him I wouldn't be going home for the holidays, and he invited me over to his family's celebration and I said I was going to spend the holidays catching up on my reading. And he laughed at me because he thought I was joking. When he realized I wasn't he told me I needed to "seize the day" and I just about had a brain aneurysm. I made him repeat the phrase many times and he finally told me to just rent the movie – The Dead Poets Society. I've seen it – of course. But the phrase allowed me to remember what your email was. Now, I did send this email to three domains, just in case I got them wrong. *(some people are in for a surprise)*

The conversation with my coworker was about two weeks ago. I convinced myself that there was no way you would want to hear from me after all this time. So, I just pretended like I hadn't remembered your email address and went on with life. But then something happened that made me realize I desperately needed to confess and the only person I've ever told my secrets to is you. So, that is where we are right now. Confession time.

Was it my turn or yours?

As of 2 p.m. yesterday I officially became an engaged man.

As of 2:01 p.m. I immediately wanted to take it back.

Remember that girlfriend I told you about? Well, her name is Liv. Her full name is Livander but, let's face it, that name is shit so she goes by Liv. I think her mother was trying to spell lavender, but she was all strung out on pregnancy drugs or something and she messed it up. This is just my theory, and I have never had the courage to try to confirm it. Liv would probably claw my eyes out if I asked her mother about it.

Back to the engagement. You are probably wondering why I would ask her to marry me if I really didn't want to. Well, that's the thing. I technically didn't ask her. We were talking. Actually, she was talking. She was going on about how we have been dating now for well over a year and it was time we "reevaluated" our relationship. I should tell you that she moved to Colorado with me. I didn't ask her to do that either. She kind of just came along and I didn't stop her. So, she keeps talking about how others in our situation would be moving on to the next step by now. After all, we had been living together for months now, it was only logical we took the next step. I guess I nodded or something because she kept on talking.

I vaguely recall her saying something about a deeper commitment to each other and announcing it to the world. Well, at the same time she was discussing a deeper commitment I signaled to the waitress that I would like another cup of coffee. The waitress held up the pot and I said, "yes", and the next thing I know Liv screams and jumps up. She's got her arms around me and the waitress is pouring me coffee and I'm thinking "what the hell just happened".

I got engaged is what happened!

We are supposed to go tomorrow to pick out a ring. Tomorrow's Christmas Eve for fuck's sake. All I wanted to do was lock myself in my study and read a damn book for the next two days. She was supposed to go home to be with her family but now we are both going to see her family – with the ring and wonderful news of course.

And so, here I am, after midnight, avoiding my own bed because how can I sleep when I am pretty much having a full-on panic attack.

I don't want to get married. And I definitely don't want to marry Livander or Lavender – whatever the hell her name is supposed to be! How do you un-engage from an engagement you never actually entered into voluntarily?

Here is the worst part – that isn't my confession.

My confession is that I have absolutely no intention of breaking this engagement. Liv already made the rounds, and both of our families know about it. My mother called me and told me how happy she was. She said this was the first good thing that has happened since my father died. She told me she couldn't wait to help Liv plan the wedding. My sister had eloped, and my mother was always hurt by that because she had wanted to be a part of the planning. Liv is her second chance and I'll be damned if I take that away from her.

So, tomorrow I will get up, smile like I mean it and pick out a damn ring.

Signed,

The Perfectly Fucked Stranger
Aka Derek
Ps. Merry Christmas

To: derekgrichards109@yahoo.com
From: seizethemoment69@gmail.com
December 25th 2007 8:05 a.m.
RE: Subject: Hello Perfect Stranger

Derek,

There is so much to say right now, and my brain is firing on all cylinders. First, I do remember you and wondered what happened to you. Despite the reasoning for you contacting me after all this time I am happy to hear from you. It sounds like you desperately needed to confess.

Second, Merry Christmas to you too. Sorry to hear you will be spending the holiday season in what I can only describe as abject horror. I am hardly the person to give relationship advice because, let's face it, I'm a relationship wrecking crew.

Liv sounds....lovely?

She may very well be the best rocking girlfriend ever and you might possibly be the worst boyfriend on the face of the planet. I just don't have enough details to give a proper lecture. So, I won't even try. Seriously though, if your heart isn't in it then maybe you shouldn't be in it either.

As for your cleverly disguised email address – I dig it. It is straight to the point and no nonsense – just like you. I remember this guy I met in the airport that was very serious and often provided one-word answers to questions. Some may call this mysterious, but I say it's evasive.

I got it!

You need to stop having such serious conversations in places where there is coffee. Coffee is your weakness, and it distracts you.

70

Next time you have a serious conversation with Liv you need to be at least 100 yards away from any caffeinated beverage. You should include tea and soda in this as well. We wouldn't want you to agree to something even crazier – like a couple swap or something.

Sorry to hear your father passed away. I understand your desire to not disappoint your mother, but I don't think you would disappoint her if you waited to marry somebody you actually wanted to marry. Something tells me she would be okay with that.

Well, since you provided a secret, it is now my turn.

I'm boinking my boss. And I like it.

Best of Luck

Addy

Ps. Dead Poet's Society gave me my mantra "Oh Captain, my Captain" and the other quote is pretty rad too.

To: seizethemoment69@gmail.com
From: derekgrichards109@yahoo.com
January 13th 2008 1:13 p.m.
Subject: Holiday Daze

Addy,

I spent the holidays and my birthday (January 9 – see email address) saying thank you to everyone that offered their congratulations on my recent engagement. Liv is ecstatic. She shows off that ring like it's…I don't know what a really expensive piece of jewelry is, but I vaguely recall something about a pink diamond when Ben Affleck proposed to Jennifer Lopez (don't judge me). She is showing it off like it's the pink Bennifer diamond. It's not, trust me. My salary is not anything to brag about.

A funny thing happened when Liv and I went home for the holidays. My brother, Drew, came up to me and shook my hand and said, "it's about time little brother". Dare I say it, but I think he might actually think I've done something right for once. I didn't have the heart to tell him that he was congratulating me because I said yes to another cup of coffee. I have no doubt had I revealed that to him he would have been back to being disappointed.

Apparently, I will be marrying a June bride. Six months away. Liv is always efficient, and the hall is already booked. Mother is happy.

Wait! Your boss!

Isn't there some company policy against "boinking" the boss? I know there is at my company, but the policy is unnecessary. My boss is a 50-year-old balding man named Ted. He's an alright guy, but not my type.

How does this work? You go into his office to give a report and next thing you know you're tossing off clothes and locking the door? I'm not judging. I am just curious for research purposes. I need to make sure I don't fall into any of Ted's honey traps. He's been eyeing me a bit funny lately.

My turn – I hate wedding cakes. I hate all cakes. They are too sweet. Frosting is gross but if I had to pick a cake to eat, it would be red velvet but you can't have a blood red wedding cake because that sends the wrong message. Wedding cakes are boring and whatever that decorative shit is on top it is so difficult to eat. If I had a pick I'd want a red velvet football shaped cake with a layer of rocky road ice cream. Get it? Because marriage is a rocky road and there is bound to be some blood at some point. The football is just because I like football. I used to play it in high school, but I was terrible. I got creamed a lot.

Hey, two confessions for the price of one.

Signed,
The Reluctant Groom
Ps. Be careful with the boss situation

Email

To: derekgrichards109@yahoo.com
From: seizethemoment69@gmail.com
January 20th 2008 6:12 a.m.
Subject: Happy Birthday!

Derek,

I am happy to hear that you and your brother had a moment together; even if it was predicated on lies. I think you should just have a genuine talk with your brother. He might surprise you. Same thing goes for your mother.

I've never been a fan of June, or the summer months. I prefer Spring. There is something refreshing about all that new life coming back into the world. Plus, I really like flowers. Especially the lilies. My yard, growing up, had all different kinds of lilies. My mother was a huge gardener. She taught me everything she knows…and I still kill every plant in sight. She really did her best but, like ballet, gardening was not in my future.

I completely understand about a measly salary. I'm not exactly rolling in the dough, but I can't ask for a raise because then it would create a whole other dilemma. Would my "boss" give me the raise because I deserve it or because he likes my lady parts? I never thought I would be this girl. The one that falls for her boss. Well, in all honesty I wouldn't say I fell for him. More like, fell into him.

That is legit how it happened. We were working late on a project, and I got up to get some files and I tripped on the carpet and fell on him. He caught me and helped me back on my feet and, I don't know, something just clicked. It doesn't hurt that he is close to my age and completely gorgeous. I hear your warnings, and they have been going through my mind too. I wondered if he had a habit of office affairs. So, I asked Janice. Janice is his long-time receptionist, and she absolutely adores me.

Janice said I had nothing to worry about. She said John was "smitten" with me. I'm not entirely sure what smitten is, but I'll take it. I'm not completely naïve. I know this has absolutely no future but I'm having a good time, and it makes me feel good. So, I'm gonna keep boinking my boss.

Secret Confession: Bunnies scare me. Ever since I saw Bambi and Thumper's eyes get all wide when he saw the lady bunny I've been terrified of bunnies. Their eyes really are just devoid of emotion and black and wide. It's creepy.

Enjoy your wedding cake, whichever you choose

Addy

Ps. Don't wait too long, soon it will be too late

To: seizethemoment69@gmail.com
From: derekgrichards109@yahoo.com
January 30th 2008 8:23 p.m.
Subject: Bunnies!!!!???

Addy,

I'm not sure I can continue our correspondence after being informed of your bunny fear. I believe your irrational fear of bunnies speaks to a deeper emotional trauma that I am simply not equipped to deal with. I highly recommend you consult a professional before this phobia impacts your daily life.

Personally, what I took away from Bambi wasn't the bunny phobia but the realization that Disney is one messed up company. The writers must have hated at least one of their parents because one of the parents in all the movies always bites the dust. Why is this?

Bambi – the mother gets shot by hunters

Little Mermaid – no one knows what happened to the mother, she's just gone, and King Triton is sad. I vaguely recall something about a fishhook (gross)

Beauty and the Beast – no mother, no explanation

Finding Nemo – Mother is killed by a predator

Cinderella – Mother is dead first, then the father dies, and an evil stepmother takes over

Snow White – see Cinderella

Sword in the Stone – both parents are just gone without an explanation and the boy is forced to endure child slave labor washing never ending dishes and the magic just makes more work for him

And the worst one of all..

Lion King – father is murdered by the uncle in front of the son and then uncle convinces the son that he is the reason the father died (animated Hamlet)

Now that I think about this some more, I think you probably haven't been paying much attention to the Disney movies. Watch them again. The best way to get over your fears is to face them head on so watch Bambi over and over again until you learn to love that cuddly rabbit.

Here is my irrational fear confession: Old ladies playing bingo. I have this image in my head that they are ruthless and cutthroat. I pity the man that comes between a bingo lady and her winnings.

Signed,

Bingo Fearing Lad

P.s. Don't get yourself fired and don't let your boss take advantage of you

To: derekgrichards109@yahoo.com

From: seizethemoment69@gmail.com

February 3rd 2008 5:10 p.m.

Subject: Old ladies playing bingo my ass

Derek,

First, thank you for the brief history on the parental tragedy that is Disney movies. As someone that has lost both parents at a young age, I am truly touched that you would point out all the horrible ways Disney has killed off or ignored the absence of parents.

Now try to imagine me saying that without being bitchy. Yeah, I can't imagine it either. But seriously, I don't enjoy Disney movies, and you probably pinpointed the reason why I avoid them (bunnies aside). Still, I must give you props on an adequate listing of Disney movies with parental tragedies.

I love making lists.

Second, I call bullshit on your irrational fear. Recent events have dictated that your irrational fear is disappointing your mother. This would explain your willingness to enter into an engagement that you want no part of. I understand we are barely friends, but I believe it would be remiss of me not to point out the obvious.

You have to break this engagement!

What happens when you marry her and then wake up one day and realize you made the biggest mistake? Are you just going to use an audible and walk away? It doesn't exactly work that way and ending an unwanted marriage may just be more painful then ending an unwanted engagement. I'm not telling you what to do. I'm just trying to be the best airport friend I can be from many miles away.

Next, thank you for your concern regarding my employment

status but I assure you that my office affair will not interfere with my employment. We no longer hook up during working hours and our encounters are far removed from the office. Aside from Janice, no one knows about it, and I intend to keep it that way. As for the raise, I haven't brought that up yet. What do you recommend? Should I put together a proposal or lock him into it in the midst of a sexual encounter? ☺ Totally kidding. I am the ultimate professional.

Proposal it is!

Oops... poor choice of words. Sorry.

Confession: I've never actually went on a date for Valentine's Day and John (that's my boss...aka sex buddy) said he had a big day planned. I'm sort of freaking out. This is all just fun for me but does planning a big day for Valentine's Day mean he is taking this a bit more seriously than I am? I need your advice relationship expert. Should I anticipate a premature proposal? Because....yikes!

Stop being a wimp,

Addy

To: seizethemoment69@gmail.com

From: derekgrichards109@yahoo.com

February 10ᵗʰ 2008 11:55 p.m.

Subject: Not a Disney hater, a Disney realist

Addy,

I must first commend you on your use of a football term to describe my relationship status. Your careful handling of such sensitive personal stuff is truly touching.

As for my "irrational fear of disappointing my mother" – I want to say you are 100% wrong, but I can't. Besides, Liv isn't bad. She is actually quite observant, and she keeps me on schedule. Honestly, I doubt I'd meet my deadlines if it wasn't for her. She pretty much has the days set out, including meal plans. I never have to waste my time on wondering what to make for dinner or where I put my keys. She's always on top of those things. I appreciate her for that, and she really is a good woman. My family adores her, and her family seems to tolerate me in small doses. Her father is a bit standoffish, but I think I'm wearing him down. Just the other day he actually, almost, smiled at me. It really was a touching moment. Wish you could have seen it. There might have been tears.

Your dig at my relationship problems was not overlooked and I must say, "ouch, that hurt". I wish I could give you some advice regarding the Valentine's Day date thing but since I didn't even know I was proposing I doubt any advice I could give would be any good. I can only tell you, from a guy's perspective, that if he is planning something special it probably involves some sort of wooing.

Do people say wooing anymore?

Personally, I think a proposal would be way too soon for you two, but I don't know John. Maybe he is a super romantic and he just fell so hard for all your lady parts that he doesn't want to see any other lady parts for the rest of his life. I have never said lady parts before. You're a bad influence on me.

Prepare yourself for a possible proposal but don't let on that you are expecting one. If you are expecting it and it doesn't happen then I can't see how that would end in any way but badly.

Do you even want him to propose? Are you…you know…there yet? God, this is definitely not a conversation I would have with any of my other friends. I swear you are slowly turning me into a girl. Is that offensive? I can never tell what is empowering and what is offensive in this new feminist society we live in. Was that offensive?

Confession time: Dark chocolate makes me fart. But I don't care, I eat it anyway. It is the only sweet confection I allow myself. Make sure you stand up wind.

Signed,
Cocoa fart monster

Email

To: derekgrichards109@yahoo.com
From: seizethemoment69@gmail.com
February 15th 2008 3:01 a.m.
Subject: Totally Panicking

Derek,

The good news is that I am not an engaged woman. There was no proposal tonight at the "big date". He brought out all the stops. I keep forgetting how much money he has. To say this evening was the best date I have ever been on would be an understatement. I was expecting a nice dinner and some flowers, but my mind was totally blown.

John told me to "dress fancy" and I did. He picked me up at my tiny one-bedroom apartment in a freakin' limo! Here I am thinking we are going to a restaurant. He had champagne ready in the limo and we were toasting and laughing and next thing I know we are at a private airport. He takes me to a waiting helicopter and we get on. I think, okay, this is kind of cool. I've never been on a helicopter before and seeing the lights from the city would be nice.

Well, not only did I see the lights from the city, but I also saw the lights from Las Vegas!

Yes...he took me to Las Vegas for Valentine's Day...in a freakin' helicopter!

So, we land and there is another limo waiting for us. We get in and he whisks (yeah, there was whisking) me away to the MGM Grand. We go through an entrance I didn't even know existed and end up in a private dining area in one of the many exquisite restaurants that particular hotel has to offer. We were waited on like

82

we were some celebrity couple. I guess John is a celebrity in his own right. I mean, he's loaded!

So, we finish dinner, and my mind is pretty much mush at this point because how could this night possibly get any more epic.

Well, it does.

After dinner he said he wanted to show me some of the artwork in the hotel. I'm like, sure, yeah okay. We get on the elevator and go down some floors and I step off. Next thing I know a song starts playing that I recognize and these three blonde guys come around the corner and I nearly shit myself. I don't know if it was a tribute group, or the actual guys because I was freaking out. Remember I told you about my juvenile obsession with the sensational boy group Hanson? Yeah, it was them, maybe.

I completely lost it!

I screamed like I was a teenager and jumped up and down I think I started crying too. This part is a bit of a blur because all I could think of was how jealous my sister would be and how my teenage self would have died.

Sorry, I'm getting off track.

After the serenade, with tears streaming down my face and incoherent words coming out of my mouth, John took me to the Belagio for the fountain show. And as I was watching the waters spring forth with all the lights set to an amazingly beautiful love song John told me he loved me. Yep...right there on the street of Vegas with my makeup all runny from my earlier crying jag.

Isn't this every girl's fantasy? To be whisked away to an exotic (I know Vegas isn't exactly exotic but run with me here) location by an attractive, rich man that is madly in love with you? And be serenaded by your teenage crush?

Well, there we are standing by the water show, with music crescendoing all around us and he is staring at me waiting for me to say something and I just blanked. I must have stared at him for a good two minutes before I blinked and said –

"What?"

"I said I love you."

And I blink again, look at the fountains now finishing their amazing show and I say –

"I liked the helicopter ride."

What is wrong with me?

John is so amazingly perfect that he just laughs, takes my hand in his and agrees that the helicopter ride was pretty awesome.

God! I am such a spazz.

John suggested we go see some piano player he knew about, and we went off to another casino. He spent the rest of the night talking to me like nothing had happened, like I hadn't just had a complete mental breakdown in front of him.

Later, he takes me back to the MGM where there is a spectacular room waiting for us that would take about a month's worth of pay for me to afford. We then proceed to have the most amazing night. I was able to not freak out about the fact he said he loved me, and I said I like the helicopter ride until much later.

So, now, here I am, hiding in the bathroom after I left him naked in the bed, and sleeping. As soon as he fell asleep, I got out of the bed, grabbed my computer (which he somehow had gotten packed for me along with other overnight items I would need because he is considerate like that) and am now naked myself and hiding in the bathroom.

Well, friend, I need your expert opinion again.

What the hell is wrong with me?

This was by far the most magical night of my LIFE and I'm hiding in the bathroom because I'm hyperventilating. This man is everything my parents wanted for me. This man is everything every woman wants and all I want to do right now is run! Run as far as I can.

I'm a fraud! I am a complete and utter fraud. I would watch those damn romance movies and blissfully wish I had what those women had. Well, here I am, experiencing a night straight out of a romantic comedy and all I can think about is how it shouldn't be me here. This night belongs to somebody else.

Please tell me what is wrong with me.

In case you didn't know this entire message was my confession/secret.

Addy

P.s. Please don't ever refer to yourself as the "Cocoa fart monster" again. It's just weird.

P.P.s. I wasn't offended but I think a feminist might be. A feminist might be offended that I'm sleeping with my boss, or they might high five me. I honestly don't know.

To: seizethemoment69@gmail.com

From: derekgrichards109@yahoo.com

February 16th 2008 7:58 a.m.

Subject: First, put some clothes on

Addy,

 It sounds like you had a pretty eventful Valentine's Day. I must commend John for his planning. And now I must curse John for forever ruining Valentine's Day for you from now on. How the hell can that night ever be topped? It's only downhill from now on. Sorry, but that is just the truth. I'm glad all I did was take Liv out to dinner and give her a necklace. I set the bar low, so she doesn't expect too much. ;) that's a winking smiley face – check it

 Well...at least it wasn't a proposal?

 Now, I must discuss this nonsense you mentioned about how that night shouldn't belong to you. Why the fuck shouldn't it!? You are an amazing woman, and you deserve everything that this guy just gave you. I cry bullshit on your theory that you don't deserve the romantic comedy ending. I say, if you have a shot at that kind of ending then take it. Take it and don't look back.

 On the other hand, if you truly don't have any affection for this man then end it, end it now before you find yourself in an accidental proposal with your wedding four months away.

 As for not telling John you loved him back, I have a bit of experience in this department. I too have been on the receiving end of the silent aftermath. I once told someone I loved them, and she never said it back. I now know why she didn't. She loved someone else. If you love someone else then please, for all the men in the world, walk away now. Don't string him along.

If you just think it's too soon then tell him that. Tell him what you are thinking so he doesn't have to guess. I don't know John, but it sounds like he thinks a lot of you. If you just let this go and don't talk to him about it then it will mess with his head. Good luck girl.

As for the Cocoa fart monster it was just a one-time thing.

Confession: Liv picked out her bridesmaids' dresses. I told her she made a great choice, because that is what she wanted to hear.

I lied. I hate the dress. Can a man hate a dress? Well, if a man can than I hate this dress. It makes my sister look like a beached whale surrounded by lace and whatever name that material is called. I lied because that is what a good groom does. They lie so their bride is happy. I am dreading the dress she picked for herself.

Signed,

The dress hating man

P.s. Second Confession: I looked up some songs by your favorite boy band and I'm not ashamed to admit that I rocked out to a couple.

To: derekgrichards109@yahoo.com
From: seizethemoment69@gmail.com
February 27th 2008 4:10 p.m.
Subject: Seizing the moment

Derek,

I am truly sorry for my 3 a.m. panic email. I'm still trying on this whole adulting thing, and it would seem, based on recent events, that I have a lot of work left to do.

After talking to my sister (her name is Julie) and reading your email I came to the conclusion that you were right. I do deserve the movie ending and I'm going to take it! I took your advice, and I spoke to John. I told him that I was blown away by everything he did and that I was grateful he cares enough about me to do all that. I also told him he didn't have to do things like that because he has already impressed me. I told him I was fond of him and that I could really see myself falling for him but that I needed more time to get to the same place he is. I told him I wasn't saying that I didn't love him. I was simply saying that, in time, the words would come because I was already more than halfway there. He told me he understood and then asked me what I wanted to do for dinner.

Am I crazy or does something just not seem right with this man? I mean, shouldn't he have broken up with me in a fit of rage and a tearful question of why didn't I love him back? Or is that just something only my girl friends did? Regardless of the reasons, I am still very much in intense like with John and things are not at all weird.

Did you buy that?

You say you aren't good at relationship advice, but I think you gave solid advice. If only you would take your own advice. Maybe you should just tell Liv you hate the dresses. Tell her you think she has bad taste. Maybe she will break off the engagement and you can tell your mom you are just as stunned as she is when the announcement is made. Or become a groomzilla and just irritate the shit out of her so she breaks it off. Or, here's a crazy thought, why don't you have a serious conversation with her just like you advised me to do with John?

And there is absolutely no way that I will be able to keep your obsession with the best boy band ever a secret. This is just too good. If I ever meet your family that will be the first thing I say to them.

"Mrs. Richards, your son is in love with the Hanson boys. It's really nice to meet you."

Yep. That is so happening.

Confession: I miss my family. I've been in Arizona for seven months. I visited them at Christmas but relying on phone calls just isn't the same. I want to be able to hug them when I talk to them. This adulting thing is way hard and all I really want is my Mommy.

Addy

To: seizethemoment69@gmail.com

From: derekgrichards109@yahoo.com

March 12th 2008 2:19 a.m.

Subject: Royally Fucked

Addy,

Well, I finally did it.

I was eating dinner with Liv, and she was talking to me about a seating chart or something and a thought occurred to me. Liv would make a really great assistant. It was like a lightbulb turned on.

Whenever I would describe her to others, I would list all these qualities she has; great multi-tasker, always sticks to a schedule, great planner, amazing at noticing the details. Do those sound like the qualities a future groom should be listing about his future bride?

No, they do not. Those are qualities you would use to describe an assistant.

So, while Liv was pointing out where the flowers would go on the chairs and tables I looked at her and said: "Liv, it's over."

She looked at me and laughed and said she hadn't finished her meal yet. Of course, I was confused because what does that have to do with ending our engagement. Then I realized she thought I meant dinner was over.

"No, our engagement is over. I can't do this. I can't marry you," I said.

The room got silent (it didn't but in my mind, it got awkwardly silent). Liv just closed the binder with all her wedding planning stuff, picked up her fork and started eating her pasta like I hadn't said anything. So, I asked her if she had heard me and she says, "Yes I heard you but it doesn't matter."

"Of course it matters," I said and then she put her fork back down and looked me square in the eyes and said –

"I'm pregnant."

Signed,
The future Mr. Livander Styverson

Email

To: derekgrichards109@yahoo.com

From: seizethemoment69@gmail.com

March 14th 2008 6:07 a.m.

Subject: WHAT!!!!

Derek,

   That can't possibly be the end of your email. What happened next? Mr. Livander Styverson? You are still going to marry her? Talk to me, Derek.

Addy

Journal Entry

March 14th, 2006

I've never written in a diary before. My father always used to say diaries were for sissy girls. I told this to the Doc, and he told me to consider this a journal and not a diary. A diary is supposed to be written every day about the events of that day, but a journal can be anything you want. I told Doc, no offense, but a diary is still a fucking diary no matter what name you call it. Doc just laughed and said I could call it whatever I wanted, as long as I wrote in it.

So, this is me, writing in my diary (aka journal).

I have no damn clue what I am supposed to write about. Doc told me to write what I feel but I don't know what I feel. I haven't known what I've felt for years now. I guess that is because of the alcohol.

When I told him that he suggested I write about what made me finally seek help for my "addiction". I should probably stop writing it in quotations. Doc says that it diminishes the importance of what I'm doing here. I don't know if I buy into that but at this point, I just might believe anything.

So, here it is, the reason that brought me to the center.

Two weeks ago, the divorce papers finally arrived. I should have seen it coming. It has been years since she moved out and went to live with her sister in Poughkeepsie. She left when our youngest, Derek, finally went off to college. She said she had no reason to stay anymore since the kids were all grown and she couldn't stay and watch me drink myself to death. She said all this while I sat in my recliner, beer in my hand. I listened to her talk, but I didn't actually hear her. I watched her take her suitcase out the front door. Heard her start her car and the retreat of the wheels as they backed out of the drive. I think I thought she would be back, that she couldn't leave me. We were a pair for 35 years. You can't just walk away after 35 years.

But she did and then the papers came.

I didn't sign them right away. I wanted to throw them in the trash and after the initial rage (I trashed my living room) I finally looked at the things around me for the first time in probably 20 years.

I was alone. All of my kids had left the house and now my wife was gone too. They had all left me. But what was worse is that I let them all go without a fight.

I guess my dad was right, only sissy girls write in diaries.

Gary T. Richards

To: derekgrichards109@yahoo.com

From: seizethemoment69@gmail.com

March 20th 2008 9:35 a.m.

Subject: Where are you?

Derek,

    Are you okay? Please tell me you are okay.

Addy

Journal Entry

March 16th, 2006

Doc told me to write about my children. I mentioned that none of them have spoken to me in years and he asked if I had tried to reach out to them. I hadn't. So, Doc said to write it down.

I have three children.

Drew is the oldest. He used to follow me around when he was little. He loved going to the station with me and I would take him with me every chance I got so I could show him off to the guys. Carol and I hadn't been married for a year yet before Drew came along. We were both just so damn happy then.

Mary soon followed and she was the complete opposite of her brother. Drew was timid and so serious. Mary was a free spirit from the start. Even as a baby she knew just how to boss me around. Drew took his role as older brother and protector seriously.

Derek came along a few years later and then there were three. Derek was a combination of his two older siblings. He was out-spoken like Mary but serious like Drew. He looked up to his older siblings and often copied them.

We were happy. Carol, me, the kids.

Those were some good years.

I've done a lot of wrong in my life, but my kids were never one of those things. If I was asked today if I had been a good father, I would say no. But during those happy years I was the best damn father, way better than my father had ever been. I used to say I would never be like him with my kids. My kids would know I loved them. During those happy times, they did know that.

Then I went and messed it all up and I'm sure those memories have long been forgotten by all three of my kids. I don't blame them.

I am a shit father.

But, for a brief moment I was the father they deserved, and the husband Carol had married.

Gary T. Richards

Journal Entry

March 20th, 2006

I spoke about my father in group today. I haven't spoken about him in years. He died while I was away. Away. That sounds so casual. I wasn't away. I was in freakin' 'Nam. I got drafted not too soon after my 18th birthday. I remember saying goodbye to my folks and my father said he was proud of me. That was the first and last time he had ever said that to me. I don't know what he was so proud of. I hadn't volunteered – I was drafted. I didn't have a choice and if I had a choice I sure as shit wouldn't have gone to war. What did I know about war? The only war I had ever known was trying to avoid my father's fists. Mom wasn't as lucky as I was at avoiding them. I didn't want to go to war because I knew that the moment I was gone he would just lay into her more since he didn't have me around to punch. I could take the punches, but she couldn't.

Dad was never one for big emotional scenes and when he hugged me goodbye, I didn't know what to do. I hugged him back. To this day I regret doing that. He was a mean bastard, and he didn't deserve a hug. I had no problem leaving him behind, but Mom was different.

I thought about her a lot while I was gone. She wrote but her letters never held the truth. I didn't know how bad things were because she never told me. I didn't know that Dad was beating her daily. I didn't know that she had finally broken. I didn't know that she had shot him until her letters stopped coming. It took me months to finally find out what had happened. She had killed him during one of the beatings and she was now in prison for it. My mother had killed my father and was in prison and I was stuck in the rain and mud in a Godforsaken country that didn't want us there and was trying to kill us. I tried to get back home but was denied. So, for two years my mother sat in a prison thinking her son had abandoned her.

98

I never hated my mother for what she did. She did what was necessary. Hell, I wish she - no, I wish I had done it sooner. She had always been stronger than me.

I thought of her often during those years.

Whenever I thought of him, I would use that anger and direct it towards the enemy. Some days it seemed like they were everywhere. The only thing that held any bit of humanity in that place was my dog, Boomer. I was his handler, and he was my dog.

Gary T. Richards

Journal Entry

March 25th, 2006

I haven't been able to get Boomer out of my head. Like my father, I try not to think about him. I've spent years trying to forget but without the booze the memories just keep coming back and Boomer is in all of them.

He's there when I wake up, curled against my side. He's there when I'm walking through the dense brush, walking ahead of me to alert us to an ambush. He's there when I'm trying to get a quick wash and drinking the cool spring water. He's there when I go to sleep, his gaze sweeping out ensuring there are no threats before he too lays his head down to rest.

Everywhere I look Boomer is there.

But Boomer isn't here. Boomer is dead.

I let them kill him.

We were supposed to leave that fucking place. Two years and we were finally free. We had both made it and were supposed to go home. They said we were all going home. But then they came for Boomer and the other dogs. They said the dogs weren't going with us. I told them I wouldn't leave without my dog, and they said I didn't have a choice. That our ride was coming and we all needed to be on it. All except the dogs.

So, I knelt down and told Boomer his ride was coming later. I told him I'd be waiting for him back home. I hugged that dog and cried until I had nothing left. He licked my face because he trusted me. He trusted that I would take care of him because that is what we did for each other. We took care of one another in that ugly hell. He saved my life so many times.

I got on that damn chopper, and I watched Boomer barking from down below, going crazy in his kennel, trying to get to me. I shouted

100

that we would see each other soon. I doubt he heard me, but I shouted it over and over again until I could no longer see him.

Boomer never came home. None of the dogs made it home. They killed them all. And I just left him there. I let them kill him.

Boomer is all around me and all I want to do is drown out the hurt and guilt.

I'm so sorry Boomer. So damn sorry I failed you.

Gary T. Richards

To: derekgrichards109@yahoo.com

From: seizethemoment69@gmail.com

March 25th 2008 6:42 p.m.

Subject: Derek…TALK TO ME!

Derek,

> *I am seriously freaking out here.*

Addy

Journal Entry

March 30th, 2006

I had to take a break away from this for a few days after Boomer. I usually have to take a few days away from everything when the memories of Boomer surface. I never told Carol about him, or about the other things that happened over there. I never wanted her to know that hell. I thought I was protecting her but really, I was avoiding the memories. I spent years trying to keep it all down and for a while there it worked. I was able to go on as if nothing was wrong. I was able to hide the voices raging inside, screaming to be let out. I buried myself in work and being the best damn family man I could be. And I got really good at faking it.

Until I didn't.

I don't know. Maybe my mistake was going into a career field that kept me around the violence, but this was all I knew. 18 and at war. Holding a weapon became necessary and being a cop gave me that lifeline. Things weren't so bad. I was able to push it all down when triggers would come up. But then that day came, and it didn't matter how hard I tried to push it all back, it just wouldn't go.

The call seemed routine enough. Some noise complaints so my partner and I answered. As soon as we got out of the squad car, I knew there was nothing routine about this call. I could hear the sounds from the front, but I wasn't prepared for what we saw. There was blood and body parts everywhere. While my partner was calling in for backup I was staring at the carnage before me and the cries kept penetrating my mind. I saw those men just standing in a circle, cheering and laughing. Nothing about this was funny. I had walked back into that jungle, into hell.

This time, I wasn't going to leave without finishing things. I don't even remember doing it, but I walked up to the closest man and

103

put my pistol against his temple. He felt the cold metal and froze. The others continued to cheer and laugh while they looked on at the dogs pulling flesh off each other. I told the man not to move or I would shoot him and feed him to the dogs. By now the other men noticed me and they started to move towards me, but my partner had returned, and his weapon was drawn. He told them not to move. They held their hands up and stopped advancing. I still had my gun to the temple of some man I didn't know.

I asked who was in charge. No one spoke. I told the man it didn't matter. That he would do. He pissed his pants and started to sniffle. My partner told me to back up, but I ignored him. All this time the two dogs kept fighting on, oblivious to what was happening around them. They were both bloodied and snarling. They weren't anything like Boomer but the others in the cages, the bait dogs, all looked like Boomer to me. It didn't matter that they were all way too small and not even the same breed. They were Boomer and this was the jungle.

I wouldn't fail him again.

Without a second thought I pulled my weapon to the two dogs in the pit and fired two quick shots, killing them both. Then, without a second hesitation I turned to the man at my side and shot him in the leg. He went down screaming and my partner started cussing. I didn't say anything. I holstered my weapon, turned, and went back to our squad car.

I don't know how it was done but it got covered up. I wasn't even reprimanded. The men were arrested, charged and released. Not a single one of them spent more than a night in jail. And the one I had shot spent his time in the hospital, on the county's dime.

Three days later I watched while all those dogs found in the cages were "put down". That wasn't justice. Justice would be me watching those men being put down, for good. I did a lot of wrong in my life, but shooting that man was not one of them. I wanted to kill him. Kill them all. I don't know what stopped me.

That was the night I turned to the drink. Boomer was all around me and all I could see were his eyes and all I could hear was him crying out to me to not leave him behind.

My kids always thought we couldn't have a dog because I didn't like them. But that wasn't the truth. The truth was we couldn't have a dog because they all looked like Boomer, and the guilt was too much. We couldn't have a dog because every single one reminded me of my failure and my broken promise.

So, I drank to forget. I drank to control the images. I drank to drown out the hurt and in turn ended up causing more pain.

Every time I picked up a drink, I would toast Boomer and all the other sorry souls that never made it out, canine and human. I would apologize for making it out and leaving them behind. A salute to fallen comrades.

This one's for you Boomer. Cheers. And I drank.

Gary T. Richards

To: seizethemoment69@gmail.com

From: derekgrichards109@yahoo.com

April 1ˢᵗ 2008 11:22 a.m.

Subject: Time to Grow up

Addy,

Sorry I didn't get back to you sooner. I had a lot to consider these past couple of weeks. So, last I wrote, Liv was pregnant. She is still pregnant, and we are still getting married. Instead of a June bride I will now have a May bride. Liv wants to get married while she can still fit into her wedding dress. You know, before the baby starts showing. And there really is a baby. I think a part of me didn't want to believe it but when we went to the doctor and there was a little heartbeat it all just smacked me in the face. She is really pregnant, and I am really getting married.

I thought, even if she is pregnant then we can still forgo the wedding thing. People manage to raise children all the time without getting married these days. I figured; how hard could it be? I was all set to tell her just that until I discovered my father's journal. I never told you about this but on the day of his funeral someone from my past showed up with this journal and said it had belonged to my father. He told me they had been in rehab together and when my father got sick, he gave the journal to this guy (this guy I hated for so long). I thought he had come to the funeral just to irritate me.

Of course, he brought her with him too (you remember the ex I told you about – the one that chose the other guy – well, there they both were at my father's funeral reception).

This guy had the nerve to tell me that my father was a 'good guy'. Like he somehow knew my father better than I did. I grew up with the man! I knew exactly who he was. I didn't need this douche

106

bag to tell me he was a good man because I knew that Gary Richards was far from a 'good man'. He was a terrible father and an even worse husband. And in all honesty, he was a questionable cop. Being drunk tends to impact your performance at work.

I took that damn journal, and I ended up throwing it in some box, never intending to look at it. After coming back from the doctor's appointment, I just needed to do something to clear my head. So, I started going through some boxes I still hadn't unpacked since moving. Luck would have it that it was sitting on the top of the very first box, marked 'books'. I thought I was opening an innocent box and then I came face to face with an object that had once belonged to the man I blamed for ruining my childhood and destroying my mother. I was going to throw it away. I had it in my hand and was holding it over the trash can when I noticed something scratched into the leather on the back. I turned it over and saw 'always for my children'.

My father was a shit dad, and he had scratched that on his journal. First, I was angry at him for bringing us into his journey of self-discovery or whatever it was he was doing in rehab. Then I started laughing because this is just something so typical of him. He's dead, gone, and he is still messing around with us. Finally, I took the journal and locked myself in my study, soon to be nursery, and I started reading.

I find I can only read one entry at a time because what my father wrote is beyond anything I ever expected to find. It turns out I didn't know him at all. I didn't know a damn thing about him. I didn't know he had been in Vietnam. I didn't know that his father was an even worse tool bag that physically abused him and his mother. I didn't know that it had gotten so bad that his mother shot and killed his father. I didn't know that my dad actually loved dogs. He loved them so much that it pained him to be near them. I didn't know how much he was hurting, or how hard he tried to keep it all together. I didn't

107

know that the good years I remembered were the best years of his life too. I didn't know.

After I read the first five entries, I realized that I couldn't walk away from my own kid. My father fought so hard to keep things together for us. He sacrificed so much, and he did the best he could. He wasn't perfect but he loved us. He loved us enough to hold on for as long as he did. I still haven't forgiven him for all those bad years. But I realize that if I walk away, if I'm not there for my child every single day then I will be no better than my father was when he picked up that bottle for the first time and never put it back down.

And so, I will marry Liv. I will be there for this kid, from day one and beyond. I will not repeat my father's mistakes. I will be the best damn father I can be, and I will do it for the rest of my life.

Confession: I'm starting to think my brother has been right about me all this time. I really have been a chump and needed to grow up. No time like the present to do that.

Signed,

An expectant father

P.s. I'm sorry I freaked you out. How are things on your end? Do you have any advice for a soon to be Dad?

To: derekgrichards109@yahoo.com

From: seizethemoment69@gmail.com

April 2ⁿᵈ 2008 6:42 a.m.

Subject: Phew

Derek,

    I can finally breathe. But first I must ask...was your last email true? You wrote it on April Fool's Day and before I go any further, I must get your word that everything you wrote is based in reality.

Addy

To: seizethemoment69@gmail.com

From: derekgrichards109@yahoo.com

April 2nd 2008 9:12 a.m.

Subject: All true

Addy,

I didn't even notice the date. Yes, everything I wrote is 100% true.

Signed,

The truth teller – Derek

Email

To: *derekgrichards109@yahoo.com*

From: *seizethemoment69@gmail.com*

April 2nd 2008 2:33 p.m.

Subject: That's heavy

Derek,

My heart is both breaking and filling for you. I know this must have been a hard decision to make but having a baby is a good thing. Really, this is a blessing. There is no doubt in my mind that you will be an amazing father to this little miracle. And I also know that you will do your best to be a good husband. Maybe you should tell all this to Liv. It might help you two connect and start off in a better place.

I think you should also keep reading your father's journal. It sounds like he poured out his soul onto those pages. Getting to know him and understand him might bring you closure. I know that sounds cliché, but I honestly believe knowing where he came from will help you decide where you are going. Or you can just ignore me. I don't know what I'm talking about. Still, it would have been nice to have discovered one of my parents' secret journal or something. To have something of them left here with me…

As for me, things are still the same. I am still seeing John. I still haven't said those three words yet but I'm trying to. I think you and your father have inspired me. I am going to get a dog. I too have never had one and I think it is time that I do a little growing of my own. Here's to growing up. May we both rock this shit!

Addy

Confession: I had to separate this because I wasn't even sure I was going to include it. Only two other people on this planet know this. I have never been able to tell my family. I was pregnant – once. In college, with that ex I told you about. I lost the baby. A few months later I got sick. I've been pregnant – once and always just that one time. Always the lost baby. So, promise me you will cherish your little miracle because they can be lost so easily.

To: seizethemoment69@gmail.com

From: derekgrichards109@yahoo.com

April 8th 2008 11:23 a.m.

Subject: Thank you

Addy,

Thank you for trusting me enough to share your secrets. It must have been extremely difficult to carry that pain with you all these years. I'm so damned sorry you had to go through that and that your ex wasn't the man you needed him to be. You deserved...hell, I'm not sure what to say next. I do know that if it had been me, I would have done everything in my power to be the man you needed me to be. I now understand why you said forgiving him wasn't about him. I get it. You won't be able to move past the pain until you can forgive him. It's your last step. Just like with my father. I'm still not in a place where I am ready to forgive him for all the bad, but I'm starting to understand why it is so important that I do forgive him. Maybe, someday, we can both utter those words – I forgive you.

Mom is beyond stoked about Liv's pregnancy. She has always wanted another grandchild, and she is finally getting one.

Surprisingly, my brother wasn't as thrilled. I thought for sure he would make some quip about being a man and finally accepting responsibility or some shit. But he didn't. After I called and told him about it, he just got really quiet and let out this long ass sigh. I asked him what his deal was, and he said having a kid this early on in a marriage was difficult. He said he was worried about me.

I laughed. What else could I do? Drew and I have never had the type of relationship where we discuss our feelings. When he was going through his divorce he never once told me about it. One day he was married and then one day he wasn't.

113

In fact, we had been over at our sister's house drinking a beer in the living room with her husband, watching a game, and Drew just blurted out – "Tammy and I got divorced. She's moving across town."

And that was all he said about it. I expected my brother-in-law to question him further, but David just nodded at my brother and went back to the game and his beer. I remember thinking David needed to say something. I know now it should have been me to say something, but I didn't. Drew and I just don't talk about those things. So, when he said he was worried about me and my upcoming marriage I just laughed. Drew didn't laugh back. He didn't shout at me either, which is how our conversations usually go.

Instead, he told me if I ever needed anything I could always call him. I was shocked and I thanked him and then quickly cracked some joke because the whole thing was just making me uncomfortable.

Let me know how the dog acquisition goes. Who knows, maybe if you have only good things to report I'll add to my growing family and get a dog too. I have always wanted one.

Take care of yourself.

Signed,
A very grateful friend
Derek

P.s. I'm so damned glad my flight was cancelled that day. I don't think I could have gone through all this without you. Thank you.

Journal Entry

April 5th, 2006

I've been here a month. I haven't had a drink in exactly 32 days. 32 long days. 32 sobering days. 32 excruciating days. 32 eye-opening days.

I haven't been living for the past 20 years. Sure, I got up, I ate breakfast, I went to work. I went through the motions. A robot on autopilot. 6,500 days that are a complete blur. 80 birthdays I wasn't present for. 20 anniversaries I ignored. Thousands of moments lost.

Doc says life is marked by moments that hold importance to us. A birth. A death. A love found. A love lost. The perfect sunset after the perfect day. Moments we recall from a sound, a scent that sparks a feeling inside that we connect too. Doc can be a poet when he wants to be.

I wonder if there will ever be a day when the scent of whiskey doesn't make my mouth water, or my fingers twitch.

I tried to think of other moments like the ones Doc described. There were some that sparked emotions of happiness. Carol's face on the day I asked her to marry me.

To this day I still don't know how I got so lucky to find her. I know that if it hadn't been for her, I would never have been able to keep everything together after I got back from that place.

I came home, believing my mother was locked up but still alive. I went to find her as soon as I got back. But I was told she had died in prison two months before my return. She had gotten pneumonia and had never recovered. A complete fluke the warden told me. I had wanted to beat the living shit out of that guy when he said that.

A fluke.

Like the death of my mother was so inconsequential that it didn't

115

deserve any title other than fluke.

The jackass picked up on what I was thinking, and he quickly called his secretary in to his office. He said she would help me with the rest of my needs, and he quickly excused himself. He left me sitting there with my anger and I was prepared to take it out on anything, or anyone, I could. Until a soft hand touched my shoulder, and a kind voice asked if I would like some coffee.

An Angel.

Carol. My Carol.

Looking into the kindest eyes I had ever seen I felt my anger just fade away. I know how foolish it was to think this, but her eyes reminded me of Boomer's eyes. Brown and wide and full of compassion and understanding. For the first time in a long time, I felt like I was in a safe place.

The pain of losing my mother just fell away because in some twisted play of fate I had ended up in that moment with Carol and my life was forever changed. If my mother hadn't killed my father, she wouldn't have been sent to prison. If she hadn't gotten sick and died, I most likely never would have met Carol. Carol lessened all the bad because she was just so damned good. I was only able to chase away the demons because I had her. I guess sometimes a fluke really could be a good thing.

We were married six months later. I promised her the world and instead I only gave her 15 years of happiness. I spent the next 20 years slowly breaking the Angel that had saved me.

In the end, it was her that gave me the world, and it was me that destroyed it.

Gary T. Richards

To: derekgrichards109@yahoo.com
From: seizethemoment69@gmail.com
April 20ᵗʰ 2008 10:58 p.m.
Subject: Operation Puppy Survival

Derek,

I'm alive!

It was touch and go there for the last week, but I believe I've finally figured it out. I didn't adopt a cute little puppy with nothing but love in his heart. Nope. I brought home a velociraptor with an appetite for destruction that matches Godzilla's. In fact, I gave him a name in homage to the Japanese created monster.

My dog's name is Zilla.

Oh, he's cute. Deceptively cute. Even when he is surrounded by the evidence of his crimes, he is still so damn cute with those sad, innocent eyes that somehow manage to look guilty at the same time. At first, I thought the shelter had simply pulled a fast one on me but then I realized this predator had simply bamboozled them too. They were so overcome by his cuteness that they didn't intentionally trick me into bringing home a lizard monster. They were scammed as much as I was.

After a week of replacing every pillow I own, repainting the apartment twice, doing the dance of cage training during the night (you know, the one where the puppy cries and you feel guilty so you take the dog out and put him on the bed with you only to wake up to wet sheets because he peed during the night), finding remnants of my best shoes all over the place and tripping over toys I have finally found what works.

One day, after our nightly walk I was flipping through the channels and a news program came on. The microwave buzzed, letting me know my dinner was ready, so I left the channel on. By the time I came back that dog was sitting in front of the tv, attention solely on the program. It was like nothing I had ever seen before. He didn't move once for the next hour. Once the program was over, he came over to me and fell asleep by my feet.

My dog likes C-SPAN!

Whenever I need to settle him down, I pop in a recording of some political commentator and he sits in front of that tv silently until the show ends. I swear to you, sometimes he even barks in response to some of the commentators. My English Springer Spaniel mix is obsessed with world events. The entire scene is absolutely bizarre to watch but it keeps him away from my shoes.

Addy

Confession: Have I mentioned that I hate watching C-SPAN? It is torture, but I can't keep buying more shoes.

Email

To: seizethemoment69@gmail.com

From: derekgrichards109@yahoo.com

May 10th 2008 1:42 a.m.

Subject: Today's the big day

Addy,

Today I will be getting married.

The reality of it hit me at the rehearsal dinner. Both our families are in town for the wedding and the night was all smiles and hugs and congratulations. At one point her father took me aside and told me I had better treat his little girl right because she was his world, and he would do anything to protect her. He stopped short of saying he would have no problem burying my body, but I understood where he was going. I told him I would take care of her.

My mother never stopped smiling all night. She told me I had made her happy and I hugged her, telling her I was glad. I smiled too. I smiled so much, my damn cheeks hurt. I've never smiled so much in my life. It was all bullshit, of course.

Drew noticed I wasn't exactly in my element. He came up to me at one point and asked if I was alright. I told him I was. He gestured to the drink in my hand and said, "That's four."

It took me a minute to comprehend what he was actually saying. My fourth Bourbon. I always stop at three. Since I began drinking alcohol at the age of 16, I have always stopped after three drinks.

I was nearly finished with my fourth drink.

I stared at that glass, then at Drew before I shrugged and finished the contents. Drew followed me when I went to the bar for a fifth drink. He asked me again if something was bothering me and I once again said nothing.

119

"Nope. What could be bothering me? I'm getting married tomorrow," I said. He narrowed his eyes at me in scrutiny, but didn't say anything before he walked away.

As I reached for my fifth Bourbon, I realized that my brother knew about my three drink rule. It wasn't something I had ever told him about but somehow, he knew. I looked for him and saw he was standing with Liv. She was laughing at something he said. She looked so happy. Her cheeks didn't hurt. Her smiles weren't forced.

My sister came up to me at that moment and said something along the lines of, "It's not too late to run little brother. I'll call the getaway car, and you can sneak out the back."

I looked at her in shock and asked what she was talking about. When she started laughing, I realized she was just joking with me, which was confirmed when she slapped me on the back and said she was just kidding. She told me Liv was great and that being a parent was the best thing ever. She hugged me and said she was happy for me.

Everyone was so damn happy for me.

After the dinner ended, I came back to the hotel room I am sharing with Drew (my best man). I came to my computer and started to write to you, and he again asked me if I was alright. I told him I just needed to get some work done and next thing I know he's looking over my shoulder and asking who would have your email as a work email.

I could have lied to him. I could have made up some bullshit about how this was a co-worker's personal email but I was just so drained after that dinner and all the fake smiling that I just couldn't find the strength to lie. So, I told him the truth. I told him about the airport and you. I told him about the emails and our friendship.

When I was done telling him he stood up and paced for a bit. It was odd, watching him react the way he did. After a bit he stopped and said, "Okay, this is what you are going to do. You are going to stop the emails. You are going to marry Liv tomorrow and you aren't going to talk to this girl anymore."

I told him to fuck off.

I told him I wasn't going to stop talking to my friend. I told him you were the best friend I had and just because I was getting married that wouldn't change things. I thought for sure he was going to yell at me because his eyes looked like they were gonna bulge out of the sockets. He didn't yell though. He just sighed and said, "I hope you know what you're doing."

Why do weddings make people crazy?

It isn't like you are an ex-girlfriend I'm secretly in contact with. I've never seen you naked. We've never even kissed and he's acting like I'm already having an affair on Liv or something. Totally crazy.

Anyway, I love that your dog is interested in politics and is also a dinosaur. Personally, I don't care what political affiliation you or your dog has. If your dog is anything like you than I have no doubt he will be just as caring as his owner.

Signed,
Your friend
Derek

Confession: I know why Drew wanted me to stop talking to you. I know because even though I haven't seen you naked the thought did cross my mind the day we met. And some days the thought returns. But that isn't as important to me as having your friendship is.

To: seizethemoment69@gmail.com

From: derekgrichards109@yahoo.com

May 25th 2008 3:15 a.m.

Subject: Lost

Addy,

I'm sorry. I know I've made this awkward and I'm sorry. I know I should have probably kept that last confession to myself but of all the people in my life you are the only one that I have been completely honest with, and I didn't want to lie to you too. I don't think I could lie to you even if I tried. You just make everything easier. I know you won't see me as a disappointment, like so many others do.

Hell, I'm disappointed with myself.

I don't know. Maybe I am a coward. Maybe I made the wrong decision. Decisions. I thought I had it all figured out you know. I thought I would come to Colorado after graduation, become some rock star in the computer programming field, get rich and land all the hot babes (okay, maybe those last two aren't exactly true).

Instead, I met you and the girlfriend I did not love came with me to Colorado. I should have stopped her. I don't know why I didn't. I don't know why I told her I loved her when I didn't. I don't know why I didn't speak up when she thought I had agreed to getting married. I don't know why I keep finding myself in the same fucked up situations.

I think I'm lost.

Who knows. Maybe I was never found in the first place.

How do you find something you aren't even sure you lost?

Signed,

A man lost in time

Confession: I'm worried I scared you away and that was the last thing I ever wanted.

To: derekgrichards109@yahoo.com

From: seizethemoment69@gmail.com

June 2nd 2008 12:18 p.m.

Subject: I'm sorry

Derek,

    After your last email I wasn't sure I should write you back. Your brother was right to be concerned. I was concerned when I read your confession. So, I pulled away. I withdrew because I believed it was the right thing to do. The last thing you needed was thoughts of me being naked in your head while you were starting life married to another woman. And I would be lying if I didn't admit that I had similar thoughts of you at the airport.

    But you weren't married then. And you weren't about to be a father. So, I told myself – walk away.

    And I had every intention of doing just that. I wasn't going to talk to you ever again. I spent the next few weeks hanging out with Zilla and John. I tried not to think about you. I tried not to think about how my withdrawal would hurt you. I ignored your email and didn't even open it. I couldn't stop thinking about it though. And one day John asked me what was wrong. He said I looked sad. I told him I missed my friend, and he asked what had happened. I told him my friend had gotten married and was starting a new life, a life where I had no place. He asked me if my friend had told me that and I told him you hadn't, that I thought it was for the best. And he said that if not having my friend in my life was making me this sad imagine how my friend must have been feeling.

    He was right. I didn't think about how you would feel. You told me you valued our friendship above all else and my response was to withdraw from it. I'm sorry I held my friendship hostage. I didn't mean to. I was wrong. I don't know how to describe that day at the airport to anyone other than you. I can't explain why I feel so much closer to you than anyone else in my life. I don't know if not talking to you is the right thing or if talking to you is the right thing. The only thing I do know is that the thought of never talking to you again makes me incredibly sad and I don't want to be sad anymore. Like you, I also felt lost.

So, again, I'm sorry.

I will understand if you want to discontinue contact, and I will honor that. But, in all honesty, I hope you don't. And you aren't a coward. You're a good man that is doing things the best way he knows how.

Addy

Confession: I told John I loved him the night he told me to talk to my friend. He knew exactly what I needed. I don't know how he does that.

Journal Entry

June 3rd, 2006

It is a strange feeling to realize that you are completely alone. When you spend 20 years driving away all who loved you it is easy to ignore the loneliness. The drink helps with that too. After a while you become so numb to everything that you don't recognize the signs of depression, or despair. You just accept it as normal and try to push it down. I can't do that anymore. I refuse to do that anymore.

I don't have enough time left to do that anymore.

I'm dying.

Cirrhosis. All those years spent in a bottle have taken their toll. My liver is shot. There is no coming back from this one. The Doc says there is no way to determine how much time I have left. The damage is extensive and irreversible. My days are numbered.

After hearing the news, I immediately wanted to call Carol. I needed my Angel to tell me it was going to be alright. But how could I call her up after years of silence? I never once tried to contact her when she left me. I just let her go.

My kids. How could I call any of my children and tell them I was dying? That just didn't seem fair. Actually, it was plain wrong to call them out of the blue and spring this news on them. I couldn't do it. I refused to do it.

Doc told me it was time I reached out. I told him it wasn't going to happen. He asked me why I was here, and I told him he knew why. He said he didn't, and I just rolled my eyes at him. He told me I had never once said aloud why I checked myself in, and why, even after hearing my diagnosis, I was still in rehab and not pouring the whiskey down my throat.

I told him to go to hell.

126

And then I met the new guy.

He was young. He was Derek's age. And I saw so much of myself in this young man. He was struggling to keep his demons at bay, and he pushed away those that loved him because he foolishly believed he was protecting them.

He was me.

He saw blood every time he closed his eyes too. He was only nine when he found his older brother dying on the bathroom floor, blood from the cuts surrounding the body.

Nine.

I saw blood at that age too. Pouring from my mother's wounds. But this young man hadn't been prepared for it, and it had forever marked his soul. He told us about how for years his brother kept trying to kill himself. He told us how he blamed himself for saving his brother and how he blamed himself when he couldn't save him in the end.

So much blame.

He also told us about the girl he loved. The girl he hurt over and over again. The one person that no matter what he did was always there for him, trying to bring him back from the abyss. He told us about his Carol. Of course, she has a different name. I know my Carol and his Kelly, are completely different people, but I couldn't help identifying with Brad's story. I knew his path if he continued to stay on it. I knew his future because I had lived it through my life.

It wasn't Doc that convinced me to reach out to my children. It was the new guy. It's never too late. I don't know how much time I have left but I'm gonna spend every last minute of it doing what I should have done years ago. I'm gonna be honest, with myself and my family. I'm not gonna hide anymore.

Gary T. Richards

127

To: seizethemoment69@gmail.com
From: derekgrichards109@yahoo.com
June 5ᵗʰ 2008 10:13 a.m.
Subject: Friends

Addy,

Please tell John I said thank you. It was never my intention to make you uncomfortable. I can't put a name to what happened that day at the airport either. I only know that your emails are something I look forward to. Just knowing you are there listening to me brings me comfort. I meant what I said. Your friendship is one of the most important things to me. Perhaps we should both agree that if there ever comes a reason for us to break off contact, we will do so quickly and without hesitation.

Revised Rules of the Game:
Reveal confessions in alternating turns
Clean break if needed

I read another entry in my father's journal. This one talks about that guy I told you about. The one my ex went back to. Actually, she never really went back to him because they had never dated. They were childhood friends or something. My father met him in rehab. I now know why he stayed in touch with him. Apparently, he reminded my father of himself. It was because of this guy my father started trying to contact us again after so many years. I never answered his letters or phone calls. I never told my mother or siblings about him contacting me. I knew my mother had taken his calls because she told me, but Drew and Mary never told me they had been talking to

128

him. It seems my father wasn't the only one keeping secrets.

How is Zilla? Still enjoying those political news programs? Tell me about your sister. Do you keep secrets from each other too?

Signed,

A guy who is glad to have his friend again

Confession: I actually enjoyed my honeymoon. The beach was nice to run on in the early morning. Liv was a beautiful bride, and I didn't hate her dress.

To: derekgrichards109@yahoo.com

From: seizethemoment69@gmail.com

June 12ᵗʰ 2008 2:53 p.m.

Subject: Secrets

Derek,

I am glad you enjoyed your honeymoon. Liv sounds wonderful. I hope she had the wedding she dreamed of.

Zilla continues to indulge in his political commentary.

I agree to the new terms of the game and will honor them.

It sounds like you are learning a lot from your father's journal. Have you spoken to your family about it and what you have learned? Maybe it is time to stop keeping secrets and just come clean. Secrets have a way of tearing things apart.

As for my own secrets…I finally told my parents and sister about my pregnancy. After your last email I knew it was time. I got on a plane and flew home and told them all together. My mother had asked why I hadn't told them before, and I said it was because I thought they would be ashamed of me. I don't think I've ever told you this, but my mother is deaf. That is how I knew sign language at the airport. Anyway, she was signing when she started to cry. I hurt her by keeping it all a secret. She wanted to know why I would ever believe they would be ashamed of me. I just said I only wanted to make them proud, and she told me they were proud of me. We all cried together as a family.

You asked me about my sister. I told you a little about her at the airport. She's virtually perfect. At least, I always thought she was perfect. I learned that she has flaws on this latest trip home. After our parents had gone to bed we stayed up in her old childhood

130

bedroom, something we used to do as teenagers.

She told me she had an affair with one of her married college professors. I couldn't believe it. My perfect, older sister – the accomplished musician and ballerina – had engaged in an extra-marital affair. And then she told me the next part – the professor was a woman. My sister is a lesbian.

My sister is a lesbian, and she hadn't told our parents yet.

So, to answer your question, yes, my family has kept secrets as well. I think all families do it out of fear that they will hurt or disappoint the others. Perhaps the real testament to a family's love isn't the keeping of the secret, but how they react once the secret is finally revealed.

My beautiful, and still perfect, sister sat with us at breakfast the next morning and told my parents her secret. She told them she had a girlfriend. Someone she had been dating for over a year now. Without missing a beat our father said, "You mean Rachel?"

Turns out, my parents already knew my sister was a lesbian. Had known since she was in high school. They just didn't want my sister to feel confronted, so they waited for her tell to them. The night prior we cried because we were sad but that morning we cried because we were happy. The secrets just came pouring out of us. I learned so much about my family and I have you to thank for that. I even learned more about my birth parents.

Thank you, friend, for everything.

Addy

Confession: My parents want to meet John. I'm so nervous.

Journal Entry

July 1, 2006

I'm able to have visitors now. Actually, I've been allowed to have visitors for a while now, but I never expected to have any. So, I waited until I reached out to my family to ask them to come. I thought for sure Carol would be the first one to answer my calls and letters, but I was wrong. The first person to respond, to visit me, was my daughter. Mary. I don't even remember the last time I had spoken to her or even seen her. To be perfectly honest, I don't remember her even leaving the house. She had gotten married as soon as she turned 18. She had eloped and I vaguely recall Carol being upset by that. I also remember that I told Carol to quit whining because the elopement saved me money.

Why Carol didn't leave me then is still a mystery to me.

Mary had children of her own now. Two boys. I couldn't remember their names, or their ages. I vaguely recall being at her house for some birthdays, but after a few I stopped going. Carol would go but she eventually stopped telling me to come along, so I didn't. I did remember the name of Mary's husband. Those two had been inseparable from an early age. David was a scrawny kid with glasses, and he followed my Mary around like she was Jesus and he was her disciple.

Today, during visiting hours, Mary showed up. She was carrying a shoe box. I was in the rec room when they brought her to me. I had been playing cards with Brad when she walked up to us. Brad noticed her first. He asked if she needed help, and she said she was just here to see her father. I recognized her voice and put my cards down. I almost knocked over my chair when I realized it was her. She hadn't written me back and I didn't know she would be coming. I told Brad she was my daughter, my Mary I said. I froze. Brad took over and asked if she would like his seat. She nodded and said thanks. Brad left and I was still standing while Mary sat down. She waited for me to sit before she talked.

She asked if what I had written was true. Was I really dying? I told her I was, and she nodded. She opened the shoe box and took out some pictures. "This is Brian and Devon. They are five. Brian likes cars and alligators. He keeps bugging David and me to take him to Florida so he can go to a gator farm. I told him we couldn't go because I was afraid of them. He told me he would protect me. He's always been like that. The great protector. He is constantly watching out for Devon. Devon thinks he's invincible. I've caught him trying to jump out of trees many times. I know it is only a matter of time before he breaks something in his mad attempts to be a superhero, but I can't watch them all the time."

She handed me more photos and kept telling me about my grandkids. She told me David was no longer in the Air Force and that they had settled back down in our hometown to be near Drew and his family. I didn't say anything until she finished. I just kept staring at the photos and at her. I couldn't believe she was really there.

"How much time do you have?" she asked.

"I don't know. Months, maybe a few years. I'm sorry, Mary," I said to her. She nodded and tears fell from her eyes. I tried to reach for her hands, but she withdrew them and placed them on her lap. It hurt to have my little girl pull away from me, but I understood.

"I know I have no right to ask you this. I probably had no right even writing to you after all the hurt I've caused. I was a terrible father to you kids. You deserved so much more than me. I see that now. I've been sober for five months now. Usually, people leave this program after two months, but I wanted to make sure this stuck. I leave next month. I'll be going back home, and I was hoping – I mean if it is alright with you and David – that I could, maybe keep calling, or writing if you prefer. I know I can't make up for all those

133

years, but I don't want to waste whatever time I have left. I want to get to know my kids and my grandkids. I don't want to leave this life still hurting you all."

She wiped her eyes and took some papers out of the shoe box. She set them down by the photos and pushed them towards me. I picked up the first paper and saw that they were letters written by her to me. There were so many of them and they went back years.

"I started writing them after the twins were three. I don't know why I never sent them. I suppose it was because I thought you wouldn't read them, or if you did that you wouldn't care what I had to say. I've read all your letters. I'd like you to read mine."

I told her I would. We sat silently for a little bit before she told me that Carol had called her to ask what she should do about me writing her. Mary told me she had told Carol not to answer yet because she wanted to make sure everything I had said was true. She told me Drew had also told her about receiving my letters. She assured me she would talk to them both.

I asked her about Derek. She shook her head and said Derek hadn't mentioned anything to any of them. She told me that Derek refused to talk about me because he was still upset about, well, everything. She offered to talk to Derek, but I told her not to. I told her he needed to come to me on his own terms and that I didn't want him to feel forced. She agreed to tell the others the same thing.

She visited with me for three hours before she said she had to get home to relieve the babysitter. She promised she would return tomorrow with David and the kids. When she left, she actually hugged me goodbye. She told me she loved me and that she was happy I had finally gotten some help. I called her Sweetpea, and she smiled. I used to call her that when she was little. It felt so good to talk to her, to hold her again and to be present for every minute of it.

I had my little girl back.

Gary T. Richards

Journal Entry

July 2, 2006

Mary came back with my grandkids. This has been one of the best days of my life. I got to play Legos with my grandchildren. I got to thank my daughter's husband for being a better man than I ever was. For the first time in a long time, I was Dad and Grandpa instead of the drunk in the recliner.

When Mary told her kids to say goodbye to Grandpa and when they complained about having to leave I started crying. This was the man I used to be. This was the father and grandfather I always wanted to be. I crushed those kids when we hugged goodbye and told my daughter and son-in-law that I loved them. Their visits made me hopeful.

I have hope that I just might be able to hold the rest of my family again before the Lord takes me away. Death may be coming for me, but he doesn't have me yet. There is still time and plenty of hope.

Gary T. Richards

To: seizethemoment69@gmail.com
From: derekgrichards109@yahoo.com
July 27th 2008 8:05 a.m.
Subject: Married life

Addy,

Sorry I haven't written in a while. Things have been a bit crazy here. Liv is now five months along and the morning sickness has finally lessened. I do think the title of morning sickness is very misleading, however. She gets sick at random times and there is no correlation to morning. Had it all been in the morning than we could have planned around it. It got so bad she had to quit her job. Her doctor's instructed her she needed to take things easy for a while. So, I've been pulling extra duty and haven't had much free time.

Do you know if the hormonal changes are the same for every woman? One minute Liv is just fine and the next she's crying because she's fat. I keep telling her she's not that big but that doesn't seem to be helping. I asked my sister to talk to her, but Mary told me I was being stupid. Drew wasn't much help either. No surprise there, he is divorced after all. Finally, my mother agreed to come stay with us for a little bit until Liv is cleared by her doctor. Thank God for my mother. She's been amazing.

I think the best part about having her here though is being able to talk to her. I decided you were right. I needed to come clean about some secrets. I told her how my dad had written to me and that I never responded. I told her I was sorry for not making it on time before he died. I apologized for the scene I made at his funeral. I even told her that I was reading his journal. I offered to show it to her, but she told me that it wasn't written for her. She told me she had known about the journal and the letters dad had written to me.

137

She apologized for keeping her secrets too. She tried to apologize for so many things and when I told her she didn't need to she said she did.

She told me she knew my father had a problem for years, but she ignored it because it was easier than confronting it. She said she was to blame too because she never pushed him to get help. She told me more things about him. Things from his youth and those early years when they were married. He used to have nightmares, but he would never talk about them. She never pressed him on them because he always said he was fine, but she knew he wasn't.

Liv and mom get along quite well. I'm glad they are close.

I wish I could say that the reason Liv and I haven't been intimate is because my mom is here, and we feel weird about having sex with her here but that isn't the case. We haven't had sex since our honeymoon and to be perfectly honest it wasn't any good. It felt forced. I'm not an expert but shouldn't newlyweds be having more sex? Sure, she's pregnant but that doesn't bother me, and she told me it didn't bother her but neither of us are quick to initiate anything. Is this normal? I can't ask my mom this because, gross. And I definitely do not want to ask my sister. Drew would probably make fun of me.

Anyway, how did the meet and greet with the parental units go? Did John hold up okay? And how is my favorite dinosaur doing? Did he destroy any major cities yet?

Signed,
A very sleep deprived and confused man
Derek

To: derekgrichards109@yahoo.com

From: seizethemoment69@gmail.com

August 2nd 2008 6:23 a.m.

Subject: Google is your best bet

Derek,

I'll start by discussing the easy things first. Zilla is growing so fast but with every passing day he seems to calm down a little more. He still loves shoes so I must keep them secured at all times. He got a hold of John's one day. Needless to say, John wasn't exactly thrilled by finding the torn pieces and my laughing probably didn't help the situation either. He had to leave wearing a pair of flip flops of mine (they didn't exactly fit him).

The meet and greet with the 'Rents went well. It went really well. I'm still trying to wrap my mind around how well it went. They adored him. Julie said she would go straight for him. The hardest part about the whole situation was leaving Zilla at the boarders. I cried like a baby leaving him there. He didn't care of course. He was so thrilled to see new people that he didn't even look back at me when they took him to the kennels. I, on the other hand, had snot dripping and no matter what John said I was a complete mess.

My dad took John golfing. Of course, I was not invited because apparently the bonding ritual of golf is only set aside for the male gender. No vaginas allowed. So, in retaliation, I went miniature golfing with Mom and Julie. I kicked their butts.

Am I crazy?

Why does the fact that everything in this relationship keeps working out makes me weary? Nothing is supposed to be this easy. We haven't even had a fight yet. I tried to pick one the other day just so we could check that off the list but no matter what I did John just wouldn't bite. In fact at one point, he flat out asked me if I was deliberately trying to start a fight. Ugghhh!!! It's like he knows everything! I came clean of course and he just said, "that is cute".

Cute! Why won't he just fight with me damnit!

Now on to the more difficult aspects of your email.

Time out – Zilla jumped on my lap and gave me his ball. Need to pay attention to the beast for a few.

Okay, I'm back. For the record, I know absolutely nothing about morning sickness, the hormonal mood swings, the feeling of being fat during a pregnancy or anything related to married life. I've had exactly two relationships in my life. The first ended in complete heartache. The second – well, I just tried to pick a fight for the hell of it so I'm sure you can picture how unqualified I am at giving advice. As my heading suggests – you'd be better off asking Google.

It is good your mother was able to come and help you and Liv out. I can only imagine how hard this all is for Liv. There is one thing I do feel confident commenting on, however.

YOU ARE A COMPLETE IDIOT!

When a woman asks you if she looks fat you do not say "you aren't THAT big". Moron! You told her she WAS fat but it's okay because she COULD BE fatter. You say she is beautiful. You hold her and ask her what she needs. You say you love her. And if you have nothing to say then you keep your damn mouth shut while you hold her. Women aren't as confusing as men think we are. Pay attention to your words and check with her regularly. See what she needs; ask her if there is anything you can do for her. Just be present. And for the love of God do NOT utter the phrase 'whatever you say' in response to a question. It's just plain rude.

As for the sex thing – I've got nothing. Maybe you should just talk to your brother about it. Or talk to Liv about it. Tell her your concerns. But do not bring her appearance into it. Frankly, I don't know what to tell you on this. I can only say that as a woman, our desire to have sex depends largely on our emotions. Chances are if we aren't there emotionally, we aren't going to be there physically. Best of luck with this one friend.

Addy

Confession: I think I've actually been in three relationships. The one from high school and into college. John. And now my dog. I am completely and hopelessly in love with my dog. Is it bad that if I were to rank them by which one fills my heart the most it would be:

1. Zilla

2. He who shall not be named (and you better know this reference, or we can no longer be long distance friends)

3. John

Journal Entry

July 30, 2006

Today's the day. The day I leave rehab – the center.

Others have left before me. They were ready to go back into the world and continue their struggle on the outside.

The outside.

That is a rather funny concept because the struggle isn't on the outside at all. No. The struggle we face is very much on the inside. The inside of everything. Inside our families. Inside our lives. Inside ourselves.

When I first started this process, I would have described my inside as very empty, hollow even. I didn't have any lasting connections tethering me to the here and now. That has all changed. My daughter and her family have reawakened the spirit I once had. The time I spend with my grandchildren has given me a second chance at redemption and I am so grateful to Mary and David for this chance.

Carol has even come to see me. I know I've written about her visits before, but I still can't seem to capture just how much they mean to me. Even though the majority of our first visit was spent in tears I know that she is proud of me. And it is absolutely wonderful to know that she still loves me. She demanded to move back home with me. I told her it wasn't necessary and that she should go back to her sister's in Poughkeepsie but she told me to stop being an idiot.

She's picking me up and taking me home today.

Another second chance.

I used to think we were only ever given one chance at everything. I looked at my life as nothing more than a series of wasted chances that I would never be able to get back again. My Mother. Boomer. My job. My kids. My marriage. Me. So many wasted chances.

I know now that nothing is finite. There are no absolutes. There are second chances all around us. It's just that we have to see them and be willing to take them when they are offered.

This time – I'm taking mine.

Gary T. Richards

To: seizethemoment69@gmail.com

From: derekgrichards109@yahoo.com

August 7th 2008 11:13 p.m.

Subject: This is why I need you

Addy,

You say you aren't good at giving advice, but you really are. I still think women are complicated beyond belief, but you have helped me crawl my way through some things lately. I will never again make the "fat" mistake. In fact, the next time the subject came up I did exactly what you suggested. I held her, told her she was beautiful and asked her if there was anything she needed. Granted, her response wasn't what I was expecting (she said she needed an enema – apparently being constipated while pregnant isn't pleasant).

I am still going to put that in the win column.

In regard to your relationship situation I don't know how I can help you. It sounds like this John guy is the perfect guy. You tell me he knows exactly what to say. He's loaded. He gets along with your family, and he bought Hanson for you – what's not to love? Okay, I know he didn't exactly buy you Hanson, but I think you can catch my meaning. Here is my best attempt at engaging in "girl talk".

Stop being an idiot!

I know I just gave you the same advice you gave me but I'm a guy and when things make sense we tend to stick with them.

Are you trying to sabotage this? The fact that you still place your ex on the top three things that "fill your heart" is a bit disturbing. This is the same guy that broke your heart and left you in a smoking heap of utter despair. I can honestly say that the thought of my ex

144

does not make my list of things that fill my heart. In fact, if she were on any list at all it would probably be the "things that make me want to punch a wall" list. Some other items on that list are baby proofing gadgets, all books related to child rearing, sometimes my brother and sometimes myself. Maybe you need to make a new list.

As always, I close with my confession. I'm pretty sure I don't like the whole marriage thing. I'm only three months in and I'm finding it more and more difficult to find any enjoyment in it. Drew was probably right. Kids this early on does complicate things.

Of course, I'll never tell him he was right.

Signed,
The guy who thinks lists are pointless
Derek

To: derekgrichards109@yahoo.com

From: seizethemoment69@gmail.com

August 14th 2008 6:45 a.m.

Subject: I love lists!!!!

Derek,

There is an art to list making and I resent your dislike for them. Many a times my lists have saved my life. Literally SAVED my life. You can doubt this but I was on the verge of dying from stress when moving to Arizona, but my lists saved me. I wouldn't have been able to get through the move without them. And to prove just how vital they are I have decided to include a brand-new list in this very email.

Addy's Brand-New List – For Derek's Benefit

Things that make me want to punch a wall
1. People who cut in line (hate em)
2. People on their cell phones in the middle of a movie theater (I mean come on people!)
3. Climate change deniers (How can all our carbon emissions and added pollution to the atmosphere not have an effect? Just saying.)
4. Misspelled tattoos (Did you not proofread it before they inked you? And if you did and you still missed it then you need to go back to school and should not be placing permanent things on your body)
5. Celebrities who think they have any right to lecture us common folk on how to live our lives (just make your movies,

146

sing your songs and leave us alone, it sure is easy to pass judgement when you can drop a cool 50k on a plate at a "fundraiser")

6. *When someone dies prematurely and without purpose (not that those deaths usually do have a purpose)*
7. *Bees that sting me (it hurts)*
8. *My car when it acts up (he's a jerk sometimes)*
9. *Bugs that decide to fly into my mouth, thus making me swallow them (yuck)*

And the final item on my list....drum roll please....

10. *Derek's stupid face when he makes fun of my lists!*

I hereby challenge you to make your very own list and share it with me. This will be your confession as mine was my confession. And just for the record, I wasn't left in a "smoking heap of utter despair". It was a normal mess of despair. No smoke.

Addy

To: seizethemoment69@gmail.com

From: derekgrichards109@yahoo.com

August 24ᵗʰ 2008 5:18 p.m.

Subject: Challenge accepted

Addy,

You think you are clever giving me this challenge, but I will crush it. I'm not going to give you just one list, nope, you, my friend will be getting two lists.

List 1 – Things I find irritating about Addy

1. *She's always right (it's very annoying)*
2. *Her laugh (really, it's like a witches heckle. You really should never laugh again)*
3. *Her obsession with Hanson (stalker alert)*
4. *Her horrible diet (how much candy have you consumed lately?)*
5. *Her utter lack of skill with throwing quarters in a coffee cup (never gamble on basketball)*
6. *The way she is able to get me to admit things like how I'm afraid of old ladies that play bingo (don't judge me, those ladies are serious)*
7. *That she doesn't have any similar ridiculous fears (you have to be hiding something- and I don't believe for a minute that you are actually afraid of bunnies)*
8. *How she can irritate me but still be cute (it's really rather disgusting – ick)*
9. *That she has a way better email address than I do (jerk)*
10. *Did I mention how she is always right? (Nobody likes a know-it-all)*

148

List 2 – Things I have done since meeting Addy

1. *Started believing in serendipity (don't laugh at me)*
2. *Begun to reevaluate what I want out of life (I hate my job. Absolutely hate it)*
3. *Read my father's journal (most of it)*
4. *Reconnected with my mother*
5. *Seriously thinking about giving Drew the benefit of the doubt and actually talking to him*
6. *Got my girlfriend pregnant (isn't there some way to prevent that? Oops, too late now)*
7. *Married my pregnant girlfriend (Go me!)*
8. *Went Surfing (I stunk)*
9. *Listened to Hanson (not my finest moment but you convinced me to give them a shot – they are not for me)*
10. *Started believing that she's right about forgiveness and the power it has*

So, there they are – my lists. My confessions.

Signed,
Someone who is starting to see the benefits of lists
Derek

To: derekgrichards109@yahoo.com

From: seizethemoment69@gmail.com

September 5th 2008 9:36 p.m.

Subject: Happy Birthday to me

Derek,

It's my birthday today.

At approximately 9:30 this morning I turned 23.

At approximately 9:45 I realized I'm a terrible person.

This marks the first birthday of mine that I have not spent with my family. Of course I woke saddened by this. I miss my family terribly and have been struggling with the distance. I know I just need to get over it. I'm an adult now and this is what you're supposed to do when you grow up – get a job and move out. I'm doing everything I'm supposed to do, and I still can't seem to be satisfied. I have an amazing boyfriend – one that surprised me with breakfast in bed. He made this amazing omelet and squeezed fresh juice with no pulp because I hate the pulp. He knows how much I hate the pulp. Nobody besides my mother has ever removed the pulp from my orange juice before. But John did.

It wasn't until I noticed he had taken out the pulp that I started crying. Full on ugly crying. John is so smooth, he didn't panic. He just pulled me into his arms and asked me what was wrong. I couldn't say anything at first other than "the pulp" and I just cried while he held me. He waited for me to calm down and asked again. I told him I missed my family, and he hugged me and said he understood.

But how could he understand? His family works with him! We spend nearly every weekend at some family function of his.

150

There is no way he understands and that was what I was thinking when he said he had something that might cheer me up.

He gave me an envelope and I opened it to find two tickets to Paris. He's saying surprise and I'm staring at these tickets holding them like they are diseased. There is definitely something wrong with me because I dropped the tickets like they burned me and just started shaking my head. I told him there was no possible way I could go to Paris now. He said the tickets aren't for another two weeks and I still said no. He laughed, made some joke about how he can guarantee my boss will let me have the time off.

Something just snapped in me.

I flipped the tray of food over when I got out of the bed and started pacing like a mad woman. I told him I couldn't do it. I couldn't leave Zilla all alone. I just kept going on about how I couldn't leave my dog again. John's response was to tell me Zilla could be kenneled again like the last time we went on a trip, and I lost it. I'm serious, Derek, I completely lost my shit and said I wasn't going to abandon my baby.

It wasn't until the words left my lips that I realized how nuts I was being. The room got awkwardly silent. Then John said it was just a dog. Of course, this only enraged me further and I yelled at him to get out. He tried to touch me, and I slapped his hand away and shouted at him to leave. I wish you could have heard the sigh he let out. It was deafening.

He got his things and went to leave but before he left, he said I wasn't being fair to him. He said he shouldn't have to compete with a dog. He said he loved me and when I was ready, he would be waiting. Then he left.

I am the absolute worst girlfriend in the world.

Who freaks out because of tickets to Paris? The tickets are still sitting on my bed, right where I dropped them.

I probably should have run after him or at the very least called him after I had calmed down. But I didn't do either of those things. I should have called my family or answered the phone when they called me to wish me a happy birthday, but I didn't.

About 30 minutes after John left, I went to the fridge and took out a bottle of wine. I have been drinking ever since, crying into my wine glass. Zilla has been by my side the whole day. He's even cried with me a couple of times. Poor guy. He has no clue what is going on, but he refused to leave me.

I know he isn't my baby.

Because I can't have babies.

Ever.

I haven't told John about that.

We haven't exactly had that conversation, but I know he wants kids. I hear him talking to his parents about the future. I don't know why I haven't told him. I know I need to. I'm not being fair to him at all, and he has been absolutely fantastic with everything. I'm the basket case and he just keeps loving me. I'm not exactly feeling worthy of that love today.

Thankfully I have my wine.

And my dog.

Addy

Confession – I tell my dog I love him all the time, but I've ever only said I love you to John twice.

Journal Entry

August 18, 2006

Love is a funny thing.

It's been over two weeks since I've been "home" with Carol and out of rehab. It only took me 3 hours to realize this place no longer felt like home. It hadn't felt like a home in many years. I told Carol what I was feeling, and she agreed. The very next day we contacted a realtor. We got a call today that there is an offer on the house. The house where she raised our children. I had a moment of slight panic when the realization hit that I would be saying goodbye to the house that held so many of my good memories. I told Carol what I was feeling.

This is new to me – sharing my feelings with my wife.

She told me she was a little sad to say goodbye to the house too, but that this was a goodbye that needed to happen. She's right.

She told Drew we were finally selling the house and he actually came over. He didn't talk to me at first. He told Carol he wasn't here for me. He was here to say goodbye to the house – the house he loved as a kid. I suppose at one point we all loved this house. These walls had witnessed it all. The good, the bad and the very bad.

It wasn't until he was finished collecting the things he wanted to take with him that he finally talked to me. He asked me how I was feeling. I told him I was feeling shame. My answer surprised him.

After years of telling everyone, I was "fine" I doubt he was expecting that for an answer. He asked me what I meant. I told him that the house that had once brought me pride now made me feel ashamed for the man I had become in it. I told him I carried the shame of what I had done to his mother, him and my other kids and that it was a constant on my heart. He didn't expect that answer either.

153

He just nodded, didn't say anything else before he went to his mother, kissed her goodbye and left.

Drew had always been our pensive, older child. Where Mary was carefree and Derek was stubborn, Drew always watched in silence. The meaning behind his choice to become a cop is not lost on me. He had been my shadow when he was little, always trying to follow in my footsteps, trying to make me proud.

When he told Carol it would be okay if we joined him for lunch one day I finally told him what I should have told him long ago – I was proud of him. Proud of the man he had become. I told him he was the kind of father I wasn't, and I told him I was sorry. Always the pensive son he just shrugged and said it was fine. I smirked at that.

Carol is right – he is my carbon copy in a lot of ways. When we parted I hugged him and told him I loved him. He hugged me back and said he loved me.

As an addict I had placed the warped love I had for my addiction over the love I had for my family. I had forgotten how comforting the love of a family is. Love has been used to justify the simplest of actions, and the most bizarre. Wars were waged in the name of love. I feel like every day is a constant struggle to fight off the allure of fake love – my addiction. Thank God for Carol and my children. I am only able to make it due to their Grace. It is because of their love that I am able to carry on. I just pray that I am able to make amends to Derek before I go. He deserves to know that I love him, even if he doesn't want me to.

Love is such a funny thing.

Gary T. Richards

To: seizethemoment69@gmail.com
From: derekgrichards109@yahoo.com
September 9th 2008 6:22 a.m.
Subject: I'm terrible, you're not

Addy,

You are not a terrible person. You are one of the kindest people I know. Everyone freaks out in relationships and if you don't want to go to Paris, then don't go. And if you don't want to tell John about your past, then don't. You don't have to do anything you don't want to do. I hope you've called your family by now but if you haven't – CALL THEM! Go see them if you have to. I know how it feels to miss family.

As for John – do you love him? If you don't, walk away. No good can come from prolonging the inevitable. Sometimes, it just isn't right. Maybe you've known that all along.

I'm struggling with this email. I want to be able to tell you that everything will be alright. I want to be able to hold you in my arms and tell you everything will be alright. I want to be able to drink wine with you and see you ugly cry. I want to be able to give you a damn cake on your birthday and show you just how special you are because you are not a terrible person. You are fucking amazing and it's pissing me off that I can't do any of those things for you.

You aren't the terrible one, Addy. I am.

I'm terrible because after I read your email all I wanted to do was get on a damn plane and go to you. I wanted to leave my pregnant wife here and go to you. It isn't my wife that enters my mind when it wanders.

It's you.

And if that wasn't enough to convince you how terrible I am this will – even though I know I need to walk away from this I can't. And I'm begging you not to walk away either. I don't know exactly why, but I need you in my life.

Signed

Derek

P.s. I'm sorry. So sorry.

To: derekgrichards109@yahoo.com
From: seizethemoment69@gmail.com
September 15th 2008 12:15 p.m.
Subject: We are both terrible

Derek,

    If you are terrible than so am I. Because I can't seem to walk away from you either.

    I ended things with John. I had to. I didn't tell him about being unable to have kids. I just told him we wanted different things. Of course he was predictably perfect about it. It was all rather civil. The nicest break-up I've ever had. I asked to be transferred to another department because I didn't think I could continue to work so closely with him, and he agreed. He even shook my hand after and told me he wished me well. It was all so civil, and it absolutely killed me.

    I needed him to shout at me. To tell me I was awful and that I was hurting him and that I was evil. I needed to be told I'm terrible because I am. I was horrible to him. The worst girlfriend ever and I'm not even a good friend. If I was, I would tell you how this is wrong. That the thought of never talking to you again frightens me more than never seeing John again is just wrong.

    I don't know when this happened, or how. How could you possibly mean more to me after only spending a few hours with you than a man I've spent eight months with? None of this makes any sense to me. I don't even know what this is. I just know that I look forward to your emails. Sometimes your emails are the only thing that cheers me up.

We need to end this. You're married. You're having a baby!

I'm an awful person.

I'm sorry too.

Addy

To: seizethemoment69@gmail.com

From: derekgrichards109@yahoo.com

September 23rd 2008 8:48 a.m.

Subject: What now?

Addy,

I'm not going to walk away. I can't. I can't stop from ending contact and I am asking you not to. You are important to me. So please, don't go.

Maybe we just need some time to…hell, I don't know…refocus or something.

Signed,

Always your friend

Derek

To: derekgrichards109@yahoo.com

From: seizethemoment69@gmail.com

September 30ᵗʰ 2008 2:35 p.m.

Subject: Friends

Derek,

I took some time. I refocused.

You are my friend. I am your friend.

We've shared things with one another that we haven't shared with others. That is bound to bring forth feelings of closeness. That is what we are feeling. A strong friendship. I would feel sad if anybody that I had shared these things with was no longer in my life.

Tell me about your life right now. How is Liv? The baby? Is your mother still staying with you? What about work?

I start my new position next week. It's actually a promotion. Guess I never had to ask John for one – I just had to break up with him.

Sorry, that's a bad joke.

Zilla is still great. He hasn't chewed on a pair of shoes in weeks. He is still favors C-SPAN but he lets me watch other networks every now and then.

Addy

To: seizethemoment69@gmail.com

From: derekgrichards109@yahoo.com

October 10th 2008 6:23 a.m.

Subject: Life

Addy,

> *I hope your new position is everything you want it to be.*

> *My mother is still here. She splits her time now between us and my sister's. After my dad died, she left the apartment they had been living in and was staying with Mary, my sister. She says she likes being by her kids and grandkids. She had been a godsend for Liv and I. Liv is having a hard time with the pregnancy and has been ordered to strict bed rest. I doubt I'm doing anything right. I feel so useless sometimes. That is usually when my mom swoops in and saves the day.*

> *Work is work. I hate it. I dread going in every day but what else can I do? Gotta pay the bills.*

> *Tell Zilla I said hello.*

Signed

Derek

Journal Entry

September 1, 2006

I don't know why I keep writing in this thing. I thought for sure I would stop this practice after I left rehab, but I find an odd sort of comfort writing all this down. It helps me clear my head and sift through the thoughts. They get jumbled sometimes. Especially on the days when I'm not feeling to good.

I have more good days than bad. The doctors say that is a good thing. It's when I start having more bad days than good when the end will be near.

The end.

It is so simple to write that and place a period – the end.

It isn't easy to picture though. I still haven't been able to get Derek to answer any of my letters or phone calls. Carol told me to call him. She also asked me to let Mary and Drew tell him that they'd been talking to me, but I wouldn't let her. I know my son. If he knew his sister and brother were talking to me, he would only be upset with them. I don't want him to be mad at them. I can handle him being upset with me because I deserve it, but the others don't. Carol said she had already told Derek she was living with me again. She didn't say but I knew he wasn't happy about that. My wife has never been very good at concealing things because her face betrays her every time.

I think I keep writing in this thing because deep down I know that I will not get a second chance with Derek. Drew may be my carbon copy, but Derek is his mother's. Stubborn, loyal and steadfast. He sticks to his ideals, and he decided long ago that I was beyond redemption. I don't blame him. I never gave him any reason to think I was worthy of his love. For the longest time I wasn't.

I can die knowing he is mad at me, that he will never forgive me.

162

But what I can't die with is him thinking I never loved him. That I don't love him today.

And that is why I keep writing. If I am never able to speak to him again then these words will be all I have left. A last ditch effort to let my son know that this broken man is sorry for what he did and that he has never stopped loving his son.

Gary T. Richards

To: derekgrichards109@yahoo.com

From: seizethemoment69@gmail.com

October 17th 2008 12:03 a.m.

Subject: Checking in

Derek,

  Just checking in. Things are going smoothly here. New position seems promising. The staff I oversee are friendly and seem to be a really good team. It'll be nice to be in charge of projects instead of assisting.

  Zilla's chew free streak was broken yesterday. Another pair of flip flops gone. At least he has become selective to just cheap flip flops. Those are easily replaced.

  My parents are coming in for a visit at the end of the month. That was a nice surprise. They will be staying for a whole week.

  What would you rather be doing for your job? It sucks that you hate it so much.

Addy

To: seizethemoment69@gmail.com
From: derekgrichards109@yahoo.com
October 20ᵗʰ 2008 4:16 p.m.
Subject: ?????

Addy,

   I have no clue what I would rather be doing. Four years of college and I never was able to figure it out. I just went through the motions of going to class and when it came closer to graduation, I just picked a major that fit with the classes I had taken. In hindsight that was not the best strategy.

   Good to hear you like your promotion. And that Zilla doesn't have expensive tastes in chewing. I'm sure your visit with your family will be good too.

Signed
Derek

P.s. Why is this so awkward now? Did I completely mess this up?

To: derekgrichards109@yahoo.com

From: seizethemoment69@gmail.com

October 24th 2008 9:55 a.m.

Subject: ???? 2.0

Derek,

You didn't mess anything up and this does feel awkward. I find myself struggling to write things to you because I can't write what I really want to. The words are in my head but every time I go to type them my hands freeze.

What are we doing to each other?

I think we need to take some time away from writing for a while. It's for the best.

Addy

Email

To: seizethemoment69@gmail.com

From: derekgrichards109@yahoo.com

November 2nd 2008 3:12 a.m.

Subject: I miss you

Addy,

I miss my friend.

Signed

Derek

To: derekgrichards109@yahoo.com

From: seizethemoment69@gmail.com

November 3rd 2008 11:37 a.m.

Subject: I miss you too

Derek,

I also miss my friend.

Addy

To: seizethemoment69@gmail.com

From: derekgrichards109@yahoo.com

November 12th 2008 5:42 p.m.

Subject: this hurts

Addy,

Nothing about us makes any sense. I've tried to figure out why I feel the way I do about you, but I just can't. That one day I spent with you at the airport has just been playing over and over again in my mind. I wanted to kiss you so bad. I wanted to touch you. I regret letting you get on that plane without kissing you just once.

Now, I can't seem to stop thinking about your lips. I think about you all the time. There isn't a moment that passes in which you are not in it. I wonder what you're doing, how you are, what you're wearing. Sometimes I imagine you sitting on your couch, Zilla beside you and I am jealous of your dog. I want to be the one sitting next to you, touching you.

I miss you so damn much it hurts.

Signed

Derek

Confession: I'm in love with you. I think I've been in love with you for a while now.

To: derekgrichards109@yahoo.com
From: seizethemoment69@gmail.com
November 15ᵗʰ 2008 1:31 p.m.
Subject: I know

Derek,

I think I've loved you for a while too. I've loved you since the day you told me chocolate makes you fart. I don't know why. Your irrational fear of old ladies playing bingo and your flatulence should be enough to send me running but I think it's things like that that made me fall for you. And then you had to go and tell me you would have been the man I needed if it had been you with me when I lost the baby. When I read those words, I wished that it had been you. You are the man I wanted by my side that day. The man I want by my side today. You are kind and loyal.

So loyal in fact you got married to a woman you didn't love for the sake of your unborn child.

You are a good man Derek, and I am no good for you.

This is no good for you.

Addy

To: seizethemoment69@gmail.com
From: derekgrichards109@yahoo.com
November 16th 2008 12:10 a.m.
Subject: Don't say that

Addy,

You are good for me. Sometimes I think you are the only good thing I have in my life. I'm not the man you think I am. If I was that man, then I wouldn't have fallen for you. I wouldn't say what I'm about to say.

I'm going to leave Liv. I want to be with you. I'll figure things out. I need to be with you.

Signed
The man that loves you
Derek

Email

To: derekgrichards109@yahoo.com

From: seizethemoment69@gmail.com

November 17th 2008 8:00 a.m.

Subject: Are you sure?

Derek,

Only say those things if you are absolutely sure. You have so much more to lose than I do. I love you and I don't want you to regret anything.

Addy

To: seizethemoment69@gmail.com
From: derekgrichards109@yahoo.com
November 18th 2008 12:10 a.m.
Subject: No regrets

Addy,

The only regret I have is losing your damn email and waiting so damn long to figure this out. I meant everything I wrote. I don't know how this is going to work but I know I want you. I promise I will figure this out somehow.

Signed
Derek

P.s. You are an amazing woman Addy. You made me fall in love with you through email.

Journal Entry

December 7, 2006

This is a day of remembrance of the greatest sacrifice one can give for their country. Lives lost in service to a nation and a people.

A day of infamy.

I spent the day at Mary's house, surrounded by my family. Derek is away at college. Carol and Mary keep me filled in on what he is doing. They told me he had recently broken up with a girl that he loved. They said she broke his heart. A father should be there for his son when the girl he loves leaves. I should be there for him. I want to be there for him, but the decision isn't mine to make.

I used to think that I made sacrifices all the time for my family, but I know now that it was always them that sacrificed. If only I could turn back time and reclaim all that I lost. I want to do right by my family now and I think I'm doing that for Mary and Drew.

Carol, my rock, my angel is still by my side, still loving me. I don't deserve her but I'm going to hold on to her for as long as she'll have me.

Sometimes I think I'm being foolish by not going to him. So much time being wasted. I would sacrifice whatever time I have left if it meant I was able to spend one full day with all of my family together.

I can only hope that one day I can realize my own personal vision of a day of infamy, one where there is only joy and laughter, and not sacrifice.

Gary T. Richards

To: seizethemoment69@gmail.com

From: derekgrichards109@yahoo.com

November 18th 2008 9:07 a.m.

Subject: Please forgive me

Addy,

Liv had the baby. I have a daughter. She's perfect. I'm a father.

I meant everything I said. I love you. I love you so damn much. I wanted to be with you, have a life with you.

Liv found our emails. I must have left my account open after I sent you the last email and she saw it when she got up to go to the bathroom. She read everything we wrote to each other. She woke me and I told her I was in love with you and that I wanted to be with you.

She went into labor. She wouldn't let me touch her while she gave birth to our daughter. She refused to look at me. Afterwards, when I was holding my daughter in my arms Liv told me to choose.

I'm so sorry, Addy. Please don't hate me. I'll always love you, but I choose my daughter.

I have to.

Love

Derek

Email

To: derekgrichards109@yahoo.com

From: seizethemoment69@gmail.com

November 18th 2008 3:02 p.m.

Subject: none

Derek,

I don't understand what is happening. I mean, I understand Liv found the emails and that she made you choose but I'm not asking you to leave your daughter. I'm not! I would never do such a thing. It's like you said – whatever it takes, we can make this work.

I can move to Colorado! I hate my job anyway and your daughter is there. I can quit tomorrow, pack my bags, get in my car and be there in a few days. Neither of us has to choose between being together or not being together. I know this isn't going to be easy but I'm in, I'm all in

.

Reasons why Derek and Addy should be together

1. *We know all our secrets*
2. *We make each other laugh*
3. *We love each other (you think that should be first, but I think numbers one and two brought us to number three)*
4. *We couldn't even go a month without talking to the other*
5. *It hurts too much to be apart*
6. *Together we can figure this out*
7. *We both secretly love Hanson and Disney movies*
8. *We belong together (it's not as cliché as you think it is because some people just fit)*
9. *We Fit*
10. *I don't want to lose my best friend*

Tell me what you need, and I'll do it. But please don't give up on us.

I love you.
Addy

Email

To: seizethemoment69@gmail.com
From: mailcentral@gmail.com
November 18th 2008 3:04 p.m.
RE: Subject: none

Email Error code 554 message. Undelivered mail returned to sender.

11 The Homecoming

Cursing, Addy slams the door to her Honda Civic and treks through the snow to examine her back tire. Sure enough, it's flatter than flat can be. Throwing her head back, Addy looks up to the overcast sky.

"Really? You just couldn't let me be, could you?" she calls up to the heavens above. The overcast sky does not respond and she lets out a frustrated grunt as she thinks about how her return home has been nothing but one giant metaphor for how twisted her life has been the last eight years. It was just one pothole after another.

This entire road trip had been nothing but a major headache. This is her third flat tire in the nearly 1,800 mile drive from Arizona to Wisconsin. The first flat tire occurred in Kansas and the second in Missouri. Her windshield had taken a rock in New Mexico and was sporting a nifty crack from one end to the other. It was a wonder how she made it through Iowa without incident. She wasn't counting the hot coffee she spilled on herself as an incident since it didn't involve her car, just her clumsiness.

Laughing, she thinks about how her love life, or rather lack thereof, also resembled this road trip. She was finally in a place where she had forgiven Clark for letting her down all those years ago. After her breakup with John she realized just how young they both had been and how terrified Clark was about the pregnancy. He never meant to hurt her and knowing everything she knew now, they were never right for each other. Just like her and John weren't right together. He had gotten married a few years back and now had two young children with his beautiful, blonde wife. She had actually gone to the wedding, and it was at that wedding she realized she needed a change.

So, here she stood on the side of the road in the snow during a Wisconsin December. As she looked around at the mounds of white, she once again asked herself why, after nine years, she had decided it was a good idea to move back home. For nine years she had only had to endure snow when she came home to visit during the holidays, and she always loved the winter wonderland during those visits, but she was thankful to return to sunny Arizona.

Well, there was no point standing here staring at the blasted tire and thinking of the sun and warmth she left behind. Squaring her shoulders she goes to her trunk and begins assembling the items she would need. Just as she's pulling the spare from its hiding place, she hears Zilla start barking. The poor dog has been cooped up in the packed car for days now. If Addy was going crazy than she was sure Zilla was too.

"It's okay Zilla. I'll get it fixed in no time," she grunts as she struggles to get a grasp on the spare.

"Ma'am, do you need assistance?" A very masculine voice calls out from her left. She freezes. She is all alone on a side street where there is virtually no civilization and her only "weapon" is locked in the backseat of the car, barking his head off.

Oh, please don't let this be the day I get murdered.

Straightening, Addy grabs the tire iron out of the trunk. She might be able to get a few good whacks in before he kills her.

"Ma'am?" the voice calls to her again, much closer.

"No. I'm ,"- Addy's voice trails off when she sees the man approaching her.

He is a uniformed police officer. His cruiser is idling on the opposite side of the road, pulled to the side to allow traffic through. She takes in the rest of his appearance and notes that while his

181

physique seems intimidating his eyes are kind. As she studies him, Addy comes to the conclusion, based on his hair cut and the way he holds himself, that he has a military background. He seems to have maintained his physical fitness as his arms are practically bulging out of his uniform. She notices portions of a tattoo underneath the sleeve of his left arm.

"Thank you, officer. I seem to have a flat tire. I would appreciate any help you can give," Addy says, still holding on to the tire iron because these days you never know.

"Very well. Let's see how bad the damage is," the officer says and kneels down by the tire. "Do you have a spare?"

"I do," Addy says and gestures to the trunk, where the spare sits. After the last flat tire, she bought another just in case. Continuous tows were not in her travel budget.

"Alright. Will your dog be alright if I jack up this side?" He asks and gestures to Zilla, still barking in the back seat.

"If you don't mind, I'm going to take him out so he can stretch. He's friendly. Please don't let this show of bravado fool you, he's a softy," Addy says and waits for the officer to tell her he is fine with the dog being free. Addy lets Zilla out and he immediately runs over to the officer, tail wagging, all remnants of menacing barking forgotten as he tries to make a new friend.

"See? My great protector," Addy jokes. The officer chuckles and pets Zilla.

"Do you mind if I get the items I need?"

"No. Please, you're saving me," Addy says and steps to the side so the officer can get the tire, jack, and other tools.

"Where you coming from?" he asks as he gets to work placing the jack.

"Arizona. I'm actually from here but I moved away nine years ago. This is officially my homecoming. Wisconsin hates me," Addy

182

says and keeps one eye on the officer and the other on Zilla, who is sniffing the ground searching for the perfect spot.

"I was stationed in Arizona many years ago. Not much grass. And too many snakes," the officer says as he secures the jack and begins to lift the car.

"That is true."

"Nice and warm, though."

"That is also true. Zilla, not too far," Addy calls to her wandering dog. He lifts his head, tongue hanging out the side of his mouth, flopping. He happily zooms through the snow.

"He seems to enjoy it here," the officer gestures to Zilla with the tire iron.

"Yeah. It's the snow. He adores it. Can I help you with anything?" Addy kneels down.

"Make sure I don't lose any of the lug nuts in this snow," he says and hands them over as he removes them. She places each one in the trunk. Once he has the flat removed, he stands to get the spare out.

"So, this is a permanent move then?" He asks, noticing the boxes in the trunk and back seat.

"Sure is. My sister and her wife had their second child, and I was tired of being the distant Aunt. Family is too important to miss out on," Addy explains. The officer smiles and she has a brief moment of déjà vu before she recovers and smiles back.

"You are right about that. My son is nearly ready to graduate high school, and I don't know where the time has gone. He was a baby yesterday. My niece and nephews are growing way to fast as well. You definitely miss the days when they are little," the officer screws the lug nuts on to the new tire as Addy hands them over.

"Yeah. I've been away for far too long."

Once the tire has been secured, the jack lowered and removed they both stood up. While the officer puts the tools and flat tire in the trunk Addy calls to Zilla. He lifts his head out of the snow and comes bounding over, tongue flopping the entire time. He is nearly ten years old, but he still acts like a young pup.

"Thank you so much for stopping and helping," Addy says after she gets Zilla back in the car.

"It's not a problem. Welcome home," he says and sticks out his hand to shake hers.

She smiles, takes his hand and gives it a friendly shake.

"Thank you, officer…" she trails off, trying to read his name plate.

"Richards. Andrew Richards. Take care, ma'am," he says and turns to walk back to his cruiser.

Addy remains stuck to the ground he left.

Richards. Andrew. Drew Richards.

His smile.

A face flashes in her memory and Addy turns to watch the cruiser drive away.

It couldn't be, she thinks.

12 The Family Gathering

December is a hard month for the Richards family. Ever since Gary passed away, the Christmas holiday held a sense of loss. Derek didn't understand it. After all, he hadn't reconciled with his father before he passed, but the others had. The loss they felt was not the same kind of loss he felt around this time of year. They mourned the man's absence due to death. Derek mourned for the time he lost while the man was alive.

The last remnant he had of his father was sitting on the dashboard of his cruiser. The journal that he continued to read over again the past eight years. After he had finished reading it the first time, he had given it to his siblings to read too. His mother said she didn't need to read it because in the last year before Gary's death he had told her everything she needed to know. Once Drew had finished reading it the journal was once again placed in Derek's care and there it remained.

He didn't just read it to himself. When his daughter was just a little baby he had begun reading the entries to her, a tradition he continued to this day. Of course he screened out the particularly dark ones. Those would be saved for when she was older. She had just turned eight and acted like she was twenty. She had her mother's spunk and her father's stubbornness. She was perfect and God save any boy that would one day come knocking, trying to date her.

Thankfully, that day was a long way off still.

With thoughts of his daughter and father in his head, Derek reaches for the journal and flips to his favorite passage. As he's reading a cold nose suddenly touches his arm and he laughs.

"Sorry, Phoenix. I know this day is shaping up to be a bit of a bore," Derek says to his K-9 partner and gently scratches his head. The dog is sitting in the passenger seat, silently looking at Derek. When he had been assigned to this dog he had taken an odd sort of comfort from the dog's name. It reminded him of a person that still, to this day, was very important to him.

Suddenly, another cruiser approaches and stops beside his. Derek puts the journal down and rolls the window down. This winter was colder than he preferred and the snap of icy air hit his face immediately.

"You heading over to Mary's after your shift?" Drew calls out to him from the other cruiser.

"Yeah. Gotta take Phoenix home first but I'll be there. You bringing Connor?" Derek asks his brother about his oldest nephew.

"Yep. Tammy is out of town for the next two weeks, so he is with me. I'm heading back to the station to finish up some paperwork. See you this evening. Don't be late," Drew calls off in parting and drives away before Derek can respond.

"Dick," he mutters to the departing vehicle.

The two brothers had gotten closer over the years, despite a rough spot nearly three years ago, but Drew sometimes fell into old habits of managing Derek. It was true Derek used to have a problem with being on time but that was over ten years ago, and he was always on time now.

Well, mostly he was on time.

It had taken Derek some time to swallow his pride and bury the resentment he had once harbored for his brother. Foolishly, he had spent years thinking his brother was simply their father two point oh. He thought Drew's drinking had driven away his ex-wife, Tammy. Turns out, she had cheated on him multiple times over the years –

hence Drew's drinking. Drew stood by her, believing their problems were due to the military lifestyle and his continued absence.

Unfortunately, his ex-wife's wandering continued after he had left the service, and it wasn't until she decided she no longer wanted to be married that they had divorced. After he discovered the history of his brother's divorce Derek actually thought about all the times he had seen his older brother so wasted he couldn't stand and he recalled how Tammy had always been cold and distant to Drew.

Thankfully, Drew was no longer that man.

The rest of Derek's shift passes without any major incidents and a few hours later he is walking up to his sister's house with a bottle of wine in hand. Christmas is next week but his sister and mother think the entire month of December is Christmas and have a few gatherings throughout the month. This one marks the fourth family gathering and Christmas Day will be the fifth. Then there is the annual New Years party Mary throws. It has taken them many years to finally have every member in the same state again and the females in the family milk every minute of it.

Mary and her husband, David, used to move frequently when he was in the Air Force and Drew was often relocating during his time in the Army. Derek had moved back home six years ago when his daughter was two and his marriage was failing. They thought being closer to family would help them patch things up, but you couldn't fix something that had been broken long before it even began.

Liv and he had separated three months after moving back home and he left his job to become a police officer. Both were decisions he had never once regretted. Surprisingly, his divorce had been very amicable. Turned out moving back home near family had been the right decision because both he and Liv were much happier. They were also much happier not being married to each other.

Sometimes it doesn't matter how much you try to force things because you can't fit a square peg into a round hole. It was that simple – Liv and he had never fit together.

He could hear the sound of laughter coming from inside Mary's house as he approached the door. Knowing it would be open; Derek turns the knob and walks into the warm foyer. He hears some running and then the voice of his sister calling out to the children to stop running in the house. Derek smiles, shakes out of his jacket, hangs it up because his sister would kill him if he didn't, and walks to join the others.

"Daddy!" he hears as soon as he enters the kitchen.

Quickly, he puts the wine bottle on the counter and opens his arms up to the love of his life. His daughter runs into his arms and clings to his neck as he lifts her and twirls her around. Derek kisses the top of her head.

"How's my little princess, today?" he asks.

"I'm not a princess today, Daddy," Molly says and laughs.

"No? Then what are you, Fairy?" he asks, using the nickname that has belonged to her since the day she was born.

"I'm a tiger!" she says and growls at him, turning her hands into claws.

"Well, I better put you back down then before you eat me," Derek kisses her cheek and puts her down. Molly growls at him one last time before turning to find one of her cousins. She is the spitting image of her mother, jet black hair and olive skin. She is going to be just as stunning as her mother.

"The two of you together is adorable," Mary says from the counter as she puts a casserole in the oven.

"Thanks. Where's Ma?" Derek asks as he steps over to his sister to give her a kiss on the cheek as well. A customary greeting that his mother started when they were younger to instill manners in her boys.

"In the living room with the others," Mary says and tilts her head in the direction of the room.

"Thanks. Smells good, Sis," Derek says. Before he leaves the kitchen, he grabs a beer, twists off the top and discards the cap in the trash. Entering the living room, he goes directly to his mother. She sits in an armchair; her knitting in her lap and her fingers busily creating her next masterpiece.

"Evening, Ma," Derek says, bending to kiss her cheek. She tilts her face towards him and smiles.

"Hello, my little boy," she says. He's nearly thirty-one years old but she still calls him her little boy.

"You're late," Drew calls to him from the sofa.

"Two minutes doesn't count," he calls back and gives his brother a shove in the shoulder.

Drew smirks, turns to his wife and asks, "What do you say, Liv, does two minutes count?"

"Late is late," Liv shrugs.

"Why did you two get married again? I liked it better when you didn't talk to each other," Derek says to his brother and ex-wife, the mother of his child.

When Drew came to him three years ago and said he had feelings for Liv, Derek's initial reaction had been anger. He felt like his brother was betraying him. There had been some harsh words exchanged and possibly a few punches. Derek lost.

After the dust had settled Derek realized he was being a jack ass. Liv was a great woman, and his brother was a decent man and they both deserved to be happy. They had been married for two years now and were that annoying couple that still acted like newlyweds. It was really rather gross to witness.

Just as he thought that Drew leaned over and started making out with his wife while Derek, their mother and David, their brother-in-law were in the room.

"Get a room!" Mary calls out as she enters. She sits down next to David, and he immediately reaches out for her hand. Derek watches as they lock fingers, all the time David's gaze is fixated on the television.

"What are you watching?" Derek asks, sits on the other side of Drew, and turns to the t.v.

"C-SPAN," David replies.

Derek is immediately taken back to a time passed but not forgotten. As quickly as the memories surface, he pushes them back down. No point dwelling on things that will never be.

He had made his choice all those years ago and while things hadn't exactly turned out as he expected he had a little girl that owned his heart. His daughter made the regret worth it. He still thought of Addy often and wondered how her life had turned out. He hoped she was happy. A few times he had even considered trying to contact her, but he knew that wouldn't be fair to her. She deserved so much more than a reappearance of the jack ass that made all these promises and broke them hours later.

"Where are the boys?" Derek asks Mary.

"Upstairs. Molly has them playing zookeeper. I swear, it doesn't matter that they are all teenagers, they will do anything that girl wants," Mary responds.

"It's because she has her mother's charms," Drew says and he pokes his wife in the side, eliciting a giggle.

"Eh, gag," Derek says before taking a drink from his beer. Drew elbows him, causing him to spill his beer.

"Ass," Drew says.

"Nerd," Derek retorts.

"Wimp."

"Pussy."

"Boys! Language!" Carol says, pausing her knitting to scold her boys.

"Sorry, Ma," they say in unison, and she nods, asserting her authority over them. The others ignore the incident because it is a common theme among the Richards boys.

"How was your day, Drew?" Carol asks her oldest.

"Uneventful. Mostly just traffic calls. I got to meet a new friend, today," Drew says and leans forward to grab his own beer from the coffee table.

"Oh? Who was that?" Carol asks; her attention back on the needles moving the yarn.

"He was black and white with a fluffy tail and an interesting name," Drew replies.

"What are you talking about?" Derek asks, his face scrunched in confusion.

"A dog. I helped a woman change her flat today and she had the cutest dog with her. Interesting name too."

"The woman?" Liv asked.

"No, the dog."

"Well, what was it?" Liv again.

"Zilla."

Derek spits the beer out that he had just been about to swallow. It cascades across the room, sprinkling David and Mary. They both start protesting and wiping at their faces.

"What did you just say?" Derek asks.

"The dog's name?" Drew asks, confused by his brother's reaction.

"Yes. What was the dog's name?" Derek puts his beer down and almost sounds desperate.

"Zilla. The dog's name was Zilla."

"What kind of dog was it?"

"I don't know. Black and white. Why?"

Derek glances around the room and notices all eyes are on him. Slowly, he picks his beer back up and leans back into the cushions, feigning indifference.

"No reason."

"You're mental," Drew says but drops the matter.

Derek only half listens as the conversations continue around him. There is absolutely no way this dog could possibly be the dog he is thinking of. What are the odds that the one woman he has never been able to forget suddenly moves into the same town as him? That would be impossible. But still, in the deepest part of him, he hopes it isn't.

13 _The Other Family_

December has always been one of the most joyous times for the Katz family. Julie and Addy had believed in Santa Claus until they were ten years old. Their parents were just that good at Christmas. Most children find out Santa isn't real by their peers but by some miracle neither Julie nor Addy had discovered the truth until a teacher had spilled the beans. Now, that Christmas hadn't been the most joyous, but it was still memorable.

This would be the first Christmas in years that Addy wouldn't have to hop on a plane a few days later and leave her family again. This time she would be present for every memory. December was definitely a joyous month indeed.

Struggling not to drop the bags full of gifts she held, Addy lifted a finger and pushed the doorbell at her sister's home. Rachel and Julie had bought the place a few years back when they decided they wanted to start a family after their marriage. Their first child, carried by Rachel, was now two years old. The second child, carried by Julie, was six months old. One boy, one girl and Addy couldn't wait to spoil them.

When the door opens, and Addy sees her father standing there she calls Zilla. He bounds out of the snowbank and runs inside the house, right at home. Mr. Katz laughs and steps aside for his daughter.

"Let me take those, Addy Kat," he says to his daughter and takes the bags from her hands.

"Thank you, Dad," Addy says, smiling at the nickname. When

her aunt and uncle had adopted her, and they officially became her Mom and Dad, her last name became Katz and her father loved to drop the 'z' from her name in a spin on "alley cat".

"The others are gathered in the kitchen, making the customary deserts," Mr. Katz tells his daughter. He takes the bags to the tree in the front room after closing the door. Removing her layers of winter gear, Addy goes to the kitchen.

"Addy!" Rachel calls when she sees her.

Rachel joyfully runs to her sister-in-law and embraces her. She is a plump woman compared to Addy and her hugs are always a comfort. When Julie had confessed to the family many years ago that Rachel was more than just her roommate, Addy gained a second sister. Rachel's presence in the family had solidified that day at breakfast when Julie tearfully told their parents she had been keeping a secret all those years. Today, those secrets are long forgotten.

"I've missed you," Addy says as she hugs back.

"We are so happy to have you home, finally," Julie says and joins the hug. Addy laughs as the three of them squeeze each other.

After the embrace ends, Addy goes to her mother, who is holding the baby. Addy signs a greeting, speaking aloud as she signs. Mrs. Katz nods, unable to respond as her hands held a feeding baby. Smiling, Addy goes to the table and greets her nephew.

"Hello Zachary. Remember me?" she asks the two-year-old.

"Kat!" he says and points at her.

"That's right. I'm Aunt Kat. I've missed you most of all," Addy says and picks her nephew up and dances with him in her arms. He laughs, claps, squeals with delight. This was what she had been missing all these years. It was good to be home.

"Don't spin him too much. He's been sneaking cookies all day and has a tendency to vomit when excited," Mr. Katz warns when he returns to the kitchen.

Heeding the warning, Addy puts her nephew back down.

"Well, the cavalry is here. Put me to work, Captain," Addy says to her sister-in-law.

"Wonderful! We finished with the sugar cookies, but we still haven't started on the snicker doodles. Would you mind getting those going?" Rachel steers Addy towards the island in the center of the kitchen where all the ingredients needed to make all kinds of deserts waited.

"Consider those doodles snickered," she says and salutes Rachel. Her family laughs and Addy gets to work.

As the family completes their tasks conversations flow, laughter rings out, and sporadic barking interject, begging for someone to drop a treat. Addy hasn't been this happy in a long time. Neither has Zilla for that matter. Zachary can't stop giving the dog bites of things that dogs should not be fed. Luckily, Zachary soon becomes bored and leaves the cooking tasks to play with the dog. Zilla was having the time of his life.

"When do you start your new job?" Mrs. Katz signs to Addy now that the baby was sleeping peacefully in her crib.

"Not until after the New Years," Addy signs back.

"Are you settled into your apartment?" Mr. Katz asks.

Everyone signs out of habit as they spoke aloud.

"Mostly. I downsized before I moved. The movers dropped everything off last week and I have a few more boxes to unpack. I like it though. It's a quaint cottage-like house. Suits me," Addy says as she places the tray of cookies she prepared in the oven. Setting the timer, she turns and sits at the kitchen table.

"Have you acclimated to the weather yet?" Julie asks.

"Definitely not. I'm cold all the time, no matter how many layers I have."

"Give it time. You'll adjust," Rachel responds.

"My car won't. I can't believe all the issues I had on the drive up here," Addy says.

"I'm just thankful that officer helped you," Mr. Katz says.

Addy had already told her family about the nice police officer that had changed her tire for her. She hadn't told them, however, that he reminded her of another man. In fact, only Julie and Rachel knew that Derek even existed. She hadn't told her parents because, well, there wasn't anything to tell anymore. He was a part of her past, not her future.

"Yes. He was very nice."

"Was he single?" Mrs. Katz asks.

"I didn't ask," Addy replies and quickly changes the subject to Zachary's potty training.

After her breakup with John eight years ago her parents had been dropping hints that they were concerned about her ever-constant single status. There had been other guys since then. Dates, a couple short term relationships but nothing ever made her desire more. She knew her parents were worried about her, but she couldn't convince them she was perfectly happy with things the way they were.

The rest of the day passes with the family finishing the rest of the customary Christmas celebrations and closes with the opening of presents. Zachary had already opened some in the morning when he woke but he eagerly tore through the rest. Addy watches on in glee. These were moments she had longed for when she had been living in Arizona. It was good to be home and surrounded by loved ones.

"This is the last one. It's for you Addy, from Rachel and I," Julie says and hands over the wrapped item to Addy.

"Thank you," Addy takes the offered gift. She unwraps the gift and finds herself holding a leather-bound journal.

"For your lists. This way you won't lose them," Julie says.

Addy stares at the book in her hands, her breath catching when Julie mentions lists. She recalls past conversations about journals and lists. Her mind wandering back in time she runs her fingers over the leather, lost in thought.

"Do you not like it?" Julie asks, concerned.

"Oh, no, I love it. I'm sorry I was just…thinking of the next list I'm going to make," Addy smiles.

Her father laughs but her perceptive sister frowns.

Later, after the kids are put to bed and their parents had departed, Julie brings up Addy's reaction to the journal.

"I know that look. You were thinking about him again," Julie says as she hands Addy a steaming mug of cocoa. The best thing about winter – hot cocoa.

"Yes," Addy admits. There was no point in denying it. Julie would just call her out on it.

"Still? After all this time?" Rachel asks.

"Always," Addy responds, and they all bust out laughing.

"Okay, no more *Harry Potter* references. This is serious. You haven't even spoken to the man in nearly ten years. He just left you a 'Dear Jane' email and disappeared. I think a sufficient amount of time has passed for you to move on," Julie says as she sits next to Rachel. They snuggle closer to each other and simultaneously blow on their hot cocoa before taking a sip. Their synchronicity sometimes scares Addy, but she loves them both dearly.

"Eight years and I'm not pinning for him. It's just that the officer that helped change my tire reminded me of him. He even had the same last name as him. And the same first name as his older brother. Then you got me the journal and mentioned making lists. I made lists with him," Addy explains.

"Bullshit," Rachel says.

"Excuse me?"

"Everything you said may very well be true, but you are pinning for him," Rachel explains. Julie nods, agreeing with her wife.

"I am not," Addy says.

At the sound of her voice rising in pitch, Zilla immediately jumps up from the floor and sits beside Addy. Instinctively, Addy reaches out and strokes Zilla's fur.

"You so are. If he contacted you today and said he was single, free and wanted to be with you what would you do?" Julie asks.

"I'd ignore him. Just like he did the emails I sent him after his horrible 'Dear Jane' email," Addy says, shoulders squared proudly.

"He didn't ignore you. He canceled his account and never received any of those emails, so that doesn't count," Julie says, rolling her eyes at her younger sister.

"Wait! You kept sending him emails, even after he completely let you down?" Rachel asks, stunned. Addy is actually surprised Julie hadn't shared that with Rachel before. They share everything.

"Yes. I sent the first one not knowing he had deleted his email account. After that, when I missed him, I would write it all down and send it, knowing no one would ever see them but me. It was a form of therapy," Addy justifies her behavior during the first few months after Derek disappeared from her life.

The aftermath that occurred after Derek withdrew was not nearly as bad as what had happened to her in college, after Clark and the baby, but it hadn't been pleasant just the same. She often sent those emails into the ether just to keep from being lonely.

"How could you possibly feel that strongly for someone you literally only spent one day with?" Rachel asks the one question Addy had asked herself countless times.

"It was more than just one day to me. Sure, we only spent a few hours physically in the other's presence, but it felt like so much more than that. I was able to tell him things I hadn't ever shared with anyone else. He encouraged me to reach out to my family when I needed it. He gave me the courage to make decisions I was too afraid to make. He was my best friend. It didn't matter that we weren't physically together. I fell in love with his soul," Addy says sadly and places the now cold cocoa on the end table beside the sofa.

"I'm sorry. I made you sad," Rachel says and leans forward, covering Addy's hand with her own. Addy smiles and pats Rachel's hand reassuringly.

"You didn't. I think I'm just overwhelmed with being back home, starting a new job, moving and everything. So many changes. Well, my lovelies, it is getting late and Zilla is wiped. I will see both of you for New Years, right? We are still going to that party?" Addy asks as she stands, taking her mug with her to deposit it in the kitchen sink on her way to the front door.

"Absolutely. The 'Rents are babysitting, and you have the two of us all night. You are going to adore Rachel's friend. She is so much fun," Julie says and hands Addy her coat from the closet.

"She's your friend too," Rachel says.

"I know, but you went to high school with her. She was actually Rachel's first love," Julie tells Addy, grinning the entire time.

"She was not!" Rachel exclaims, horrified that her wife would share such a detail.

"Oh pish, posh. You had a huge crush on her and was devastated when she ran off with her boyfriend and eloped. It was quite the scandal back in the day," Julie jokes.

"I'm sure I will love her as much you two do. Thanks again. I had a wonderful time." Addy hugs them both goodbye, calls for Zilla and carefully walks back to her car. She manages to avoid the ice and get Zilla in with ease.

See, she thinks, *I'm acclimating.*

Journal Entry

February 13, 2007

I don't know how many more second chances this life is going to give me. I nearly died last week. I was so sick, and the doctors pretty much told me my days were numbered. Carol and the kids freaked but I rallied and managed to pull out of it. My lungs cleared up and they said I was well enough to go home.

I'm home now, with Carol. She is knitting right now, sitting in the chair beside my bed while I write this. I have cherished every moment I have spent with her, Mary, Drew and my grandkids.

I'm running out of time and there is still so much I need to do, need to say. I kept writing Derek, but the letters came back unopened. He refused my calls. I know there isn't anything else I can do besides respect his decision. So, I've stopped writing. I've stopped calling.

This journal will be the last piece of me left when I leave this earth. The last link to all that has defined me. I have asked Carol not to read it until after Derek has, if he ever chooses too. She said there was nothing written in here that she didn't already know. That woman has always held my heart and she still continues to surprise me.

I haven't told Drew or Mary about the journal. I've spoken to them about things I've written but for some reason I have not told them I am writing this. I was so worried this was a sign of relapse I actually called Doc Stone about it. He did what he always used to do and asked me why I thought I couldn't tell them. Really, I don't know why I bother to call him when all he does is ask me questions.

I told him that I wasn't writing it for them. He asked who I was writing it for, and I said, Derek. I think I've always known, even before starting this, that I would never speak to Derek again.

Everything I've written has been all the things I wanted to tell my son about. All the things I had never been able to talk about before.

I'm all out of second chances and I'm trying not to be angry. I don't want to leave this world bitter.

I know what I have to do.

Gary T. Richards

14 *The Party*

As Julie, Rachel, and Addy got out of the car their laughter carried out into the quiet night. There was still a gathering of snow on the ground, but the weather had warmed, and the cold wasn't as biting as it had been. The ladies had decided to indulge in a few pre-party drinks and were bustling by the knowledge that this would be the first New Years party they had all attended in years. Addy was particularly excited to be attending an event that would, hopefully, allow her to make some community connections. Public relations was one aspect of her appointment with the Township. She was, after all, a government employee now.

"I sure hope her brothers are here. The two of them together are a riot," Rachel says as she wraps one arm around Julie and the other around Addy.

"They are funny. When they aren't trying to beat each other up," Julie agrees.

The three of them stop at the door and Rachel rings the bell. Music can be heard through the walls and the front window shows people already mulling about in the home.

This is going to be a good night, Addy thinks as the door opens.

"You made it!" the woman that answers the door proclaims, a glass of wine in one hand. She moves forward and embraces Rachel with her free arm. "Come in, come in. Get out of the cold."

"Mary, this is my sister," Julie says as they all step through the doorway and begin removing their jackets.

"Welcome to my home. I am so glad you moved back. Julie and Rachel couldn't stop talking about it," Mary says and steps forward.

She embraces Addy and Addy laughs as she hugs the woman back. Her short hair is being held back by a thin band and the bob almost dances when Mary laughs. She is a woman that is clearly comfortable in her own skin and well on her way to enjoying more wine. She is not shy with her greeting at all.

"Wow, thank you. This is the most welcoming greeting ever," Addy says and smiles at her sister standing behind Mary.

"Oh, sorry if I'm being to forward. My family is very affectionate and I tend to forget that not everyone likes to be touched. Plus, I'm on my second glass of wine and according to my husband I'm a lightweight. I love everybody right now!" Mary shouts as she steps back, her hair dancing the entire time.

"Yeah, you do you, sexy minx," a scratchy voice growls behind them.

Addy looks past Mary and sees a tall, lanky man with wire rimmed glasses approaching them. He comes up behind Mary, puts his arms around her and nuzzles his face in her neck. She laughs and reaches her arm behind her to stroke his neck.

"David, how many beers have you had?" Mary asks the man.

"Not nearly enough my scrumptious white chocolate," he says into her neck.

"Please forgive my husband. Sometimes I think his tolerance is lower than mine. Isn't that right my brown sugar bear?" Mary says and gently pulls away from her husband.

Addy, Rachel, and Julie watch the scene before them. While Rachel and Julie are acting like this is nothing they haven't seen before, Addy shuffles her feet a little in discomfort. She can't help but feel like she is encroaching on a private moment between a loving husband and wife. She softly clears her throat, trying not to be inconsiderate.

"Sorry. I just can't keep my hands off this beauty," David says and steps forward, holding out his hand to Addy. "I'm David Weber."

"Addison Katz. Thank you so much for welcoming me into your home," she says and shakes his hand. He smiles at her and turns to Rachel.

"Rachel. Please don't be jealous. You know if my wife had other desires, you would have been her first choice," he teases. Julie, Addy, and Mary laugh at Rachel's expression of feigned hurt and amusement.

"Oh, please David. Don't fool yourself. If I wanted her, she would have been mine," Rachel says, snaps her fingers and walks away.

"And that is how you make an exit," Julie says and follows her wife.

David chuckles, kisses his wife's cheek and also disappears down the small hallway.

"If we haven't scared you away yet then I think you are going to fit in just fine. Come on, I'll introduce you to the rest of the brood," Mary says and grabs Addy's hand. She gently tugs her down the hall and takes her into a kitchen. Various people are scattered around, chattering and having a grand time.

"Would you like a drink? We have wine, beer, mixed drinks, water, soda…well, pretty much anything," Mary says as she releases Addy's hand and goes to the fridge.

"I'll just have the same you're having. Thank you. Your home is lovely," Addy says as she takes in the homey kitchen décor and the various photos lining the walls of the hallway they had walked through.

"Thank you. After David left the Air Force we came back here and have been in this house ever since. We have no intention of ever leaving. In fact, I insist on dying here," Mary says as she uncorks a

205

bottle of red wine and pours a serving into a long stem glass. She passes the glass to Addy and pours some more into her own dwindling glass.

"Cheers," Addy says, and they clink their glasses. After they both take the customary sip Mary turns to the people gathered in the kitchen.

"Let's see. You already met David. He's not as crazy he seems, I promise. Sitting at the table is Joan and her husband Keith. They work with David. Joan is a bit of a bore, but we love her anyway," Mary whispers, causing Addy to chuckle. "Standing by the back door pretending like they aren't itching for a cigarette are Deshawn and Conrad. They are on the force with my brothers. My mother, brother, and his wife are in the living room. I'll introduce you to them."

Addy follows Mary into the living room that is full of more people. They walk to a small group gathered around a lit Christmas tree. There is an older woman who seems to be in her sixties and a younger couple that have their back to Addy. The man has is hand on the woman's back and he is caressing her as they talk to each other. Addy feels a pang of jealousy.

After she broke things off with John all those years ago, and Derek disappeared from her life, she had dated casually here and there but nothing had ever approached the level of commitment she had with John, or even her college boyfriend Clark for that matter. She missed those familiar touches, and she gazed longingly upon the couple before her.

"Guys, I have someone I want to introduce you to. This is Addison, Julie's sister and Rachel's sister-in-law. She just moved back and plans to stick around so don't scare her off. Addison, this is my mother, Carol, my brother Drew and his wife Liv," Mary says as she introduces her family.

Addy's heart stops.

Those names.

It isn't until the man turns around and she comes face to face with the same officer that helped change her tire that panic starts to set in. The others are oblivious to her mini panic attack, and they all smile and greet her. Stunned, she stands there and doesn't hear their words. She notices a look of concern flash across the older woman, Carol's, face.

"I'm sorry. I had a brain freeze," she says and shakes her head.

"I remember you," Drew says, and he points a finger at her. "Liv, this is the woman I told you about. The one with the dog with the cool name. How is Zilla? And your tire? Still holding up?"

Addy stares at him.

Drew. Liv. Carol. Mary.

Derek.

Names she knew once upon a time.

"Sweetheart, are you alright?" Carol asks, stepping forward and placing a hand on Addy's shoulder.

Addy jumps back in fear. It's silly. Her reaction is completely silly but all she can think about is that this can't be real.

"I'm so sorry. It's just, well, you look like someone I used to know," she says to Drew. He grins, puts his arm around his wife who smiles up at him lovingly.

Liv. Derek's wife. No. Drew's wife?

Addy's head is spinning, and she takes a long drink from her wine glass, nearly finishing it. As she swallows the wine sticks in her throat, and she coughs to clear it. Four sets of eyes turn to her.

"Addison, are you sure you are alright?" Mary asks concerned.

"Oh, call me Addy. Everyone does. And I'm fine. Just fine. Oh, I think I need another drink. It was really lovely to meet all of you and I promise when I return, I won't be so spastic. Drew, thank you

207

again for helping me that day. It's been a really long week, and I think another glass of wine is just what I need. Please excuse me," Addy says and turns to go back to the kitchen to find that bottle of wine.

She knows she is reacting poorly but she can't seem to stop her heart from pounding. She downs the rest of the wine in her glass and is grateful when she finds the bottle still on the counter where Mary left it. She grabs for it, pours some in her glass, drinks that down and then pours another glass. She hears laughter and turns to see her sister and Rachel talking to the men by the back door – Deshawn and Conrad.

In fact, all the people here have smiles on their faces or are laughing. Even boring Joan is having a good time, and all Addy can think about is how none of this makes any sense.

She knows she can't stay here forever and if she wants answers she is going to have to go back into that living room, apologize, and assure these people that she isn't crazy. But this whole scenario is completely crazy. Grasping onto the possibility that this is all just one big, crazy coincidence she tightens her grip on her wine glass. She closes her eyes, breathes in deep, tells herself to grow a pair and turns on her heels to walk back through the fire.

The family she just walked away from is still standing by the tree, talking quietly to one another. She swallows her pride and walks right back up to them.

"I am sorry about that. I don't know what came over me. I'm not normally this socially inept; I assure you," Addy says as she takes the place she had abandoned moments before.

"Oh, don't you worry about us dear. If we ran at the first sign of abnormality this one wouldn't be here," Carol says and gestures to her son, Drew.

"That's true. I'm fortunate that the women in my life overlook my flaws. I'm a lucky guy," Drew says.

"Yes. I can already tell how much love is in this family. Really, Mary, your home is lovely. All those photos show how much love this house has seen. And I really am grateful that you raised such a kind hearted son, Carol. I probably would have frozen out there if it wasn't for Officer Richards," Addy says to Carol. The woman smiles at her and puts her hand over her heart letting Addy know she appreciates her words.

"Carol is the best. I only hope I am half the mother she is," Liv says, her arm still linked with Drew's. Addy looks over at her, shouting in her head to keep her expression kind. The last thing she wants to do is show what she is really thinking. If this is the same Liv, Derek's Liv, then something isn't right here.

"You all give me too much credit. I don't do anything special. And you are an amazing mother, Liv. Molly is just the sweetest little girl and the new baby is blessed to have you. Look at all of us, getting all weepy. This is supposed to be a party. Mary, stop us," Carol says to her daughter. Mary had always been the peacemaker in the family. A role she happily embraced in adulthood.

Liv smiles appreciatively at Carol and placed her hands over her midsection and Addy trails her eyes over the woman, noticing the slight telltale bump of an early pregnancy. Her eyes widening, Addy looks quickly at Drew, then back to Liv.

What was happening?

"Right. Well, I say we aren't nearly drunk enough. How often do we all get a night without the kids? No more mushy stuff. Addy, tell us about you. Julie said you were living in Arizona?" Mary turns to her, a smile on her face.

Addy jerks her head towards Mary and says, "Yes. I grew up here though. I went to Roosevelt High."

"Really? We went to Jackson. How strange is that? We must

209

have grown up just a few towns away from each other. Isn't that strange, Drew," Mary says.

"It is a small world," he says and takes a drink from the beer bottle in his hand.

Addy stares at him, her eyes still wide. Out of uniform his features resemble Derek even more clearly. They have the same jaw, the same eyes. Of course, all of this could just be in Addy's head. She had only ever spent a few hours with Derek and the time that had passed since then could have altered her memories. Perhaps, she was just imagining the similarities.

"What about you, Liv? Did you grow up here?" Addy is extra careful to keep her true intentions out of her tone. She doesn't want Liv to think she is prying. But she is also wondering why Liv hasn't recognized her yet. Maybe, hopefully, these aren't the same people that her Derek had told her about. Maybe this all really was just some strange coincidence.

"Oh, no. I'm actually not from Wisconsin. But my parents ended up moving here after I graduated college and my first husband and I moved here to be closer to family," Liv responds.

She smiles sweetly at Addy, and it surprises Addy until she remembers that Liv doesn't know who she is. Not really. Liv had discovered the emails between her and Derek but that was years ago and there was no reason to think the Addy standing before her was the same Addy from the emails. But then, Liv's comments register with Addy. She said she had a first husband. Drew, then, would be her second.

"First husband? I'm sorry. I don't mean to be rude. That was rude," Addy says, scrambling to cover her embarrassment. Liv just laughs kindly.

"Don't worry about it. It is actually a rather strange story. I was married to Drew's younger brother. We met in college and when I became pregnant with our daughter, Molly, we got married. We really should have known better, but we were young and unsure. We divorced about seven years ago and four years after that Drew and I realized we had feelings for each other. I think if this had been any other family this would be weird, but I lucked out. I married into the best family, twice," Liv jokes and the members of said family all laugh.

Addy smiles awkwardly but does not join in the laughter.

Holy crap! Holy crap!

"You were destined to be one of us," Mary says affectionately and Addy watches as Liv's eyes glisten with tears.

"I love you," she says to Mary and then they both start crying and hugging.

"Don't worry about this, Addy. They do this all the time. So, what brought you back here?" Drew asks, drawing Addy's attention away from Liv. The stunning Liv with the dark, exotic features and legs that seem to go on forever.

"I missed my family. After ten years away I decided I'd rather be making less money and living closer to those I loved than living in a place I had no connection to."

"Family is important," Carol says, her voice dropping softly.

"Oh, Ma. Dad is here. He is," Drew says and pulls his mother into his side in a quick embrace.

"Yes. He is. Every day. Oh, Addy, I'm sorry. This is supposed to be a celebration, and you have three of the Richards women crying," Carol says as she wipes the tears from her eyes.

"I'm a Weber now," Mary chimes in, still hugging Liv.

"You will always be a Richards," Drew says.

Addy looks on at the people before her and before she knows it, she starts crying too. They remind her so much of her own family and all the emotions she had when Derek disappeared just comes flooding back.

"Oh. Look what we did. We broke Addy," Mary says and stops hugging Liv so she can embrace Addy.

"I'm sorry. This is stupid. I'm being stupid," Addy says. Without realizing it, she is hugging Mary back, holding on to her as if her life depended on it.

"I'm gonna go see what Conrad has going on," Drew says, clearly uncomfortable with how emotional the women around him have become. He slowly walks around them and leaves the crying women in the living room.

"Men," Liv says. Mary and Addy both snort, pull out of their embrace, and wipe their eyes.

"Your girls have fun. I'm going to check in with Joan and see what we are going to quilt for the next charity auction. Addy, it was lovely to meet you and welcome home," Carol says. She places her hand on Addy's shoulder and gives her the most welcoming expression Addy has ever seen.

"Thank you, Carol. It was lovely to meet you," Addy returns.

After Carol excuses herself Mary declares they must have a change of scenery and the three of them go into the dining room. A quick detour through the kitchen finds each of them carrying a bottle of wine and they sit at the dining room table. The first bottle is opened, glasses filled, and Mary breaks the ice.

"Addy. You are gorgeous," Mary says.

Liv laughs and then quickly apologizes.

"I'm sorry. I didn't mean to laugh. You are beautiful. I wasn't laughing at that. I was laughing at Mary. She tends to flirt when she drinks," Liv explains.

Addy really wanted to hate her. She wanted to say Liv was a

terrible person, worse than both her and Derek, but the woman before her wasn't terrible. She was kind. She was loving. She was perfect.

Life just wasn't fair sometimes.

"It's okay. Thank you, Mary. You are particularly attractive as well," Addy says, lifts her glass in salute to Mary and takes a drink. Mary snorts.

"You are definitely Julie's sister," Mary says and salutes Addy back.

15 *The Women*

An hour passes and Addy finds herself laughing more than she had laughed in years. She spent nearly ten years in Arizona but had never found someone there she could call friend. Sure, she had people she associated with, but they were mostly business associates. The only other being she ever *socialized* with was her dog and, in the early days, John.

Sitting here with Liv and Mary was reminiscent to her adolescence and college years. She never doubted who she was back then, and she reveled in the relationships she had with her friends. Even Brad, a man who had helped her through her darkest period, had been able to give her more in such a short span than ten years in Arizona had.

"I haven't had this much fun in a long time," Mary declares as she pours the remnants of the second bottle of wine into hers and Addy's glasses. "Don't get me wrong. David is the best but there is something nice about spending quality time with females. Sometimes I just want to escape the farting that living with three men brings."

"Oh God. It's that bad?" Liv asks.

"You have no idea," Mary says, looking her sister-in-law square in the eyes.

"Mary has two teenage boys," Liv explains to Addy.

"What about you Addy? Do you have any children?" Mary asks, slurring the word children slightly. She leans over and uses her right hand to rest her chin on.

"No. No children. Just my dog, Zilla," Addy answers. She looks at Liv out of the corner of her eye to see if her dog's name sparks her memory. Liv continues to smile on, oblivious to whom Addy really is.

"Is there a *man* in your life?" Mary asks and she snickers when she looks slyly at Liv.

Addy smiles, even though she is silently breaking inside. "No, no man."

"Well, balls. How are we supposed to live vicariously through you if you aren't having crazy monkey sex?" Mary asks, sitting up straight, reanimated by her frustration.

"Mary! Addy doesn't have to have crazy monkey sex," Liv says, astonished by Mary's reaction.

"Well, somebody has too!"

"Mary!" Liv scolds and Mary pouts before picking up her wine glass to hide behind it.

Addy smirks as she takes a sip from her wine glass. She has missed this. Just talking to other women about life and everything in between. She isn't thinking about how these people were connected to her in ways they had yet to discover. None of that mattered right now.

"I wish I was having crazy monkey sex. Honestly, I haven't had sex in two years," Addy admits.

"What?!" This time it is Liv that seems shocked. She looks at Addy, eyes wide.

"I just didn't have an opportunity." Addy explains with a shrug.

"How does that even happen? You are in your thirties. You aren't dead!" Liv says and Addy busts out laughing. She covers her mouth with her hand and gains control before responding.

"I know that. I've had sex. It's just these last two years were more about figuring out what I wanted and a man didn't factor into that," she says.

"Bullshit. Sex is sex. If you want it go get it," Mary says and burps. Liv looks over at her and pats her hand.

Addy sits at the end of the table while Liv and Mary sit across from each other. The hour they had been sitting here the house had filled up with more people and Addy had a clear view of the front door from her seat. Occasionally, people came in to greet Mary and Liv. As the time passed Mary continued to drink wine and her greetings had gone from joyous words to slight waves and crooked smiles.

"You doing okay?" Liv asks.

"Yep. I'm good. It's only," Mary looks down at the watch on her wrist and squints, "11:30. Plenty of time. And this is only my… second bottle?" she asks, her eyebrows raised.

"Yeah, something like that," Liv says, her voice dripping with love.

Before she can help it, Addy snorts. It wasn't a laughing snort, but a condescending one. She doesn't know why she did it. Just moments ago, she had been thinking about how nice Liv is and for some reason her most recent display of just how nice she is made Addy upset. It didn't make any sense. Liv had never done anything wrong in any scenario. She had been a completely innocent by-stander in the whole mess that was Derek and Addy.

But, for some reason, the love in her voice when she spoke to Mary elicited a feeling of utter contempt in Addy. Immediately, Addy feels shame.

Both Mary and Liv look at her questioningly. Feigning ignor-ance, Addy smiles and takes a drink from her glass. It is then that the front door opens and a familiar voice rings out, confirming every fear Addy had been having over the last hour.

"Mary! I'm here. Sorry I'm late. Work kept me longer than I

expected," the voice says.

Addy freezes immediately. Her back tenses and she holds her breath.

Mary, on the other hand, perks up and claps her hands.

"Oh, perfect. Addy that is my other brother. You are going to love him," she says and stands from the table.

I already did, Addy thinks and waits for all her fears to come crashing down around her. She knows that her deception will be revealed once he confirms who she is to his family. So much for female bonding and making friends.

"We are in here!" Mary shouts as she calls out to her younger brother.

Suddenly, he appears in the archway.

Derek walks to his sister, kisses her cheek and pulls her in for a hug.

"Please don't be upset with me. This time I really couldn't help it," he says, looking into her eyes. He can clearly tell she is drunk and that is something he knows will work in his favor. His sister is a happy drunk, unlike their father.

"Don't be silly. I'm not mad. Come on. I want you to meet Rachel's sister-in-law," Mary says and grabs his hand. She pulls him into the dining room.

"Rachel? The girl from high school that was in love with you?" Derek asks.

"It was just a silly crush. Don't be stupid," Mary says.

The two of them stop at the table and Addy stares down at her wine glass. She didn't want this moment to happen. She wanted to go back to just being Julie's sister and another girl having a good time. Derek's presence changes everything, however.

"Derek, this is Addy. She just moved back from Arizona. Be nice to her," Mary says.

Seeing no way around this, Addy lifts her head and stares into the eyes of the man she has tried to forget about for the last eight years. He starts to speak to her but his voice catches when he recognizes her. He stands there, stunned into silence. It is Liv that breaks the silence.

"Geez, Derek. You look like you've seen a ghost," Liv says.

"I have," Derek replies.

His voice is all it takes for Addy to break. She quickly stands up, stumbling a little bit because she has had a few too many glasses of wine than she is used to. Mary tries to reach out to steady her, but she holds up her hand, warning Mary to stop.

"Mary, thank you for inviting me into your home. I had a good time. Liv, you're perfect, absolutely perfect. I'm sorry. I have to go," Addy says and immediately turns away.

She rushes to the front door and runs out into the night and away from that house, those people, that man. She runs from the past eight years and all those unanswered emails she sent out in a desperate attempt to cling to something that had never been hers to keep.

She just runs.

16 The Catalyst

Running out into the cold night, Derek quickly glances around, desperately searching for the woman he thought he would never see again. When he saw her sitting at his sister's dining room table like she belonged there he just about had a coronary. She looked exactly the same as the day they had met at the airport in Vegas. She was still completely stunning and just the mere sight of her had him wanting to touch her because he didn't trust his eyes. He was about to do just that when she suddenly bolted from the room. He didn't even think about it or offer an explanation to his sister and Liv. He just bolted out the door right after her.

He couldn't see her anywhere, so he started walking down one end of the sidewalk and called out for her. He hadn't heard or seen a car pull away, so she still had to be around here somewhere. He kept calling out but the only sound that answered him was the neighbor's dog barking. After walking a little further down the sidewalk and not seeing her he turns and goes in the other direction. As he passes each car he ducks down to see if she's inside any of them. He comes to a dark colored Blazer and is about to walk on when a movement on the other side of the car catches his attention. He moves around the car and finds her leaning against the SUV, her eyes closed, and head tilted back. There are tear streaks running down her face. Seeing her like this rips at his heart. He moves closer to her and starts to reach for her, but her voice stops him.

"Don't!" she warns, her eyes still closed.

He immediately drops his hand and takes a step back.

All these years, he had often thought of what he would say to her

219

if he ever saw her again. And now here she is and it's like he has lost his ability to speak. Moments pass with them remaining still in the silent night.

"I had hoped it wasn't you. I didn't want that family to be your family. I didn't want her to be your wife. No. She isn't your wife, not anymore. She's your *ex-wife*. Why couldn't they have been somebody else's family?" Addy asks, her voice breaking and a fresh set of tears falling.

She opens her eyes and tilts her head towards him. He is standing a few feet away from her, his hands in his pockets. He simply shrugs at her question but does not offer a verbal response. A small laugh escapes her lips. It isn't fair that he is still as attractive as she remembers. He has some lines near his eyes, showing he has aged from the responsibilities of fatherhood. His face is no longer clean shaven, however. He now has a short, trimmed beard and she silently curses him for that because it only makes him more attractive. His hair is cut shorter than she remembered it being. He is like the embodiment of a men's fitness magazine model. The same kind of magazine he had bought that day at the airport.

He probably still runs, she thinks.

"I'm sorry," Derek finally answers, and she laughs again, harshly this time.

Turning away from him, she wipes her eyes and steps away from her sister-in-law's vehicle. She had every intention of getting in the car and driving away from this house, from him and his perfect ex-wife and perfect family. But she hadn't driven because her sister insisted on picking her up so they could all drive together. So, after she ran out of the house and realized she had nowhere to go she just stayed by the car and hoped he wouldn't come after her.

But he had.

"You're sorry? You made all those grand declarations and then disappear without a second thought. You just walked away and went on living your life like nothing ever happened, like I never mattered and you're sorry! She's perfect Derek. Absolutely perfect and you were going to leave her, for me? But that's okay. Everything's okay because you're SORRY!" Addy shouts, the words coming out of her mouth in a mad rush. With a grunt she turns and walks away from him.

"Where are you going?" Derek calls to her and runs to match her, step for step.

"Away from you!" she says and continues to walk down the road, her arms folded in front of her. In her rush to get away she had forgotten to get her jacket, and the cold night wind was making her shiver.

"You're cold," Derek says and once again tries to touch her shoulder. She jerks away and glares at him.

"Don't. You don't get to touch me," Addy says and takes a few steps away from him.

"Okay. I won't touch you, but you are cold. Come back inside. Please Addy," Derek says softly. He can see that she is shivering, and her teeth are chattering. She will certainly freeze if she stays out in the cold much longer. He has so much to say to her, but his only priority right now is getting her warm.

"I can't go back in there, to them. They will know who I am by now," Addy says as she looks back at Mary's house. She has no doubt now that Liv knows who she is and is probably telling the rest of the family about the hussy that broke up her marriage. Of course, Addy is forgetting that Liv is now happily married to Derek's brother. None of that matters right now because all she can think about is the humiliation of being the other woman.

"They won't care. Come on, please. You're shivering," Derek says and takes a step towards her. She takes a step back. He sighs and glances back to his sister's house.

"At least tell me where your jacket is. I'll go get it and bring it out to you." He hopes she will take the compromise and not disappear on him while he's gone. He can tell she is contemplating her options because her expression changes from upset to frustration to defeat.

"Fine. It's the navy-blue, button down sitting on the bench in the front hallway. My gloves and hat are tucked inside the sleeve," she says.

"Do you have a bag or anything else with you?"

"No. Just the coat. My sister-in-law drove."

"Okay. I'll go get your coat. Don't disappear. I'll be right back," he says and waits for her to nod in agreement before he jogs back to the house.

Never.

He had never expected to see her again and seeing her sitting in his sister's dining room had shocked his system. At first, he hadn't been entirely sure she was really there, or if his emotions had been taunting him. When she ran passed him and out of the house he hadn't thought twice about going after her. He had lost her once.

No, that wasn't accurate. He had let her go once. He wouldn't be making the same mistake twice.

As soon as he enters the front door he is met with the faces of his sister, brother, ex-wife, and two other women: Rachel and her wife. He ignores the questioning looks and goes straight to the bench and sifts through coats until he finds the one she described. Once he has it, he starts to leave again but his sister stops him.

"Oh no you don't. What is going on Derek? Who is she?" Mary asks, blocking the front door with her body.

"Mary, I love you, but if you do not move out of the way I will move you myself," he warns, glaring down at his older sister. His menacing stare does not faze her. She knows he would never put a hand on her.

"Derek, why did that woman run out of my house at the mere sight of you?" Mary asks again, her voice stern. It is the same voice she uses on her boys when they are lying to her.

"Is that her?" Liv asks from behind him.

At the sound of her voice, Derek sighs and his shoulders sag, all tension leaving. He turns to look at her, meets her eyes then casts his gaze downward in sorrow. Liv had moved on and was happy now, but she had been hurt by his actions all those years ago. He doesn't want to hurt her again, but he knows he had to get out of this house before Addy disappeared. He and Liv had reconciled the past many years ago, but he knows it couldn't be easy for her to have it all shoved into her life once again.

"Yes. It's her," he says softly. He hears Julie gasp and watches as she reaches out to take hold of Rachel's hand.

"Oh my god. You're him," Julie says. He just looks at her and nods.

"Mary, I need to get out there. Please," he begs his sister.

"Let him go Mary," Liv says from behind him. Silently, he thanks Liv for understanding.

He sighs with relief when his sister purses her lips, nods and gives him a quick reassuring hug before she steps aside. He quickly rips the door open and runs to the spot he had left Addy. Nothing else matters right now to him but her. He relaxes when he finds her still standing there, shivering in the cold and trying to warm her arms up by rubbing her hands on them.

"Sorry it took me so long. Here's your coat," he says and goes to put it on her shoulders. She snatches it out of his grasp and steps away to put it on. She removes the hat and gloves from the sleeve and puts them on before the coat. Once she is settled, she rubs her gloved hands together.

"Now what?" she asks him.

"I don't know," he says honestly and puts his hands back in his pockets because all he wants to do is touch her and he knows he will reach out for her again if he doesn't restrain his hands somehow.

"God, this has to be one big cosmic joke the universe is playing. Of all the places for me to be tonight it had to be your family. Why did you leave Colorado?" Addy asks when she suddenly remembers that was where he had lived the entire year they had exchanged emails.

"Things weren't going so well between Liv and me, and I really hated my job. It just made sense to come back home, be near family," he explains. He keeps his distance because he doesn't want to scare her away. The fact that she is still here, talking to him, has him feeling hope.

"You're a cop now?" she asks and shuffles her feet a little.

"Yeah. For the last seven years or so. I work with the K-9 unit. Drew and I belong to the same station," he says, watching her reactions closely. She squints her face a little at his answer.

"So, the little boy got his wish," she says. His brows lower in confusion and she rolls her eyes at him. "You're childhood Halloween costume," she explains.

"You remember," he smiles at her.

"Don't be daft. Of course I remember," she says and turns her back. She takes a few steps forward, then turns around and closes the distance between them.

"I've hated you," she says when she stops before him and pokes him in the chest with her index finger.

"I know. I've hated me too." He keeps his gaze locked with hers, his expression calm.

She once again turns her back to him and paces away before returning. Her movements remind him of a dance of indecision. She clearly wants to run but she has nowhere to go. She is uncomfortable but stubborn enough to see this confrontation through.

"Liv married Drew," she says when she has stopped her current pacing.

"Liv married Drew," he confirms.

"That's weird," she says softly, and he chuckles.

"Yeah. I thought it was too. But oddly enough they are good together. They are a much better couple than her and I ever was," he says, his eyes twinkling with humor.

Addy smiles briefly as she looks into his eyes. Then she realizes she's smiling at him and frowns before pacing away again.

"Do you want to go somewhere? Talk?" Derek asks hesitantly. He sees her glance back at his sister's house and knows exactly what she is thinking. "Not there. Somewhere else."

She nods her head once in agreement and when he turns towards his car she follows silently behind him. Neither of them say anything when he opens the passenger door for her. They are silent when he gets in the driver's side, turns the key and pulls out into the road. He sort of just drives aimlessly for a bit because he isn't sure where to take them. It's New Year's Eve and there will be a crowd at any place open at this time of night. He doesn't want to have this conversation surrounded by other people. Seeing her again is a once in a lifetime chance and one he never thought would happen. He wants to be alone with her.

"Turn right here," Addy suddenly says. He glances at her but does as she requests. For the next ten minutes she provides him instructions until he pulls into the driveway of a small house on a private street. He turns the key, silencing the car's engine and waits for Addy for a cue to move.

"This is my house," she says, staring straight ahead at the house, not looking at him.

"Okay," he says, still waiting for her to move first. She waits a few minutes before sighing and reaching for the handle of her door.

Derek exits the car at the same time she does. He follows closely behind her and waits while she pulls keys out of her coat pocket and unlocks her front door. She starts to turn the knob but suddenly stops and turns to face him.

"I'm not going to sleep with you," she blurts. Her face is already red from the cold wind hitting it but underneath the top layer of redness she blushes.

"I mean, I'm inviting you in to talk. Nothing more," she explains in a rush.

"Okay," Derek nods his head in understanding. When she turns back around, he grins behind her.

God, he had missed this woman.

17   *The Talk*

As soon as they enter the house Zilla is bouncing around their feet with excitement. Addy is thankful for the distraction her dog presents to a tense situation. She watches as Derek laughs, kneels down and scratches Zilla behind the ears. The dog lathers his face with slimy kisses, tail wagging the entire time.

"So, this is the infamous Zilla. It's nice to finally meet you," Derek says to the excited dog. Zilla offers a playful bark in response.

"I need to let him out," Addy says when she is finished hanging up her jacket on the pegs near the door.

Derek looks up at her, still crouched on the floor and nods. She wishes he would stop looking at her like that. Like he wants to push her up against the wall and kiss her. It doesn't matter that a part of her wants him to do just that. A bigger, saner part of her said he needed to keep his distance.

"Come, Zilla," Addy says, and her dog immediately turns and follows her to the kitchen. She opens up the sliding patio door and he charges out into the night. She tenses when she feels Derek's presence behind her.

"Would you like something to drink?" she asks and walks to the fridge in an attempt to avoid being close to him.

"Water is fine," Derek says. He watches her as she takes a pitcher from the fridge, walks across the kitchen to glasses drying on the counter and pours them each a glass of water.

He walks over to her, and she holds out his glass. He takes it, deliberately brushing his fingers on hers. He notices her breath catch at their touch and as he brings the glass to his lips he continues to stare into her eyes. She stares right back, refusing to back down, and the longer he holds her gaze the more annoyed she appears. He takes a long sip before lowering the glass.

"Thank you," he says to her. She nods and breaks their stare so she can sit at the small kitchen table in a corner near the patio doors. She needs to not be so close to him. He follows her, sits across from her and waits.

"Did Liv know who I was?" she asks, staring down at her water glass.

"Yes. She knows," he answers.

"What a mess," Addy sighs and then she sits up as she remembers she forgot to tell her sister she was leaving. "I need to call my sister. Let her know where I went," she says, starting to stand so she can get her cell phone from her coat.

"She already knows you're with me," Derek says and stands as well.

Addy stops, turns and curses.

"Do they all know about me?" She is referring to the rest of his family. He just nods. Defeated, Addy returns to the table and sits back down.

Derek does the same. She is slightly perturbed that he keeps mimicking her movements. It strikes her then that this little cottage house she had once looked at as her safe haven was now being invaded by a past she thought would never again resurface.

"Do they hate me?" she asks.

"No. They have no reason to," he responds, shock in his voice at her question.

"I broke up your marriage. I'd say that's a pretty good reason."

"You didn't break up my marriage. No one did. There wasn't anything to break. Liv and I were all kinds of wrong together. She's married to my brother now for God's sake. The last thing on anyone's mind is my marriage and divorce from Liv," Derek explains.

"You're just saying that to spare my feelings. You don't have to. I can take it," Addy says. Zilla comes running back in, his business complete, and Addy reaches behind her to close the patio door. Her loyal dog comes to her side, sits down and puts his head in her lap. She lovingly strokes his ears, grateful for his presence.

"Addy, no one in my family, Liv included, blames you for anything. You never did anything wrong. *We* never did anything wrong," he tries again to convince her.

"Derek, we were having an affair."

Derek chuckles at her and she glares at him.

"No, we didn't, Addy. We've never even kissed. We were never in the same state, let alone room, together."

"You don't have to touch another person to be having an affair. We had an emotional affair," she says with her eyes narrowed at him.

"Okay, maybe we did. But we still didn't do anything wrong. Addy, none of that matters now. What matters is that you're here and I'm here. We're here together. You were right about the cosmos having something to do with this, but it isn't a joke Addy, it's a second chance," he says and reaches out, folding his hands over her free hand resting on the table. She doesn't pull away and he takes it as a good sign.

"A second chance for what?" she asks sadly. She is staring at their joined hands, not sure how she feels about seeing them touching. This is the first time they have ever touched, and her heart cracks from the cruelty of fate.

"For us. Addy, I still love you. I've never stopped loving you. I meant everything I said to you then and I still mean it today," he confesses, wishing she would look at him.

"How could you? It's been eight years. Everything is different. I am different. And so are you."

"The time hasn't changed anything. The only thing that is different, is that we can finally be together. There's nothing in our way this time. Please Addy, look at me," he pleads.

Slowly, she lifts her eyes, and he sees they are filling with tears.

"Don't cry. Don't be sad," he says and wipes away a tear as it spills across her cheek. "We can start again. We still love each other and can start again."

Addy closes her eyes and takes a deep breath before responding.

"I don't love you," she says.

"What?"

"I don't love you anymore," she repeats and opens her eyes. He is staring back at her, still smiling at her like she hasn't said what she did.

"I don't love you anymore Derek. Things have changed," she says and slowly removes her hand from his grasp. She watches as his face drops and his eyes become clouded with hurt.

"You don't mean that," he shakes his head at her.

"Derek, it's been eight years. You just disappeared out of my life. You didn't expect me to just wait around for you, did you? I thought I was never going to see you again. I didn't know you lived here. We had never shared those details with each other. I never expected for us to ever meet again," Addy says.

"Is there someone else?" Derek asks.

She was speaking like she was involved with someone else. That she had *moved on* with someone else. Immediately he thinks of John.

Did she get back with him after he had written that last email?

Of course she did. Why wouldn't she? She had described the guy as the perfect man. Any woman would have gone back to him.

Addy doesn't answer. She doesn't want to lie to him, but she knows if he believes there is someone else then he will leave. So, she just continues to stare silently at him until he accepts that she isn't free to do anything with him.

"I just keep missing my chance with you, don't I?" Derek leans back in his chair, removing his hand that covered hers, and glances around her kitchen, avoiding her gaze.

"Derek," she says and leans forward. He holds up his hand, stopping her.

"I don't care. Whoever he is we both know you don't belong with him. We belong together, Addy, and I'm not going to give up on us this time. This time I'm going to fight for you." Derek's expression is set and stubborn and Addy knows there is no possible way she can let him do this.

"Derek, there is no point. You and I just weren't meant to be. Please, let me go. Forget you saw me tonight." It had taken her eight years to get to a place where the thought of him didn't destroy her. She wasn't about to open those wounds again.

"Addy, I love you. I've always loved you. And I know you still love me, even if you aren't ready to admit it. I am reinstating the game. No dodges this time. No more excuses. No clean breaks. You can't push me away. I'm not going to let you run from this. I'm going to fight for you, Addy, and this time. I am going to win."

18 The Fight

One week passes and Derek once again disappears from her life. This is what she wanted. This is why she alluded she was involved with someone else. She wanted him to disappear again so eight years of healing wouldn't be unraveled. She didn't want to be reminded of the guilt she had felt all those years ago when Liv had discovered their correspondence.

Yes. This is what she wanted.

"No, it isn't," Julie says to her for the thousandth time.

"Yes, it is Julie. This is what is best for both of us. Think about this logically for a minute. How in the world could I possibly fit into his family with our history? It just wouldn't work. There is too much pain there," Addy says as she washes the vegetables for the salad.

"I think you're scared," Rachel says. She is setting the table while Julie feeds their youngest her dinner.

"Scared?" Addy laughs, dismissing her sister-in-law's claim. "What could I possibly be afraid of?"

"That you are still in love with him," Rachel answers.

"Don't be ridiculous. It's been eight years. I don't love him anymore," Addy says. Once she has finished adding the vegetables to the salad bowl, she brings it over to the table.

"Weren't you just in this very house a month ago quoting *Harry Potter* in reference to this man and your feelings for him?" Julie asks. The baby, Eve, has finished eating and is now being gently burped.

"Those were jokes," Addy says and sits next to her sister at the table. Julie rolls her eyes letting Addy know that she never once believed her sister was joking about her feelings for Derek.

"So, if he showed up right now, tonight, you wouldn't see him?" Rachel asks.

"Why would he show up here? You didn't invite him, did you?" Addy asks, horrified that her sister-in-law took the situation into her own hands and is trying to play matchmaker.

"No. But your reaction proves our point. If you were truly over him, it wouldn't matter if you saw him again. You want him to stay away because it makes things easier for you. Denial is swallowed better when the object of said denial is absent," Rachel states and goes to the living room to get Zachary, their son.

"Why did you marry a psychologist?" Addy glares at Julie.

"She was good in bed," Julie shrugs.

The sisters share a laugh and Addy is glad when the topic at dinner shifts away from the upheaval in her life and to the daily schedule of the children.

Later that evening Addy is back at her house, cozying up on the couch with Zilla when there is a knock at her door. She glances at the clock and wonders who could possibly be knocking at ten o'clock at night on a Saturday. She laughs briefly at this because in her twenties ten o'clock was still early. Now in her thirties she is already in her pajamas and ready to head to bed. She follows a barking Zilla to the door and cracks it slightly, ensuring her latch is still in place.

"Don't close the door," Derek says in a rush just as Addy is about to do just that.

"What do you want, Derek?" she asks. Zilla has stopped barking and is waiting for the stranger to be let in so he can play.

"You are a lot of things Addy but one of those isn't a coward. Let me in," he pleads.

Cursing, she closes the door and unlatches the final lock. Her sister-in-law's words are running through head. She will show them that she is capable of moving on from this mess of a man. She opens the door and walks into the kitchen, leaving Derek to secure the entrance. After he closes and locks the door he follows her.

"What do you want?" She repeats, her arms folded over her chest as she glares at him.

"To read you something," he says and takes a piece of paper out of his pocket. He unfolds it and waits for her permission to continue. She waves her hand before her, giving permission for him to continue.

"Reasons why I am the biggest idiot on the planet. One: I let the most amazing woman get away from me, not once but twice. Two: It took me too damn long to admit my feelings to you. Three: I confused duty with honor and married the wrong woman. Four: I hurt the woman I loved and then just pussied out and left her hurting. Five: I held on to my anger and never forgave my dad when I had the chance. Six: I never got on a damn plane and went to you. Seven: I foolishly thought happiness didn't matter if you were doing what was socially accepted as the right thing to do. Eight: I spent years thinking I had lost you and never tried to find you. Nine: I left your house the other night when I was terrified that I'd never see you again. Ten: I took you for granted," Derek finishes, folding up the paper.

"Okay. No one doubts you are an idiot. Can I go to bed now?" Addy asks.

"I'm not done." Derek takes another piece of paper from his pocket and unfolds that one. "Reasons why Addy should dump her boyfriend. One: He's stupid. Two: She doesn't love him. Three: He's ugly. Four: He hates dogs. Five,"-

"You don't even know him!" Addy exclaims, interrupting the recitation of his second list. This is the most ridiculous list she had ever heard.

"Don't interrupt," Derek scolds, holding up a finger. He continues to look at the list as Addy grunts in frustration. He smirks and continues reading. "Five: He smells like rotten fish. Six: The sex is bad. Seven: He has a lazy eye. That's just weird, Addy. You can never tell if he's looking at you or another woman. Eight: He says words like axiomatic and protean. Really, he's just a snob. Nine: He hates the all-boy band Hanson and mocks you behind your back. Ten: He isn't me." Derek folds up the list and puts it back in his pocket.

Addy just continues to stare at him and raises her eyebrow.

"Finished?" she asks.

"Finished," he says.

"You hate Hanson too," she points out, her arms still crossed.

"On the contrary, I used to hate Hanson until you showed me the error of my ways."

Without thinking, Addy laughs. Shaking her head, she uncrosses her arms and goes to the fridge. She takes out two beers and hands one of them to Derek. He takes it, not sure what to do next.

"Sit," she orders, gesturing to the kitchen table. He does as she instructs, as does Zilla because he heard the command in his human's voice, and he knew better than to ignore her. Reflexively, Addy takes a treat from the counter cookie jar and gives it to Zilla.

"Do I get one?" Derek jokes.

Addy gives him a look of exasperation and replies, "Only good boys get treats."

"That's fair," Derek says.

Addy sits across from him, and they both sip their beers silently for a few minutes. Derek knows the next move is hers and so, he waits. He is just grateful she hasn't thrown him out of her house yet.

"Your list making skills need some work," she finally says.

"Yeah? I have been out of practice," he smiles at her and for the first time since being reunited, she genuinely smiles back at him.

"Where did you get your information about my boyfriend?" she asks.

"Well, I figured that after knowing me there was no way you could possibly find someone more attractive, so I played the odds."

"You're very confident in yourself," she remarks.

"Oh, not at all. I just hoped he was ugly and that was why you left him back in Arizona."

"I don't have a boyfriend," Addy confesses softly. She avoids his gaze and picks at the label on the beer bottle.

"I know," he says just as softly.

"I'm not sure I can do what you want."

"All I want is a chance. Give me two – no, one month. One month to convince you that you and I still have something. If, after one month, you can still say you don't love me then I will walk away. For good this time," Derek leans forward in his chair and pleads with her.

Addy sighs. She had lied to her sister and Rachel earlier. She did have feelings for him but some of those feelings were still very rooted in pain. She isn't sure she can forgive him for hurting her. She isn't sure she is strong enough to let go of the hurt. But she also knows that if she doesn't do this she will regret it. Second chances don't come along that often.

"One month," she says.

Suddenly, Derek stands. She looks up at him in surprise.

"May I take you to dinner tomorrow?" he asks.

Still reeling from how quickly he stood up she nods in response.

"Good. I'll be here at seven. Okay, I'm going to go before you change your mind. Lock the door behind me. And Addy?"

She looks up at him, still processing everything that just happened.

"You are still my favorite person," he says and quietly exits her house.

He isn't there to hear her say, "You are mine."

19 *The Panic Attack*

Here she was, over thirty years old and panicking because she couldn't decide what to wear on a date. She had been on many dates, over the course of thirty-one years, and the last time she was this nervous was when she was a teenager and went on her very first date. She supposed this was very much like that day when her high school boyfriend picked her up at her parents' house that long ago night. She hadn't dated anyone for a couple years so, in theory, this night was another first date in a sense.

Her first date with Derek.

Addy isn't crazy. She kows it didn't exactly work that way. Born again virgins were just kidding themselves. Once a line was crossed there was simply no going back. She used to think she would never find herself in this position. Then again, she never thought she would ever see Derek again, let alone consider dating him. Fate had once again stepped in and took over her life, derailing her plans.

She is perfectly content to continue on with her life finding fulfillment from her family, her career and her dog. Derek is simply a complication that she needs to endure for thirty days. There is that number again. Thirty. It is like fate is enjoying this moment and laughing at her. She doesn't have any friends that are over thirty and not married with kids. Society is constantly reminding her that she is over thirty, not married, and childless. If one more person asks her what she is waiting for she is going to implode and take a couple people out with her.

With a frustrated growl Addy throws the dress down she is holding and angrily stomps to the telephone beside her bed. She violently punches the screen with her index finger until she finds the number she needs. Waiting, she taps her foot.

"What's wrong?" her sister asks in greeting.

"I can't do this. This is insane. I'm thirty freaking years old and I can't decide what to wear. What is wrong with me, Julie? I'm too old for this. I'm cancelling," Addy says as her foot tapping morphs into pacing; a task that required she navigate around the various clothing items she had strewn across the floor.

"Calm down. You aren't going to cancel, don't be stupid," Julie tells her.

"I'm not like this. I'm not a nervous wreck. I'm levelheaded. I don't care what I wear on dates. I don't date! Nothing good can come from this." Addy runs her free hand through her hair in an attempt to grasp onto something. When Julie's laughter rings through the phone, however, all of the nerves melt away and confusion takes its place.

"What is so funny?"

"You are. You are absolutely like this. I remember when Clark would come to pick you up from the house. For like the first two months you dated you were a nervous wreck every time he came to pick you up. A total spazz. Mom and I used to get a kick out of your antics. Dad and I would place bets on how many times you would change your outfit," Julie reveals.

"You did not! That is a horrible thing to admit."

"Oh, stop being so dramatic. You were ridiculous back then and you know it. Look, Addy, you need to just think for a minute here. Nothing terrible is going to happen tonight. You are going to put on that royal blue dress you wore to Rachel's birthday dinner. Wear your hair up in a twist and show off your neck. Put the silver necklace on I got you for Christmas. Do all this, not for him, but for you. You deserve a night where you feel beautiful and like the old you again. You think she was someone to be embarrassed about, but I used to envy that girl. The same girl that danced naked in our hallway to that awful music she listened to."

Addy listens to her sister's words and takes comfort from them. Blinking, remembering the girl her sister had just described, a single tear fell. Quickly, she wipes it away and turns to her closet to get the dress her sister had described.

"Have I told you lately how wonderful you are?" Addy asks.

"Not today. No need. Addy, I know you are scared but you don't have to be. This is Derek. Don't spend the night worrying about what happened yesterday. Promise me you will go out tonight and just be you and allow yourself to have fun."

"I don't know, Julie. Too much time has passed. What if we are just too different now?"

"Of course, you both are different than before. Life shapes people and a whole lot of life has happened since the last time you talked. But just because life happens, that doesn't mean you should give up on something if it's good. Maybe I'm biased. I've known Derek for years now and I know he is a good man. And I've known you for longer and I know how much you loved him. This night doesn't have to mean forever if you don't want it to. It is just a chance for you to close a chapter or start a new one. Whatever you decide I will be here for hugs and lots of late-night hot chocolate," Julie tells her.

"Rachel is the luckiest woman ever. And I am the luckiest sister ever," Addy says. The nerves have completely gone thanks to the calming affect her sister always has. Of the two of them Julie was by far the most grounded.

"That is true. But really, I'm the lucky one because I got both of you. Now, get ready and call me later to tell me all the details."

The sisters say goodbye and Addy spends the next hour

getting ready for her first date in two years. Her first date with Derek – the man she loved and lost so long ago. When the knock sounds on her door promptly at seven she feels the nerves returning but she pushes them back down and confidently walks to her door.

Addy opens the door and finds Derek on the other side, flowers in hand and a box of dog biscuits in the other. He grins at her as he shakes the box of dog treats. She laughs and steps aside so he can enter the house.

"I wasn't sure what your favorite flower was, so I went with the cliché roses," Derek says as she closes the door.

"Thank you. They're beautiful," she says and takes the flowers from his extended hand.

"You're beautiful. They are just adequate," he replies as he steps closer to her, maintaining eye contact the entire time.

If heat could enter a moment with a single look, then it definitely entered this moment. Addy looked away from his penetrating gaze, the nerves returning. He hadn't made her nervous all those years ago in the airport and she doesn't know why it is happening now. Stepping aside, she goes into the kitchen to find a vase for the flowers. He follows behind her.

"Where is Zilla?"

"At my sister's place. My nephew likes having him stay the night sometimes," Addy says as she removes a vase from a cabinet and fills it with water.

"Well, that foils my plan," Derek says and places the box of biscuits on the counter.

"What was that?"

"To get him to fall in love with me through treat bribery and enlist his help to convince you to love me again," Derek says.

She hears the grin in his voice before she turns around to see it on his face. At first, she is taken aback by his words. But when she sees the playful shrug of his shoulders she relaxes. This is the man she remembers from the airport and the emails.

"Is that so?" she returns, grinning herself.

"I'm no fool. I know that dog is the key to your heart. Next time, I'm bringing flip flops. Fair warning."

"Always the planner." Addy finishes filling the vase and places it on the kitchen table where the sun's light can reach it. "Ready to go?" she asks.

As she is turning to head back towards the front door, she is surprised by the hand that reaches out and grabs a hold of hers. Derek gently pulls her back to him and she finds herself pressed up against his chest, looking up at him in surprise.

"Almost," he says and leans down to press his lips against hers.

Her head is screaming at him.

First kiss.

They were kissing and she wasn't sure how she felt about this. She should step away. She should slap him for being so forward. She should...shut up and enjoy it.

That is exactly what she does. She stops the thoughts and simply falls into him and meets his every movement. The kiss is gentle and not at all forced. Once he realizes she isn't pulling away he steps further into her, places one hand on the side of her face and the other wraps around her waist, pulling her closer. Addy places her hand on his chest, closes her eyes, and melts.

When he pulls away, her eyes are still closed. The hand on her face moves and she feels his fingers in her hair, gently massaging. She tilts her head into the touch and sighs. Her insides are warm and for the first time in a long time all she feels is comfort.

Opening her eyes she finds him staring down at her face, a slight smile at the corner of the right side of his mouth. Chocolate eyes stare back at her and she suddenly thinks of her sister's words promising hot chocolate, her favorite warm comfort drink.

"I didn't want to risk never kissing you. I have always regretted not kissing you last time," Derek says as he continues to move his fingers through her hair. The loose twist she had put it in is now in tatters, but she couldn't care less.

"Oh," she says in response to his words which makes him smile completely.

Stepping back, he disengages from their contact and pulls his keys out of his pocket.

"Are you hungry?"

And just like that Addy is standing in her kitchen alone, reeling from the encounter that just transpired. She is still wrapping her head around it when she hears Derek call out to her from the front door. She turns and sees he is holding her jacket for her. Silently, she walks to him and allows him to help her put the jacket on. She follows him out the door and with a final shake of her head she closes the door behind her and prays she isn't in over her head.

20   *The Date*

The restaurant is one of those where couples go to celebrate Valentine's Day or an anniversary. It is fancy and romantic and everything Addy hates. It reminds of her the dates she used to go on with John. All pomp and circumstance, devoid of anything familiar to her. While John had often done grand romantic gestures, they had usually made her uncomfortable because she felt expected to perform. She much preferred spontaneity to planned out romantic gestures. That is probably also why she dislikes surprise parties. A specific reaction was expected, and she hated feeling forced to react in certain ways.

"You are uncomfortable," Derek says to Addy across the table from her.

She turns her wandering gaze over to him, her eyes wide and stunned. He notices her expression shift and sees the moment she puts on her mask.

"No. Not at all. This is a nice place," she says and picks up her napkin to shake it out and put it on her lap.

Derek laughs and stands up. Taking out his wallet he pulls out some cash and throws it on the table. Addy is staring up at him in confusion. He walks over to her and holds out his hand.

"Come on. Let's get out of here," he says and waits.

Slowly, she places her hand in his. Derek once again notices the moment when the mask disappears. She smiles and allows him to pull her to her feet. Quietly, they walk out of the restaurant into the winter chill.

"What now?" Addy asks as she pulls her gloves out of her pocket.

"Now I'm going to stop trying to impress you. Do you like tacos?" he asks as he reaches out to hold on to her elbow to keep her from slipping on the ice.

"Are you mental? Who doesn't like tacos?" she asks.

Derek suddenly stops walking and looks at her, grinning. The time that had passed hadn't diminished his love for this woman.

"Crazy people," he answers. They resume walking to his car, and he helps her in.

"I know this great taco place. I usually eat there every time I'm on shift," he says as he settles into the driver's seat.

"That's a lot of tacos," Addy laughs. She keeps her gaze on him. She decided after the kiss that she was going to take her sister's advice and just allow herself to have fun. This night was not about yesterday and all that had happened before. All that matters now is what would happen next.

"They're really good tacos. Seatbelt," he says. She rolls his eyes at him but puts the seatbelt on.

"Yes sir, mister trooper," she teases.

"That's mister sexy trooper to you," he teases right back.

"What made you finally decide to give the whole law enforcement thing a go," she asks as they drive on.

"My Dad actually. His journal. After things ended with Liv," he quickly glances out of the corner of his eye to gauge her reaction and sees the slight wince she makes, "I started reading his journal again. I came across an entry where he talked about how the job had been his salvation during the years my mother had left him. He wrote about how even in the darkest moments some light would shine through because of some person he had helped. He basically said the job was what kept him waking up every day. The day he was forced into early retirement was not a good day. That was also the day he got the divorce papers from my mother. He went into rehab right after that. I figured if the job had brought him joy then maybe it could do the same for me. So, I joined the force," Derek finishes.

"And, does it? Bring you joy?"

"More. I know I'm doing good and that what I do matters. It's a good feeling. What about your work?"

"I don't know if I would say it brings me joy. I'm good at it and when I finish a project, I do feel triumphant, I suppose. But if I had to pick what brought me joy then that would be my family and Zilla."

"Tell me about your family," Derek says and looks at her. She is sitting with her head resting against the seat, staring at him. She smiles when he asks about her family.

"They are amazing. You know Julie and Rachel. They just had their daughter a few months ago and she is the perfect baby. Zachary, that's my nephew, is two and he is a little rascal. Him and Zilla are best friends. Mom adores them and can't seem to stop buying them toys. Julie hates it because they are running out of places to put the toys, but she won't ever tell Mom that. Dad, well, he's like a cuddly bear. He has a beard too. Except his is like a mountain man's, much longer than yours. When did you grow the beard?"

"I don't know if I'd call this a beard. I'm not allowed to grow it too long. Regulations. I started keeping it about three years ago. I thought it would help keep my face warm in the winter. I shave it for the summer months."

"Does it keep you warm?"

"No. Not at all," he says, and she laughs.

"Then why keep doing it?"

"Habit," he shrugs and announces they have arrived at the taco joint. It's a tiny place with only four tables inside but it is warm. Addy follows him to the counter.

"What would you like?" he asks her.

"Hmm. I will trust your judgement since you know this place," she says and takes a seat while he orders for them. She would never admit this to him, but she checks out his ass as he stands at the counter. She definitely likes what she sees.

While he orders, she watches him, cataloging the changes in his appearance since the last time she saw him. Despite only ever having that one encounter with him, she can recall exactly how he looked then. When he finishes ordering, he brings two bottles of water to the table, and she thanks him.

"After Liv, did you date anyone?" she asks suddenly as he is settling into his chair.

Derek swallows and leans back in his chair. He knows this is something they need to talk about. Hell, there is much they need to talk about.

"I did."

"And?" she asks.

"And none of them were you." He says it so plainly, so smoothly, that it causes Addy to intake a quick, sharp breath of shock.

"Did you date after John?" he asks.

"I did," she replies.

"And?"

"None of them were you," she repeats his words.

Lifting her gaze, she finds him studying her. Neither of them is smiling. This is a serious and somber moment as they acknowledge the years they were apart.

"I'm sorry, Addy. For the rest of my life, I'm sorry," he says as they hold their gazes.

"I know. I want to say it's okay. I want to say I forgive you, but I don't know if I'm there yet," she says honestly.

He nods slightly. "I understand."

"I want to be there," she reveals.

"We have time now. I'm not going anywhere," he promises and they are interrupted by the teenager from the counter bringing their order to them. The tacos and chips and salsa are placed on the table and once again they are left alone.

Straightening in his chair Derek slides two tacos over to Addy and takes the remaining four.

"This one is chicken tomatillo, and the other is a beef and potato one. I like to put the red salsa on the beef taco," Derek explains.

"Alright. Then I will do the same," she says and unwraps her tacos. Addy spoons some of the red salsa on the beef taco. Derek waits for her to take her first bite before he prepares his own tacos.

Addy tries the beef taco first and is pleased with the juicy meat and slight spicy flavor in the potatoes. The salsa adds a kick that has her reaching for her water. It's spicy, but not too hot for her. The taco is exactly what she needed.

"It's really good. I can see why you come here so often," she says and takes another bite.

"Drew thinks they are too spicy but he's a sissy," Derek says and unwraps his food.

"How did your brother and Liv end up together?" Addy asks and then quickly takes another bite. She isn't sure if he would be bothered by this topic and is surprised by a lack of reaction from him. He just continues to set up his tacos as if the topic doesn't cause him any irritation.

"Well, they had become friends from spending so much together at family events over the years. Even though Liv and I divorced it was never the typical resentful divorce. There was no fighting. We just finally accepted what we had both known all along. We didn't fit. So, after we split, she still came to all the family events. My Mom adores her. In fact, Mother said she would disown me before she would disown Liv," Derek laughs as he pauses to take a bite.

Addy averts her gaze. She has seen how close his family was to Liv. She isn't jealous – okay, maybe she is a little jealous. All these years she had told herself Liv was a horrible wife, but she hadn't been. She is also a really good person, which makes Addy feel like a terrible person.

"So, Drew and Liv started doing things with his kid and my sister's kids and then they started meeting up without the kids. That went on for a couple weeks and my brother finally realized he had feelings for her, and he told me he wanted to date her."

"What did you say?"

"I hit him."

"What?" Addy asks as she coughs down her food. She takes a gulp of water and swallows down the last bit. She waves away Derek's concern and waits for him to answer.

"He told me he had feelings for her and said he hadn't planned it. He said he wanted to know if I would be alright with him asking her out. I don't know why I did it. We were sitting at this bar and I just blanked. I turned and hit him, knocked him off the stool. I thought for sure he would get back up swinging, but he just said that was a free punch. He said if I wanted to hit him, we could go outside and finish it that way but at the end he would be the last one standing and he was still going to ask Liv out." Derek took another bite of taco.

Addy starts to tap her finger in anticipation. When he goes in for another bite she rolls her eyes. "And?" she asks.

249

"We went outside. He kicked my ass, and they went on a date the next night."

"Why were you mad? Did you still have feelings for Liv?" She holds her breath as he answers.

"No. I don't think I ever really had those kind of feelings for Liv. I wasn't mad that he liked her. I think I was upset that he would be the man I couldn't be. I was afraid they would fall in love, and he would take my place with my daughter. He's a damn good father and I didn't want to compete with him for my daughter," Derek explains.

"I don't think he would have stood between you and your child," Addy says.

"Yeah. I know that now but in the moment all I felt was fear and Drew and I usually settle our differences with fists."

"That's horrible."

"Nah. It's okay. He always wins. But one day, I will best him," Derek grins.

Shaking her head and snickering, she finishes the second taco and watches as he eats all of his. Once they have finished clearing up their mess, they venture back out in to the night.

After dinner they are back in his car, and he is driving them to some surprise destination that he won't reveal to her. She leans her head back and realizes that the night has gone well.

"Tell me about your daughter?" she asks.

"She's my everything. Her name is Molly. She is eight, going on twenty. She looks just like Liv and is her twin. She's smart as hell and already knows how to charm the boys. She lives with Liv and Drew mostly but I live on the same street a few houses down, so I see her nearly every day."

Addy bites her lip when she learns he lives so close to ex-wife and sees her practically every day. Even though he said he no longer had feelings for Liv, Addy can't help but feel inferior. Liv is exotic, tall, and thin. She has a model's body. Addy isn't awful looking, but she isn't model ready. She is shorter and definitely stockier. A real woman her sister would say. Standing next to Liv, however, Addy only feels inferior.

"That's good that you live so close to her," Addy says.

"Yeah. You'll like her," Derek says and turns to her.

Blinking, it takes a moment before Addy realizes what Derek has said. He wants Addy to meet his daughter? Already? That is serious and not something a single parent usually did so early. Feeling the earlier panic returning, she turns her head away from him and remains silent until he announces they have reached their destination.

Derek notices her reaction when he mentions meeting his daughter. He also notices the way she reacts when he says Liv's name. He knows he needs to convince her that she has nothing to fear from Liv. He has a plan for that but tonight is not about Liv.

"Where are we?" Addy asks as she removes her seatbelt.

"It's a park. Come on," he says and gets out of the car. She does the same.

Derek offers his hand to her, and she takes it. He walks her to a cleared out path and she meets his pace. They turn a corner and her eyes light up when she sees the rows of trees all adorned with twinkle lights for the holiday season. Derek watches her as she releases his hand and takes a few steps forward, her head tilted back as she examines the lights.

"They are taking it down tomorrow. I wanted to make sure you saw it," he says, puts his hands in his pockets and just watches her spin around.

"It's beautiful."

"You're beautiful."

Addy stops spinning and meets his gaze. She inhales deeply and then slightly lifts her shoulders in a shrug that says she accepts defeat.

"I don't know how to do this," she admits.

"Me neither. But I know that this night has been one of the best nights of my life. I want to spend as much time with you as I can. I'm here, for as long as you'll have me."

Addy wraps her arms around herself to stabilize her nerves. Briefly, she glances at the decorated trees before she responds.

"What if we're making a mistake?" she asks.

"Then it will be the best damn mistake I'll ever make."

She rolls her eyes at him, and he steps forward so he is within inches of her. He reaches out and unwraps her arms. He takes hold of her hands and catches her gaze.

"You were never a mistake. *We* were never a mistake. The mistake was walking away from you. I don't know what will happen next. All I know is that I don't want to lose you again. I know you're scared. I'm scared too. I'm afraid of messing this up again. I'm afraid you will realize you can do so much better than me and tell me to take a hike. Despite all that I know, you and I make sense. For the longest time you were the only thing in my life that did make sense. I'm not going to force anything on you. I'll go at your pace. You decide what happens next," he says and remains where is, holding her gloved hands.

Addy breaks his gaze, tilts her head back to the sky before closing her eyes and taking a deep breath. Finding her courage, she looks him squarely in the eyes and admits the one thing she had refused to admit all these years.

"Loving you once almost destroyed me. I don't know if I can do that again."

"Then let me put the pieces back together. Give me the chance to prove that I am the man you thought I was, the man you deserve."

After a beat Addy softly whispers, "Okay".

Derek smiles and squeezes her hands.

"But I'm not sleeping with you," Addy quickly adds.

Chuckling, Derek pulls her to him and tucks her into his side.

"You're the boss," he says, and they continue walking down the path among the twinkling lights.

21 The Run

She doesn't know what is wrong with people in this town knocking on her door at inappropriate hours but once again she finds herself stalking to the door in her pajamas.

It is Saturday. This is her day of rest. She had gone to dinner with Derek again two nights ago and they usually spent the other days talking on the phone or texting each other. He often works the night shift, and her sleep has certainly suffered since she decided to give him another chance. It is her new normal to fall asleep with her phone in her hand and the pinging of an incoming text in her ear. She enjoys those conversations but she also looks forward to sleeping in on Saturdays.

"I'm coming, stop knocking," she calls out to the person behind her front door. Zilla is still just as sleep-confused as she is and he hasn't even started barking yet. He walks by her side though, ready to protect her if need be.

"Addy, it's me."

She recognizes Derek's voice, groans, and looks at the oven clock in her kitchen.

7:32

He is knocking on her door at 7:32 in the morning on a Saturday! Who does that?

"It's Saturday," she says to him as she opens the door. The jerk has the audacity to grin at her and hold up two to-go cups of coffee.

"I brought energy," he says and takes advantage of her tired state to step into her house without being invited.

Groaning, she closes the door and follows him into her kitchen. Dramatically, she falls into a chair, puts her head down on the table and reaches one arm out, hand extended. Derek chuckles and places the coffee cup in her hand. He sits in the seat next to her and watches as she slowly lifts her head from the table to drink some of the coffee.

Coughing slightly from the first sip, Addy reaches behind her and opens the back door to let Zilla out. He shoots out the door and into the melting snow. The sun is peaking out and Addy can swear she hears it laughing at her.

"Not that I'm not thrilled to see you," she starts.

"Yeah, I can see the joy all over your face," Derek jokes behind his coffee cup. She shoots him an impatient look and waves him off with a flick of her wrist.

"Why are you here so early? Didn't you work last night?" she asks and puts her head back down on the table.

"I did. I just got off shift and wanted to see you," he says, trying to charm her. It doesn't work. She just grunts at him.

"Hey Zilla," he says when the dog comes charging back inside. "Want to go for a run with me and your mom?"

"What!?" Addy sits straight up in her chair, all remnants of sleep instantly gone and replaced by panic.

"Look at his tail wagging. He wants to go for a run. Are you gonna deny him this experience?" Derek grins at her.

"You can take him. I don't need to be there," she replies.

"I wouldn't get two steps with him before he realized you were missing and shoot back to the house looking for you. Come on Addy. Go running with me," he begs, his eyes resembling those of a puppy wanting a snack.

"Don't. Your charms won't work on me," she says and starts to leave the table to return to her bed.

Derek stands behind her and pulls her into his warm body. He leans down and breathes in her ear. She isn't sure if he knows what effect he is having on her, but she does know nothing about his closeness is fair right now.

"If you come with us, I'll let you do whatever you want to me later," he promises, his voice sultry and seductive.

"Anything I want?" she raises an eyebrow and glances up at him.

He nods.

Addy grins. He has no idea what he has gotten himself into.

"Okay. One time. Don't go making a habit of this," she says and walks up the stairs to her bedroom. She hears his triumphant call behind her and laughs.

Thirty minutes later her footsteps are pounding on the pavement, snot has frozen to her face, and she is cursing Derek with everything she has. He is ahead of her with her traitor dog, and she is panting. She was a decent runner, but she had never taken to it like others in her life had. What she wasn't good at was running in the cold winter months. The ice hardened her lungs and only made her want to keep running back to Arizona where she never had to worry about icy lungs.

"Come on, slow poke," Derek calls to her. He turns around and is jogging in place, waiting for her to catch up. Zilla is happily running circles around him and yipping.

"I hate you," she says as she reaches his side.

"No, you don't. You secretly like this," he teases her and matches her pace.

"Why do you like running so much?" she asks.

He shrugs. "I don't know. I used to do it competitively in high school and college. I've always liked how my mind just clears. It's peaceful," he explains, and she shoots him a dirty look as she fills her lungs with cold air.

"There is something wrong with you," she says, and he chuckles again.

"Probably. What do you like to do, Addy? Kickboxing? Skateboarding?"

"Now you are just making fun of me." She pushes him on his shoulder, but it has no effect on his stride.

"I'm really interested in your hobbies. Tell me."

"I don't hate exercise. I do it. Just not on any set schedule or because I feel the need to have muscles."

"Okay. I didn't just mean exercise. What do you enjoy doing with your free time?"

"Sometimes I take Zilla to nursing homes to visit with the patients. He gets a kick out of it, and they like to cuddle with him," Addy answers, smiling at all the memories she had of the visits.

"Really? That sounds great. Have you done it since moving here?"

"Not yet. I haven't reached out to any of the homes yet."

"Well, I can give you some suggestions. The department also has a program about educating school age children about the proper way to approach dogs if you are interested in volunteering. Zilla would be good at that," Derek suggests.

"I am interested."

"What else do you do to pass the time?"

"I make lists," Addy says but something in the way she says it has Derek glancing at her questioningly. She catches his gaze and suddenly stops running. Derek stops too and waits for her to say what is on her mind.

"I make lists," she repeats.

"Okay."

"And then I do what's on the list. Once I've finished the list, or finished as much as I possibly can, I make a scrapbook of the list," she reveals.

Derek just smiles at her nervousness. She is cute when she is embarrassed. He reaches out for her and pulls her into his side and hugs her.

"Show me," he says and kisses the top her head.

She groans. Then immediately darts out of his arms and runs full speed back to her house. Zilla runs after, barking his head off. He stares after her in disbelief. She had been holding back. The girl could run.

He isn't able to catch up to her until they are a block away from her house. She smiles up at him as he matches her stride, and he notices the smugness behind it. She had fooled him into thinking she was a terrible runner but here she was, breathing back under control and her legs pumping. She picks up her pace when her house comes into view, and she pulls ahead of him. He realizes she is trying to beat him, and he picks up his pace. She shoves him when he catches back up and he stumbles slightly but stays upright.

Laughing, he returns, and they both push themselves to their limits. They are neck and neck until they reach her driveway. At the last second, he pulls ahead and manages to reach her front door a couple of milliseconds before she does.

"Victory!" he says breathlessly. She walks up to him and pats his cheek with her gloved hand. He is grinning until he realizes she isn't even winded. "Who are you?"

"Wonder woman," she says as she unlocks her door and steps inside. She is certainly a wonder to him.

"Water?" She offers him as they enter the kitchen. He nods and she pours them both a glass of water. They drink the contents down and she waves him into the living room. Her house is a tri-level and the living room is down a small set of stairs off the kitchen. She tells him to sit on the couch and he does. His gaze follows her as she takes what appears to be a photo album off a bookshelf and bring it with her back to the couch. She sits next to him, and he watches her flip through the pages.

"Here. You'll appreciate this one," she says and places the book on his lap.

He looks down and is face to face with the Hanson brothers in all their teen glory. Quickly, he glances at her and finds her grinning sheepishly. The page is decorated with photos of the boys and calligraphy like handwriting of their song titles, glitter, photos of her with her sister and other drawn designs. In the center is a tempered paper that holds one of her lists.

1. *Go to one of their concerts*
2. *Sit in the front row*
3. *Get Taylor to wave at me*
4. *Join the fan club*
5. *Become president of the fan club*
6. *Start a band*
7. *Meet Taylor*
8. *Kiss Taylor*
9. *Marry Taylor*
10. *Live happily ever after*

They were the scrawlings of her adolescent dreams, but they were filled with the promise of happy times and even though the list was absolutely comical Derek couldn't laugh at it. He simply pictured teen Addy sitting on her bed, making this list, one of her Hanson CD's playing in the background. He wished he had known her then. If she was even half as amazing as she was today, he knew he would have loved her, even then.

"Well?" she asks beside him.

"I think I can guess which one was your favorite," he jokes, and she nudges his shoulder with her own in response.

"I obviously didn't complete this list, but it deserved to be included in the book. That was taken at one of their concerts," Addy says and points to the photo of her and Julie.

"Did you ever start a band?"

"I tried but I had a hard time finding members to join a Hanson tribute band."

This time he did laugh at her. She takes the book back and ignores his chuckles as she returns it to its proper place. When she comes back to the couch he calms down, and she pulls her feet up underneath her and leans into him. He put his arm around her, and they sit like that in silence for a few moments.

"Come to my house tomorrow for lunch," he suddenly says

"Okay. Now, it is time for you to pay up."

"Pay up?" he asks.

"Yep. You said if I went on a run with you, you would let me do anything I wanted with you. Well, I know what I want to do with you," she says in a sultry voice.

"Do you now?" he lifts an eyebrow suggestively and tries to lean in for a kiss, but the palm of her hand stops his advancing lips. He laughs against her warm palm.

"I want to make a snowman."

"What?" he asks, his lips still smashed against her palm.

"It has been years since I've lived in a place with snow and have made a snowman. You are going to help me make one. Right now," she commands and jumps off the couch. She holds her hand out to him and he reluctantly takes it. She pulls him up the stairs and to the foyer, where she puts all his winter gear back on him, then puts on her own.

"Zilla," she calls, and the dog comes bounding over to them. He is off in a flash as soon as she opens the door.

"Don't we need a few things?" Derek asks.

"Oh, right. No snowman is complete without his accessories. Get started, I'll be right back," she orders him and quickly dashes up the stairs that lead to the two bedrooms her small house has.

Caught between laughter and growling, Derek does as she instructs and goes into her front yard to begin collecting the snow. He starts with a small, compacted ball and gets on his knees to roll it through the snow on the ground to make it bigger. Zilla runs circles around him, barking and trying to get at the snowball he thinks is a toy.

When Addy returns, she finds him wrestling with Zilla and throwing snow in the air so the dog can try to catch it in his mouth. She smiles at them and is pleased that they get along. Phoenix and Zilla also got along. In fact, Phoenix settled Zilla and she looked forward to the walks she and Derek took with their dogs. But today was not about their dogs, it was about a snowman.

"I don't see much progress," Addy scolds them. She puts down the plastic bin, she put the snowman items in and begins to make another ball for the middle part of the body.

"Don't blame me, it was your monster of a dog that kept running into the ball and destroying it," Derek says.

"Sure," Addy replies and receives some snow thrown in her face.

"Hey," she retorts and throws some back.

Derek grins.

"Oh, no, don't you dare," she says and tries to scoot away from him, but it is too late. He grabs a hold of one of her ankles and pulls her to him, then he smashes snow in her face.

"It's cold!"

"You wanted to make a snowman. How about a snowwoman?" Dereks asks and begins to roll her in the snow.

Addy laughs, begs him to stop, laughs some more, then tries to get Zilla to attack him. The dog barks, jumps, lunges, and barks some more, but never attacks.

"Ok, ok," you win," Addy concedes.

Derek stops rolling her, then joins her on the ground, laying on his back. They both turn to each other, smiles on their faces, snow covering them. He opens his mouth to say something, and a handful of snow is shoved into his mouth.

Addy chuckles and Derek spits most of the snow out and swallows some.

"There better not be any of your mess in this snow," Derek says to Zilla. The dog has lost interest in them and is now running his snow through the snow.

"We are both wet, and cold, happy now?" he asks Addy.

"Very happy. But I'd be even happier if we made that snowman."

For the next hour they bend, crawl, roll, and assemble a very lopsided snowman that has a crooked grin and a top hat that had seen better days. His buttons were strawberries, his nose a zucchini, and his eyes were gumballs. The scarf wasn't a scarf at all, but was a series of old, tattered socks they tied together. It was the worst crafted snowman, but it made Addy happy, and making Addy happy made Derek happy.

He leaves shortly after and kisses her gently goodbye at the door. She stays there and watches him drive away. She has no idea where this is going but she does know that she loves every minute she spends with him.

So, this is what I missed out on.

22 The Mission

Derek is no fool.

Correction, he is no longer a fool. He had made many foolish decisions where Addy was concerned but he was determined to end that streak. The dinner they had gone on a few nights ago had gone better than he could have hoped. She continued to return his calls and answer his texts. She went on that run with him and agreed to meet today for lunch.

What he hadn't told her was that his family would also be at his house. He knew blindsiding her like this may not be the very best tactic, but he also knew her. If he had told her ahead of time that his family would be here, she wouldn't have come. She would have convinced herself that she should stay away. Derek wanted her to be a permanent fixture in his life and if that was going to happen then she needed to be comfortable around his family. His family was very important to him, and it was also important that those he loved could all be together.

Perhaps this may be rushing things a bit, but he had given himself a thirty-day moratorium and he was already down one week thanks to conflicting work schedules. The clock was ticking, and he didn't have the luxury to ease her into things. This would definitely be a baptism by fire type of situation, but he knew Addy could handle it. She was scrappy like that.

His family, on the other hand, was being a bunch of turds. They kept asking him questions about whether or not she knew they would be there, and he kept dodging them but they wouldn't let it go. He knew if they knew Addy wasn't expecting them, they would just leave because they didn't want to scare her away. He had spoken to them all since the New Year's party and explained how he was trying to convince Addy to give him another chance.

They were all supportive – of Addy!

They were rooting for her and kept reminding him to not screw things up again. His family didn't exactly adhere to blood loyalty.

Traitors.

"Derek, I don't know about this. It seems a bit overwhelming to have us all here," Mary says to him as she nervously moves various food items on the table in his kitchen.

His family had all done a pot-luck meal for this gathering. The kids are out in the backyard playing with Phoenix. His brother, Liv, mother, and David are sitting in the living room together waiting for Addy's arrival. As usual, Mary is playing the host, even though this technically isn't her home, and ensuring every little detail is properly seen to. At the current moment she is sharing her doubts about the gathering with Derek. His sister always had an uncanny ability to know when he was lying, and he is sure she knows he has misled them all.

"Don't worry, Mary. Everything is going to be fine," he says and avoids her gaze.

"Oh my God! You haven't told her we are going to be here," Mary suddenly says and before he can stop her, she rushes to the living room.

"Guys, Addy doesn't know we are going to be here," Mary shouts in a rush just as Derek reaches her. He tries to cover her mouth with his hand, but she is able to get all the words out before he can stop her.

"Derek? Is that true?" His mother asks as she turs to him. Sighing, he nods.

"What were you thinking?" Drew asks.

265

"I was thinking that I love her, and I love you guys and I want everyone I love to be able to be together. I told you guys I only have thirty days. I don't have time to do things with finesse," he says and glances out his front window to make sure she hadn't arrived yet.

"Finesse? This is a damn train wreck," Drew says and stands from the sofa. Liv stands with him.

"Come on. Let's get Connor and go before she gets here," Drew says to Liv and takes his hand in hers. As they are walking out of the living room a car pulls into the driveway.

"Too late," David says, his face moving along with the movement of the car.

Cursing, Derek turns to see Addy parking her car.

"Don't go anywhere," he says to his family and rushes to the front door. He runs out the door and almost knocks into Addy as she is letting Zilla out of the back seat.

"Woah, slow down there killer," Addy laughs as she catches him before he crashes into her.

"Don't be mad," he says in way of greeting.

She blinks at him and her shoulders sag slightly. A movement inside his house catches her eye and she tilts her head slightly to see around him. She is greeted with many pairs of eyes staring out at them from the living room windows. She recognizes every person staring at her and her own eyes widen as she looks at him briefly before indignation takes over.

"We can't put this off. This needs to happen," Derek says.

"And you just decided it for the both of us?" she asks, her head shaking in disbelief as she talks.

"Okay. You are absolutely right. This was a dick move. I should have thought this through, but I didn't. And you're here. They're here. Walking away now is not in your blood," he says, hoping the challenge in his words is enough to make her stay. He recognizes the moment he knows he has her and does a mental high five with himself.

"I hate you," she says and walks around him to the front door, her faithful dog following on his leash.

Grinning at her departing figure he silently gives a cheer for the stubborn woman that he knew wouldn't back down from a challenge. He took a gamble and so far, things were working out. The rest depended upon his family.

Addy waits for him at the door and before he opens it he turns to her.

"They are going to love you as much as I love you. All you have to do is let them," he says and takes her free hand. Her other hand holds Zilla's leash.

"I'm still mad at you," she replies, and he laughs at her pursed lips.

Derek guides her into the house, and he is grateful his family doesn't come to the entrance. They stay in the living room to give them space. Zilla proceeds to sniff every nook and cranny as they make their way into the living room. Addy still has him on the leash to prevent him from running off to explore on his own. Secretly, she is glad to have Zilla at her side for this. She is not ready to be face to face with these people for the first time since the party she had run out of.

Even though Derek assured her they didn't hold any animosity towards her she still dreaded he was wrong.

"Everyone, this is Addy. You've all met her before, at the party," Derek announces, his hand on Addy's shoulder to provide support.

"Best party ever!" Mary says and walks up to Addy. She puts her arm around her and steers her away from Derek.

"Definitely one for the ages," David remarks and comes away

from the windows.

"Addy, you come sit here by me and just ignore those buffoons," Carol says from her seat and pats the cushion next to her.

Dazed, Addy does as Carol says.

"Who is this?" Liv asks and she bends down to let Zilla sniff her hand.

"This is Zilla. My dog," Addy says.

Stupid! Of course, they know he is a dog.

"Aren't you just the friendliest thing," Liv says and laughs when Zilla licks her face.

"Zilla, no," Addy commands and the dog immediately stops to heel by his human.

"Oh, I don't mind. I love dogs," Liv says and stands to go sit by Drew on the other sofa.

"How long have you and Zilla been a family?" Carol asks.

Derek watches the scene before him and gives thanks to every member of his family for being the amazing people they are. They all recognize how nervous she is and they don't miss a beat by drawing her in and talking about a topic she is comfortable with. His mother leads the conversation and gets Addy to relax by telling them stories about Zilla's antics and before long Addy is laughing right along with the others.

"It sounds like you picked the perfect name for him," Liv says after Addy finishes another story about Zilla tearing through the dog park and terrorizing the other dogs.

"Yes, he is a character," Addy says and actually smiles at Liv.

"I owe you an apology, Addy," Carol says, and Addy turns to her, stunned.

"Why?" Addy asks.

"I never got a chance to invite you to our Sunday dinner the last time we saw each other. Please accept my invitation for next week's dinner. Liv is hosting this time," Mary says.

"Yes, please do come," Liv seconds the invitation.

Derek watches as emotions play over Addy's face. She is confused by this turn of events, and he can tell she isn't sure what to say. In a panic, she looks over to him. He stayed back and sat on a kitchen chair they had brought into the living room. He hadn't wanted to interfere with the magic that his family was creating.

"Will you go with me to dinner next Sunday?" he asks her. She turns to glance at the rest of the faces in the room before turning back to Carol.

"I'd be honored to," she finally says.

"Wonderful. Now that that is settled, let's eat. I'm famished," Carol says and stands. The rest of the family follows the reigning matriarch into the kitchen, leaving Derek and Addy alone with Zilla, who is now curled up at Addy's feet.

"What is going on in there," Derek asks as he sits beside Addy. He gently places a hand on her head and begins to caress her, running his fingers through her hair. He expects her to pull away from the intimate touch, but she doesn't. Instead, she leans into his touch.

"I'm not sure. This is all so…surreal. It's like I've done this before, with them, with you," she says softy and looks around the room she sits in. This is her first time here but everything about it feels so familiar.

"My family has a way of drawing people in. Are you doing okay with all this?" Derek asks and takes her hand. She turns her face to him, an expression of pure bewilderment upon her.

"I – don't know. I'm still processing. Why are they being so nice?"

"Because they are nice people. And they like you."

"They don't even know me," she says and shakes her head at him.

"Yes, they do. I've told them everything," Derek explains.

"Everything?" she asks, her eyes wide in shock. Derek just shrugs.

"Why? Why would you do that?" she asks and stands, pulling her hand from his.

"Because I love you."

"Stop saying that," she groans and starts to pace. Zilla lifts his head and watches her, but he does not go to her, content to watch the scene before him. Derek does go to her, and he pulls her into his arms.

"I'm not going anywhere. And neither are they. They know how I feel about you and if you would just let them, they would see how amazing you are. Addy, stop worrying about things that happened in the past. I guarantee you no one in there is thinking about anything other than lunch," Derek says as he runs his hand up and down her back to soothe her.

"Liv?"

"What about her?"

"Why did she have to be so nice?" Addy asks and Derek laughs.

"I'm sure Drew could fill us in on her not so nice moments," he says to lighten the mood.

"So, what now?"

"Now, we go into the kitchen, eat some questionable food my family brought and hopefully, make it through this day without a food fight," he says and releases her.

"Okay. No promises on the food fight," she replies and calls to Zilla. Now free of his leash he follows his human into the kitchen, tail happily wagging the entire time.

Derek also follows her, smiling. Operation Convince Addy was now in full swing.

Journal Entry

April 10, 2007

Mary doesn't understand why I just don't let her give this journal to Derek. She wants to give it to him now, before it's too late. She doesn't understand that it was too late years ago. Against my wishes she attempted to convince Derek to come see me but, just as I expected, he refused and stopped talking to her for a couple weeks. He eventually gave in and answered her call but told her he would not see me and asked her to stop asking him to. She finally agreed and I know she is hurting. I would give anything to take this hurt from her, but it is outside my control. Dr. Stone taught me well. I must accept this as beyond my control and live within this reality.

So, in the spirit of living in reality, I have reached out to another young man that has impacted my life. My rehab companion, Brad. I called, after getting his contact information from Dr. Stone's son – something Dr. Stone gave me an earful for. I'm not a complete moron. I knew Dr. Stone couldn't give me Brad's details – doctor/patient confidentiality and all that. But that does not extend to the Doc's son, and Brad's good friend. I think Dr. Stone regrets teaching me too well those coping mechanisms. Matt gave me Brad's number and the young man agreed to meet with me.

At first Brad wasn't thrilled about what I wanted him to do. He didn't have any kind of relationship with his parents and told me he wouldn't take too kindly to some stranger stepping into their mess. I told him the fact that he was a stranger was the only way this would work. If I had Drew or Mary approach Derek with my journal, he would only see their betrayal. But, if a stranger did it, then there would be no betrayal.

Eventually, Brad agreed, that when the time came, he would come and collect the journal and deliver it to Derek upon my death.

My death. That doesn't scare me anymore. I've come to terms with my fate. I was one of the lucky ones. I was able to love my Carol again and have her love me. Mary and Drew have opened their hearts and their homes to me so I can get to know my grandchildren. Most with my condition do not get this kind of time with those they've wronged. I am fortunate.

Hopefully, between Brad and my own words Derek is able to take some comfort in knowing that his father was repentant. In the end, I owned my failures and did what I could to atone for them. I recognize that what I have done is not nearly enough, but I will spend whatever time I have left righting the wrongs I have caused.

For now, I am going to hold my Carol tight and thank God every day for another minute with her.

Gary T. Richards

23 *The Daughter*

Addy enters the kitchen to find a small army of Richards' family members gathered around the table placing food on plates and shoving each other in the process. She is taken back by how the male family members fill the room. Drew clearly worked out and could only be described as a body builder, but there were three other young men in the kitchen that seemed to be following in his footsteps.

Derek must have picked up on her hesitancy because he comes to stand beside her and begins telling her who everyone is.

"The tallest blond headed giant in the corner standing next to my Mother is Drew's son, Connor, from his first marriage. He just turned seventeen and is determined to join the Air Force. David is thrilled but Drew likes to pretend Connor will change his mind at the last minute. Since he just got a scholarship to play football for the Air Force it doesn't seem likely he will be changing his mind. The two boys by Mary are hers. They are twins but lucky for us they aren't identical. Devon is the one that just stuck is finger in the potatoes and Brian is the one that told on him. According to Devon, Brian is a mama's boy but don't let him fool you. Devon is usually the one that is attached at the hip to Mary," Derek explains, pointing out each boy as he talks.

"Devon looks just like David," Addy says looking over to David as he scolds his son for sticking his finger in the food.

"He sure does."

"Mom! Mom! I want watermelon!"

Addy turns to the sing-song voice and sees Liv stoop down to talk to a little girl that is excitedly jumping.

"That's Molly, my daughter," Derek says softly.

Suddenly, Addy inhales a sharp breath and turns her back on the scene in the kitchen. Derek follows her movements and leans towards her to whisper in her ear.

"What are we doing?" he asks.

"Hiding," Addy responds, closing her eyes briefly before letting out a long breath.

"Addy, we aren't doing a very good job of hiding. They can still see us," Derek chuckles.

"I know. Of course, your daughter would be here. Why wouldn't she be? I don't know why I'm acting like this. I've been around kids before. I like kids. This is silly. I'm being silly," she says it all, barely pausing between sentences to breath.

"She's going to love you. She is really into zoo animals lately. If you get stuck just talk about tigers and giraffes. She'll eat it up," Derek says and gives Addy's shoulders a reassuring squeeze. She nods and the two of them enter the kitchen together, hands clasped.

"You better get in here Addy before the boys take it all," Mary says when they walk into the kitchen.

"Hey! Dad has more on his plate than we do," Brian says and calls out his father, who is currently chewing on a chicken leg while using his free hand to scoop some macaroni salad on top of his already overflowing plate.

David swallows his bite, shrugs and continues to scoop more food.

"What do you like?" Carol asks Addy as she hands her a plate.

"Thank you. I'm not picky. I'll eat pretty much anything," Addy replies.

"That's what she said," Devon replies, and his brother joins him in laughter.

"Apologize," Mary says as she smacks Devon in the back of his head.

"Hey," Devon wines and is rewarded with a second smack on the back of the head by his father.

"Don't talk back to your mother," David says, pointing his chicken leg at his son in reprimand.

"I'm sorry," Devon finally says. He leaves the kitchen with his brother close behind him, laughing at him for getting into trouble.

"Forgive them, Addy. They are heathens," Mary says. "Unlike this one, who is absolutely perfect," she says and pinches Connor's cheek. He brushes off her hand and blushes.

"Ah, Aunt Mary cut it out," Connor says and turns to Addy. "Are you sure you want to be in this family? They are nuts."

Addy is stunned by his question. Be a part of the family? She isn't there yet and she nervously glances at Derek, hoping he isn't there yet either. This was just moving too fast for her. Derek catches her eyes and slightly shakes his head. His easy brush off of Connor's words puts her at ease and she turns to Carol.

"Some chicken would be fine," she says, and Carol begins placing items on her plate. Before she finishes, Addy has enough food on the plate for three meals. She smiles at Carol but knows there is no way she would be eating all that.

During this exchange, Molly proceeds to tell Liv what items she wants to eat. Addy watchs the mother and daughter interact and feels a pang of jealousy. She would never be able to have this with her own child. Something as simple as preparing her child's plate would not be in her future. Just as she always did when she felt this way she blinks away the feelings and puts a smile on her face. There is no need dwelling on what could never be.

"We usually just eat in the living room because Derek's kitchen is too small to hold all of us. When you have finished, come join us,"

Carol says to Addy before she follows the rest of her family that had already departed the kitchen.

This left Addy, Derek, Liv, and Molly alone in the kitchen together. Molly catches Addy staring at her and the little girl smiles widely.

"Hi. I'm Molly," she says.

Addy smiles back. "I'm Addy. It's really nice to meet you," she says.

"I know," Molly replies and turns to her mother. "I can hold the plate."

"I know you can Sweetie, but I need you to carry the drinks," Liv says and gestures to two water bottles sitting on the counter. Liv's mini copy skips over to the counter and takes the bottles and immediately drops one. Laughing, Molly picks up the dropped bottle and skips out of the kitchen.

"Now imagine if I had given her the plate," Liv says over her shoulder to Addy.

Addy smiles at her and watches Liv follow behind Molly.

"She's adorable," Addy says to Derek when they are left alone.

"Yeah. She's the best part of me. I'm glad you are here," he says and comes up behind her.

Addy feels his breath on her neck as he dips his head down to place a soft kiss on the spot between her shoulder and neck. She is still holding onto her plate and quickly puts it down on the table before she drops it. His short beard scratches her skin as he continues to kiss his way up the side of her neck. She tilts her head to accommodate his path. When his lips reach her jaw, she turns and steps into him. Addy waits for the kiss to meet her lips but when it doesn't, she opens her eyes to see him staring at her with a soft expression upon his face.

"What?" she asks nervously.

"I'm just trying to convince myself that this is real. That you being here isn't a dream. I dreamt about you for so long that a part of me thinks I'm still dreaming," he answers.

Addy bites her bottom lip briefly before responding.

"What kind of dreams?" she asks and winks at him.

Suddenly, Derek is laughing and pulls her into a tight hug.

"When you guys are done making out can you grab me a beer?" Drew calls out from the living room, interrupting their laughter.

"He's my brother and I love him but sometimes I just want to kill him," Derek says as he moves away from Addy to get the beer his brother requested out of the fridge. Withdrawing the can he proceeds to shake it vigorously. Addy looks on in amusement.

When they join the others in the living room, Addy keeps her face blank as Derek hands Drew the beer can. All around them conversations are happening and no one except Addy and Derek watches as Drew places his food down to pop open the beer. As soon as he does, he is showered with a spray of frothy beer. Both Addy and Derek break into uncontrollable laughter as Drew freezes, his face and hands dripping with the frothy beverage.

"Seriously? You knew he was going to do this?" Drew turns his attention to Addy. She chokes down her laughter and coughs a couple times before gaining her composure.

"I don't know what you are talking about," she says innocently.

By now the rest of the family has stopped talking and are watching the scene unfold before them. Liv hands some napkins over to Drew and tries to hide the smirk she has on her face but she can't stop the laugh that escapes between her lips. Drew takes the napkins but glares at his wife. Liv just looks sheepish and continues to smile.

"She's perfect for you," Drew finally says to Derek as he uses the napkins to wipe his face.

"Yeah, she sure is," Derek says and turns to Addy sitting next to him. She is still laughing slightly as she looks down at her plate and brings a forkful of macaroni salad to her mouth. As he watches her, Derek realizes that for the first time in a long time, he truly feels like his world is absolutely perfect.

He had shaken his head no to comfort her when his nephew had inadvertently mentioned marriage in Addy's presence, but that is exactly where his thoughts were going. To be able to fall asleep next to her every night and wake up beside her was his idea of heaven. He still couldn't believe she was back in his life, but he wasn't about to take it for granted. His life was perfect, and it was all because of the woman sitting next to him, trying to hide her snicker every time she looked at his beer-soaked brother.

24 The Apology

Molly hands her a lion figurine as the two of them create their very own zoo for all the wild animals that didn't have mommies and daddies to look after them. Addy is in charge of the cats and Molly is in charge of all the other animals.

After the beer exploding incident the rest of the day consisted of various family events. Apparently, this was a very competitive family and during gatherings a variety of games were played to determine who were the winners and who just didn't measure up to the Richards' genetic material. That was how Connor had described the scene to Addy when Mary and Derek got into a shouting match during charades. The clue had been *The Flying Nun* and Mary didn't think Derek had done the movements correctly. Addy had been told she was spared being on Derek's team because he wasn't the greatest at this game and they didn't want her to suffer. So, she had been paired with David, and Mary had *sacrificed* herself. Derek, of course, disagreed with their assessment of his skills.

After many family-friendly games Connor took leave to join his friends for a late-night movie. Mary, David, their boys, and Carol left soon after that. When they left, Mary hugged Addy goodbye and happily told her she was excited about family dinner on Sunday. Carol told her she was glad to see her again and thanked her for her patience with her crazy family. Even the twin boys had made her feel welcome as they argued over who would get Addy to be on their team next time. Apparently, she was pretty good at family-friendly games.

Once the only adults remaining were Addy, Derek, Drew, and

Liv, Molly had laid claim to Addy and pulled her into her room. For the last hour she had been sitting on the floor with the little girl and learning all the names of the various zoo animals she had. They discovered that they both claimed the tiger as their favorite wild cat.

"Did you know that pandas eat bamboo?" Molly asks Addy as she moves a giraffe to a different location.

"I thought they liked bananas," Addy replies and earns an eye roll from Molly.

"No, silly. That's monkeys."

"Well, I'm glad you corrected me," Addy smiles at Molly. She still couldn't believe how much she looked like Liv but there was no denying this little girl would grow up to be just as stunning as her mother.

"Molly, sweetheart, it's time to go," Liv says suddenly from the doorway.

"But Ma, we haven't finished fixing the zoo," Molly whines up at her mother.

"I know but it's late and you have to get to bed soon," Liv steps into the room and kneels down by her daughter. She absentmindedly reaches out and plays with her daughter's hair.

"I want to stay at Daddy's tonight," Molly says and turns to her mother. The little girl brings a pout to her lips as if she already knows her mother is going to deny her request.

"Your Daddy has company. You are staying with me and Uncle Drew tonight. You can come over to Daddy's tomorrow," Liv says. Molly's eyes start to water and Addy's heart breaks. There is no way she is going to stand between this little girl and her Daddy.

"I need to get home anyway. I'm sure Zilla is ready to go to bed too. I've had a good time playing with you Molly," Addy says and starts to stand.

"No! I want you to stay too! I want us to have a sleep over," Molly says and reaches out to grab hold of Addy's hand, stopping her from leaving the room.

Not sure what to do, Addy looks down at Liv for assistance. Liv gently smiles and tries once again to convince her daughter that she needs to give her father some privacy tonight. Molly will not be convinced, however, and she suddenly jumps to her feet and runs out of the room calling for her daddy.

"I'm really sorry about this. She likes you and when my daughter wants something she tends to keep going until she gets it," Liv says to Addy as they walk towards the living room.

"I like her too. She is a special girl," Addy says.

Just as they are about to exit the hallway and enter the kitchen Addy stops short, surprising Liv. Turning to Liv, Addy says the very thing that she had wanted to say to Liv since meeting her.

"I'm sorry. I'm so unbelievably sorry for everything I did to you," Addy admits. She does not look Liv in the eyes because the shame she carries for her actions is still very near the surface. She waits for the onslaught she had always expected Liv, the wronged woman, to give her. The onslaught never comes.

"You have nothing to be sorry for, Addy. I admit that I was hurt when I discovered those emails. I was mad at Derek for a long time. And I suppose I was mad at you too. Maybe even blamed you a little bit but the truth is if anyone was blameless in all this it was you. I read every word you two wrote. I could tell how much pain you were in and how many times you tried to convince him to talk to me.

"The truth is I knew long before you even entered his life that he didn't love me. I knew before he moved to Colorado, but I ignored the signs and followed him anyway. I was young and I thought I was in love. I thought I could convince him to love me too. And then Molly happened. I can't say I regret any of it because that little girl is my world but I do regret keeping Derek from being happy.

"When Drew and I happened, I hoped Derek would allow himself to finally be happy. But it seemed like he thought he didn't deserve it. You, showing up again in his life is a blessing. Please know that I do not have any ill wishes towards you or Derek. Don't let me or the past keep you from him," Liv finishes and reaches out for Addy's hand. She smiles at her gently and with a squeeze of the hand gives Addy the forgiveness she had been looking for.

"Why did you have to be so perfect?" Addy blurts out and immediately blushes from embarrassment.

Liv laughs. "Oh, I am far from perfect. Just ask Drew."

The two women finish the rest of the walk towards the living room arm in arm and laughing together. They are greeted by a crying Molly in Derek's arms. He looks up at his ex-wife and silently begs for assistance. Liv goes to him and sits beside him on the couch and whispers to her daughter.

"Did you have a good day?" Drew asks Addy as they give the parents and child some privacy.

"I did. I really did. Your family is…" Addy's voice trails off because she isn't sure any words can provide justice to how incredible this family is.

"I know. They are one of a kind," Drew acknowledges. They are plunged into an awkward silence before Drew speaks again.

"I told him to walk away from you," he admits softly.

"I know," Addy says just as softly.

"I didn't know how much you meant to him. He tried to tell me, but I didn't want to hear it."

"I know. He told me," Addy says and turns to Drew. She has a soft expression on her face letting him know there were no devils here. They were all simply just people trying to do the best they could in a difficult situation. He thought he was doing what an older brother should have done and there had been nothing wrong with his actions. There was no blame to be placed here.

"He loves the shit out of you. He deserves to be happy. Make him happy, please," Drew begs. All Addy can do is nod because Derek is slowly making his way over to them.

"Molly is going to stay here tonight," he says to Addy.

"Well, this is her home. Let me just get Zilla and then we can get out of your way," Addy starts to go to the kitchen to bring the dogs in from outside when Derek stops her.

"She wants you to stay too," he says.

"Oh," she looks at Derek, then Drew, then back to Derek. "I'm not sure that is a good idea," she finally says.

"I understand." Derek starts to go back to Molly who is now sitting in her mother's lap, the tears drying. Before she can second guess herself Addy is lunging forward and she grabs Derek's arm, pulling him back to her.

"I'll stay. As long as it's okay that Zilla will be here," she says. Derek's somber expression morphs into a smile, he cups her face in his hands and gives her a quick peck on the lips.

"You're a life saver," he says and turns back to Molly.

"Molly, Addy and Zilla are going to stay the night too," he says and sits down next to Liv. Molly suddenly brightens and jumps out of Liv's lap to rush to Addy and put her arms around Addy's legs. Addy laughs and leans down to return the embrace.

"Can we finish playing zoo now?" Molly asks, her face turned up to Addy.

"Sure," Addy says as she looks to Derek and Liv for help.

"You have twenty more minutes and then it is time to get ready for bed," Derek says to Molly.

"Okay," she replies and pulls Addy by the hand and down the hallway back into her room.

Addy laughs the entire way.

25 *The Confession*

Zilla turns in a circle once, twice before finding the spot on Molly's bed that he thinks is just perfect before plopping down and resting his head on the girl's stomach. She laughs at the dog and pats his head. Derek is on the bed with them, book in hand and ready to read to his daughter. Addy is standing in the doorway watching the scene quietly from a distance.

"Addy, come sit here," Molly says and pats an open spot next to her.

"Oh, it's okay," Addy says and shakes her head.

"Get in here," Derek says and gestures towards the spot Molly had identified. Jaw set, Addy pushes off the door frame and sits next to Molly's head. The girl snuggles into Addy's side and absently continues to pet Zilla's head as Derek reads her a story of a kitten and her family.

Addy swallows down the feeling of sadness that starts to creep up at the extremely domestic scene.

Hold it together.

Derek finishes the story, kisses his daughter goodnight, and the two of them quietly leave Molly and the snoring Zilla to a room lit by a nightlight.

They go back to the living room and Derek pulls Addy to him as they sit on the sofa together. Phoenix is already resting in his designated sleeping area, a spot set up for him behind the couch. He is a police working dog and has a clearly defined regiment. Molly was excited to have Zilla sleep with her, because her daddy wouldn't let Phoenix sleep in the bed with her.

Addy leans into Derek, pulling her feet onto the sofa and bending her knees. She catches a glimpse of their reflection in the front windows and allows herself a moment to enjoy the embrace before reality sets in. This whole day had been completely wonderful but a constant reminder of the very things she couldn't give Derek. While she now feels her past sins have been forgiven there are still concerns about the future, she knows they need to discuss. She isn't sure how, or when, she had stopped thinking about this as a temporary relationship, but she knows, after today, things need to be said before they both got hurt again.

"Derek, we need to talk," she says as she slowly sits up.

"Uh oh. The last time a girl said that to me she broke my heart," he jokes. His expression falls when he sees Addy is serious.

"This day, your family, your daughter…you," she begins, "everything was just perfect. You were right. I adore your family. Even Liv. All of you make falling in love with you so easy," she sniffles as tears start to form.

"Hey. What is going on? Why are you crying?" Derek asks and starts to reach out for her, but she stops him.

"I need to say this. I can see how important family is to you. And you are just wonderful with Molly. You're a great father."

"Thank you."

"A life with me, a future with me, would take away any chance of you having another child and that just isn't fair. You deserve to be with someone that can give you that." The tears were flowing freely now. She waits for him to agree with her. She waits for him to say the words she knew would come but he says nothing. Finally, with great reluctance, she looks up at him. She finds him grinning at her and that stuns her so much that she stops crying.

"Why are you grinning?" she asks, accusatory.

"Because, for someone that is so smart, you are being really dumb," he replies. She blinks at him a couple of times before regaining composure and smacking him on the chest. He laughs, rubs his chest and adjusts his position on the couch so he is fully facing her.

"Addy, when I look at you, I don't see a baby factory. I see the woman that has captivated my soul since the moment you cursed like a sailor and tried to speak to me in sign language. I didn't stand a chance against your charms," he says, and she snorts at his comment.

"I love having a daughter and I wouldn't say no to more kids, eventually, but Addy, all I want is you. And nowhere is it written that you and I can't still have children. A family can be made in other ways. If that is our future then so be it but all I need to know is that you will be there with me, building that family together," he says and pulls her back into his arms.

Addy falls into him, crying against his chest. This stupid, stubborn, handsome man was everything she has wanted. All of the sadness, all of the guilt, all of the pain she has been holding on to for so long just drifted away. She continues to cry but it is no longer for the lost child she never got to know. This time she cries because she is finally thinking about the moments she still had ahead of her. She cries because she finally feels like she found a place she belonged.

Derek continues to hold her while she cries. He doesn't try to stop her. Instead, he waits patiently for her to get all the emotions out. She clings to him and he waits.

"What now?" She speaks into his shirt.

"What do you want to happen?" he asks and strokes her hair.

"Will you" *sniffle* "make love to me?" Addy nervously waits for his response. She is surprised when he pulls away from her. She averts her gaze, hurt by the rejection. Suddenly, she is scooped up into his arms and he is carrying her through the house.

Derek doesn't say anything to her as he brings her to his

bedroom. He closes the door with his foot. Leaving the room in darkness, he uses the sliver of moonlight to find his way to the bed.

Gently, he lowers her to his bed. Neither of them says a word as he looks down at her. He silently removes his shirt, maintaining eye contact with her the whole time. When he sits down on the side of the bed she scoots over and sits up.

Addy moves towards him, her fingers outstretched. This will be the first time that she has ever touched his body in this way. They had kissed a few times since reentering one another's lives, but this was the most intimate they had ever been. With shaking fingers, she touches his chest. He lets her get acquainted with his body and keeps his hands to himself while she explores.

After she has familiarized herself, he takes hold of one of her hands and brings it to his lips. He kisses the inside of her palm, and she moves closer. This time it is her that kisses his neck and breathes in his scent. She can hear his heavy breathing and uses one hand to cover his chest. His heart is beating as fast as hers and she smiles in his neck.

Pulling back, she brings her lips to his. Slowly, softly, they get to know each other in another way. The moments seem to move in frames. He is removing her top. She is leaning into him, feeling skin against skin. He is dipping her down towards the bed and she is closing her eyes from the pleasure of his touch. They are joined, together, physically for the first time since their souls had touched all those years ago.

26 *The Dodge*

Addy is woken by a slobbery tongue on her cheek. Smiling, she wipes the drool from her face and absently reaches out to stroke Zilla's fur. He nuzzles against her hand and gives a quick bark in greeting when someone enters the room. Addy feels the bed dip as a body joins her. Stretching, she rolls to her side and smiles at Derek.

"Morning," he says and smiles down at her.

"Morning."

"Would you like some breakfast?" he asks and brings a hand forward to caress her cheek.

"Yes. Food is good," she replies.

"Come join us after you get dressed," he says and stands. He is about to leave the room when Addy calls out to him.

"Um. Where are my clothes?"

"I laid out some things for you over there. Your other clothes are in the dryer right now," he says and points to some folded items on his dresser. She thanks him and waits for him to close the door behind him before rushing over to the dresser.

There are her under garments, a t-shirt and a pair of sweatpants. She picks them up and smells them. A little disappointed that they smell like laundry soap and not him, she puts them back down. Now that there is light, she is able to view the room and its items. It is a typical male room. The necessities are there. A bed, a nightstand, a dresser. She notices a connecting bathroom and decides a quick shower is in order.

She is still basking in the glow of last night when she steps out of the shower, wraps a towel around her and searches the items in his medicine cabinet for some toothpaste. She quickly locates it and uses her finger to brush her teeth. With a chuckle, she is reminded of her college days and doing the exact same thing then.

She quickly dresses and is looking for a laundry basket for the used towel when something on his dresser catches her eye. It is a leather-bound journal and there is a photo sticking out of it. Without thinking, she picks up the journal and flips the front cover open. She sees a scrawled name on the first page – *Gary T. Richards.* Below that is an inscription that reads – *For my son.* Addy realizes what she holds and is about to place it back where she found it when a face on the photo inside the folds of the pages catches her eye.

Removing the photo from the journal, Addy finds herself staring down at a face she never expected to see again. The face of someone from her past that had once brought her solace during dark moments. A friend that had shown her that pain didn't have to last forever.

Brad.

A man she had turned to when her world had fallen apart around her. He is standing in a group, arms draped around an older gentleman. The majority of the people in the photo are smiling or waving at the camera. All except the older man and Brad.

"Did you get lost?"

Addy jumps at the sound of Derek's voice. The photo falls from her fingers and flutters to the ground. She turns to Derek, standing inside the doorway, and her face flushes from embarrassment.

"I'm sorry. I didn't mean to pry," she says.

Derek, still smiling, walks over to her. He picks up the photo, his brow furrowing slightly, before taking the journal from her hands. He tucks the photo back into the leather book.

"My father's journal. I told you about it," he says and places it back on the dresser.

"Yes. I'm sorry. I just saw the photo. I didn't mean to pry," she says again. Her mind is reeling. Why would Derek have a photo of Brad? Did he know him?

"It's alright," he says and takes her hand so he can kiss the palm. He continues to hold her hand as he walks with her to the kitchen. Molly is sitting at the table, Zilla diligently at her side, waiting for a scrap to fall. Phoenix sits nearby as well, but not shamelessly begging like Zilla.

"Would you like some pancakes?" Derek asks Addy, startling her out of her daze.

"Yes, please."

"Addy! Morning!" Molly says and jumps out of her chair to give Addy a hug.

Addy laughs and hugs the girl back.

"Come sit next to me," she says and pulls Addy to the table.

Addy spends the next few minutes answering Molly's many questions, but her gaze remains fixed on Derek. How does he know Brad? Why would his father have a photo of Brad in his journal? Addy continues to observe Derek as Molly prattles on. As her mind races, Addy is reminded of how she had felt recognition that first day she met Derek in the airport. Was it possible that they had met before, and she just couldn't remember?

"Pancakes and sausage coming through," Derek announces. Molly claps as he places food on her plate. He winks at Addy as he puts some food on her plate as well.

"Syrup Daddy," Molly calls when Derek has put the pan in the sink.

"Yes, my Fairy," he replies and gets the syrup before returning to the table. "Is orange juice, okay?"

"What?" Addy asks, lost in her thoughts.

"Orange juice?" Derek repeats. He is holding the carton in his hand and gives it a shake.

"Oh, yes. That is fine. Thank you," she says and watches as he pours some juice into a glass for her. She takes it from him, smiles, and takes a sip.

"That's enough syrup, Molly," Derek says and takes the dispenser from his daughter. She ignores him, picks up her fork and stabs a sausage with it.

Derek sits and looks at Addy with concern. She has been jumpy since he caught her holding his father's journal. He wasn't upset with her and thought he had handled the situation well. Yet, here she is, jumping every time he speaks to her. She is slow to pick up her fork and keeps her gaze fixed on her plate. She looks at Molly when Molly asks her a question, but she quickly returns her gaze to her food. The food that she isn't really eating. She is massacring it, though.

"All done, Daddy," Molly says proudly when she is finished.

"Great job, Fairy. Why don't you take Zilla and Phoenix to your room and get ready for school," he says. Molly does as he says and as soon as she disappears, he turns his attention to Addy.

"Is everything alright?" he asks, noticing the slight way she jumps at his voice.

"Oh, yes. Everything is fine." She finally looks at him, but the smile seems forced to him.

"It's okay you looked at the journal. I'm not mad," he says, hoping this will help her relax.

"Oh. Yes. Sorry. Who was in the photo?" she asks.

The photo?

Derek isn't sure why he kept that all these years. His father had placed it in there and even though the photo held no sentimental value to him, he hadn't rid himself of it.

"It was my father's group in rehab," Derek answers. Quick to discontinue talking about that, he stands and begins removing the plates from the table.

Addy remains seated at the table. She has begun to fiddle with her hands, wringing her fingers. A movement Derek has noticed. She is trying to figure out how to ask him more questions about the photo without seeming nosey when he suddenly appears by her side and takes hold of her hands.

"What is going on in there?" he asks and taps her forehead.

"I just,"- she doesn't know how to answer him. "I'm just worried you think I was snooping. I honestly didn't mean to. I just picked up the photo without thinking," she supplies.

"It's alright. My father left the photo in the journal," Derek says, and he suddenly laughs.

"What?"

"I doubt he would have left it in there had he known."

"Known what?" Addy asks, confused.

"That Brad, the one standing next to him in the photo, was the guy that my ex left me for," Derek says and laughs again. He is oblivious to the horror that is playing out inside of Addy at that moment. All he sees is a woman that is nervous about the day after an intimate night. He doesn't realize that Addy is panicking.

Brad.

The same Brad she had been involved with. The same Brad she credited for helping her to heal after everything that had happened to her back in college. The same Brad she had helped steal somebody's girlfriend from.

Suddenly, she recalls why Derek had seemed so familiar that day at the airport. He had been Kelly's boyfriend. She had seen him with her one day at a diner. The very same diner Brad and her had gone to when Brad had approached Kelly to tell her about his addiction and going to rehab. Derek had been on the track team with Brad and her ex-boyfriend, Clark.

Why hadn't she recognized him before? She must have crossed paths with him frequently at college. Then again, after her breakup with Clark she rarely attended the track meets. And she only did so a few times when she was hanging out with Brad. She never stuck around the team for fear she would run into Clark. As she recalled, Derek had joined the team after she and Clark had split.

As she was running through all the possible ways they could have come in contact with each other, another, more devastating thought pushed its way to the forefront.

Derek hated Brad.

What would Derek do once he found out that she had a history with Brad? Would he hate her too?

"Addy?" Derek's voice breaks her from her thoughts.

"Huh?" she asks.

"I was asking if you wanted me to pick you up next week for the family dinner at Liv and Drew's."

"Oh. Yes. Please, that would be nice."

Get it together Addy Kat!

"I would love to spend the rest of the day with you, in bed, naked," he says and pulls her up from her chair.

Once she is fully standing, he bends down and kisses her softly. She returns the kiss, willing herself to snap out of her haze.

"But I'm on shift today," he finishes saying. She smiles at him, trying to show she understands but her smile is crooked and his brow furrows.

"Are you sure everything is okay?"

"Yes. I'm sure. I just think I'm still trying to wrap my head around everything," she explains and puts her arms around him. He mimics the embrace and kisses her neck.

"As long as you aren't having second thoughts," he says.

Addy's heart cracks a little. She most definitely is having thoughts but none of them involved walking away from him. If anything, her thoughts are centering on how she could keep from losing him once he finds out the truth.

"Never," she responds.

Journal Entry

May 25, 2007

Doubt has this uncanny ability to creep in when you least expect it. I experienced doubt many times as a soldier and a cop. Many more times as a father. Doubt haunts you when you aren't sure if what you are doing is the right thing for your children.

For so long I felt confident that I was going about this the right way but now I am not so sure. Derek is graduating from college. Carol wanted me to go with her, but I said no. I said no because I know he doesn't want me there. But here I am, coughing up blood and doubting I made the right choice.

My days are numbered now and there is fear inside me that perhaps it isn't Derek that is the stubborn one. Perhaps it is my pride that is preventing me from doing as Carol asks. I keep saying I can't go to him because he would only turn me away and then be upset with his mother. Maybe I am wrong though. Maybe if he saw me, he would change his mind. Dare I risk the rejection?

No. I know my son. If I went to him when he wasn't ready, he would turn from me forever. The words I leave him are what are important.

So, son, if you are reading this know that it wasn't pride that kept me from you. It wasn't stubbornness. It was love. I loved you enough to respect your wishes. I loved you so much it hurt to stay away. I wrestled with this doubt and found myself going to you many times.

I also want you to know that I was there on your graduation day. I missed your high school one, but I wasn't about to miss your college graduation. Drew took me. That was why he was late. He had to help me since I was wheelchair bound by then. I know you were probably mad at him for arriving late, but it wasn't his fault. It was mine. Please forgive him for that.

I was so proud of you that day. And even though I couldn't tell you then, know that I am so damn proud of you son. There is one thing I do not doubt and that is you. I know you will be a fine man. I know one day you will find a beautiful wife and be the best husband, the best father you could be. I know this because even as a young boy you demanded so much of yourself. I have no doubt you will be a better man than I.

Then, now, always, I am proud to call you son.

Gary T. Richards

27   The Truth

After she left Derek's house Addy called in sick to work, drove straight to her sister's and confessed everything that had transpired over the last twenty-four hours. Rachel and Julie listened intently. Their every reaction was timed perfectly. They sighed with relief when Addy told them how well it went with his family, they said "aw" when she described her interaction with Molly, they swooned when she told them the things Derek had said to her, and their mouths fell in surprise when she told them about the photo and what it meant for her and Derek.

"This can't be happening," Julie says when Addy finishes telling her story.

"Oh, believe it Jules. Your sister has one fucked up relationship with the universe. Do you hear me universe! Stop messing with me!" Addy shouts at the ceiling.

"Addy, sit down," Rachel says as her head follows the pacing movements of Addy.

"I can't. I can't sit down. If I sit down, then this is all real. Jules, I need alcohol, stat!" Addy points at Julie. Julie starts to stand but Rachel pulls her back down.

"Addy, it's barely nine in the morning. You don't need alcohol. You need to sit down. Breath," Rachel says and goes to Addy. She gently steers Addy towards the armchair and gets her to sit down.

Addy leans back, her legs splayed out in front of her and slouches in the chair. Releasing a disgruntled breath, she throws her hands over her face and screams into them.

"Why me?" she asks no one in particular.

"What did he say when you told him?" Julie asks.

"Tell him? Are you kidding me? I didn't tell him. I got out of there as soon as I could. I can't possibly tell him that once upon a time I slept with the very man he blames for ruining his relationship with the woman he loved," Addy says as she peeks between her fingers at her sister.

"Loved. Past tense. He loves you now," Rachel says.

Addy turns to gaze at her through her fingers. Rachel can't see it, but Addy is scowling at her. Right now is not the time for logic and level-headedness. Right now is the time for alcohol and panicking.

Curses on her sister-in-law and her psychology training.

"I don't think that will matter much to him. He told me how devastated he was by his Ex leaving him for Brad. It destroyed him so much that he ended up engaged to Liv and we all know how the rest of that story goes. Nothing good can come from me telling him I too have a connection to Brad," Addy says, grunts and sits up.

"I don't think you are giving him enough credit. Remember, he is not the same man you once knew. Many years have passed since he told you all those things. He is a father now. He's been through a lot and the last thing on his mind is some ex-girlfriend that is no longer in his life," Rachel explains. Julie nods along in agreement.

"But what if you're wrong?" Addy whispers.

"Then he was never the man for you," Rachel concludes.

Deep down Addy knows that Rachel is right but on the surface all she can see is how hurt he was nine years ago by Kelly's rejection. Derek has blamed Brad for so much back then and she can only imagine how he would feel by learning, yet again, another woman he loved had been involved with Brad.

Granted, her involvement with Brad had nothing to do with love and was simply a way for them to cope with the pain they were experiencing regarding personal losses. The time she had spent with Brad had simply been a time for healing. At no point did either of them believe it would be permanent. In fact, they both knew and wanted it to be a temporary connection. She hadn't seen or heard from him in nearly ten years. He is far removed from her life now, but she doesn't think Derek will see it that way.

"I'm scared," she finally admits. Julie and Rachel immediately come to her. They each perch on one of the armrests and offer reassurance with embraces and soothing touches.

"It is easy to be scared when faced with the possibility of losing someone we love. But if you don't tell him then it will always be between you. What is more important to you? Being honest with him or keeping your secret?" Rachel asks Addy.

Addy sighs, looks at her sister-in-law out of the corner of one eye and shakes her head.

"I hate when you use your training on me. Why did you have to marry a psychologist?" she asks Julie.

This time, Julie doesn't give her customary answer. Instead, she hugs her sister and says, "For times like these."

Addy knows she shouldn't wait too long to tell Derek the truth. She is supposed to go to a family dinner with him the next week and she admits that there is no way she could make it through that dinner with this secret. So, she asks him to come over after he completes his shift. He agrees he will come over after he takes Phoenix home.

She hasn't told him that something is wrong, but Derek already knows she had been acting off. He knows something is going on as he drives over to her house that evening. He is worried that she is having second thoughts about him. He has already decided that he won't let her walk away so easily.

When he arrives at her house in the early morning hours she has a robe on and her eyes are bloodshot. He can tell that she is tired but has been battling sleep, most likely from a restless mind. She lets him kiss her in greeting but steps away from him when they enter her house. Zilla happily greets him, but the dog looks at Addy with concern. Derek pats the dog's head and also looks at Addy with concern.

"Let's go into the kitchen. Would you like something to drink?" Addy asks Derek. She goes to the refrigerator, opens it and nervously begins shuffling items aside. "I have water, juice, and beer. You probably don't want beer. Tea! I also have tea," Addy says and begins pulling the pitcher out of the fridge.

Derek comes up to her, takes the tea from her, puts it back in the fridge, closes the door and takes her hands. He guides her to the table and they both sit down. With their hands still linked on the table Derek asks her point blank, "What is wrong?"

"I-I have something to tell you," she stammers. She is looking down at their linked hands. He is looking at her face and the regret he sees on it.

"Alright."

"You aren't going to like it," she says painfully.

"Alright."

"The reason I picked up that photo from your father's journal is because I recognized someone in the picture. I knew him from before. From college," she begins. Finally, she looks up at him. He waits for her to continue.

"I think we went to the same college," she says.

"Okay. So, you and the person you recognized went to the same college," he repeats, confused.

"No. You and me. *We* went to the same college," she says and pulls her hands from his to gesture between the two of them.

"Okay. So, that means we, you and me, went to college with the guy you recognized?" Derek connects her thoughts.

"Yes."

"So?" Derek shrugs.

"You hate him," she blurts. She sees the moment he connects another dot, another thought. His expression goes from mildly amused to narrowed anger in a matter of seconds.

"Brad," he confirms.

"Yes."

"Okay. Why does this upset you?" he asks carefully.

"Because I know how much you hate him for what he did to you. And I was *involved* with him," she replies, avoiding his gaze again.

"Involved?"

It's a single word. One question. But his voice betrays his emotions. He is upset, confused, and unsure of what his happening here. She is sitting before him looking like she has betrayed him. She is avoiding his gaze like she is ashamed and all he can think is *'she is still in love with Brad'*.

And then, his next thought is, *'I'm going to kill him'*. Because, in his mind, Brad is the guy that got her pregnant and then left her after she miscarried.

"We were there for each other when no one else was. He was my friend. At one point my lover. I was the one that convinced him to tell Kelly how he felt. For as long as I knew him, I had always pushed him to be honest with her. I helped break you two up," she finishes, her head cast down.

"Was he the guy from college you told me about? The one that got you pregnant?" Derek manages to get out.

"What? No! That was Clark. You had to have known Clark. He was on the track team. He was the one that got me pregnant. Brad was Clark's former roommate. We were friends. After everything happened with Clark, Brad and I…we were…he was my friend," she finally decides. She isn't sure she can describe the relationship she had with Brad in terms others would understand, least of all him.

Addy is now looking at Derek, but he is no longer looking at her. His gaze is staring out in the distance and his expression is emotionless. She can't decipher what he is thinking, and this brings forth the panic. She can't help but think she has lost him.

"A friend you slept with?" he finally asks.

"Yes."

"Did you love him?" This time he does look at her. His expression is still rigid.

"I loved what he did for me. He made me believe in life again. He was my fr,"-

"Friend! I got it," Derek says and suddenly pushes away from the table.

"Derek, I'm sorry. I didn't know. I remember thinking you seemed familiar, but I swear to you I didn't know who you were," Addy stands and starts to reach out to touch him but he pulls away from her.

"The diner. You were the girlfriend," he says, connecting the final dots.

"No. I was *not* his girlfriend," she says pointedly.

"You were fucking him! You were his girlfriend," he says and turns for the door.

"Derek, wait! I didn't know!" She rushes after him, ready to stop him but he abruptly breaks his stride and turns to her.

"It doesn't matter Addy. Don't you see it? Everything in my life that I thought was mine has been his first! Her. My father. You! It's like I can't escape him. He's in every crack. The ghost that keeps haunting me."

"I'm sorry," she cries, her voice breaking. She reaches out one hand to him, but his words disrupt her reaching out.

"I know. I'm sorry too," he says and turns away from her.

As soon as the door closes behind him, Addy crumbles to the floor and breaks. She is crying in aguish when Zilla comes to her, nuzzling her with his wet nose. She grabs a hold of his fur and cries into the softness that is her faithful companion. Zilla puts his head on her shoulder and does what he does best, be there for his human.

28 The Advice

The family didn't understand why Addy was absent from Sunday dinner. It was obvious that Derek didn't want to discuss it but letting things be was not the Richards' way. After many secret conversations it was decided that Drew would be the one to approach Derek.

So, under the guise of having work related things to discuss with him, Drew convinced Derek to go to into the study. The rest of the family remained in the kitchen while Drew talked to his brother. As soon as they were alone Drew wasted no time.

"Tell me the truth. Why isn't Addy here?"

"I don't want to talk about this," Derek says and starts to leave the room. Drew immediately slams the door closed.

"Too bad. Talk," he says and points at a chair, demanding Derek sit. Much to Drew's surprise, Derek doesn't argue, and he sits in the chair. He doesn't speak but he still sits down. Drew decides that is progress and continues.

"Did things go south after we left your house?"

"No. Things were amazing that night," Derek half laughs as he says this.

"Okay. So, they went to shit after that?"

"Yep."

"Derek! You gotta give me something, here," Drew says in exasperation.

"Brad," Derek scoffs.

"What about him?" Drew had known Brad due to their father. Gary had introduced them during the last few months of his life. In fact, Brad and Drew had often talked to each other during those last months. Drew knew now that Gary had enlisted Brad's help in giving Derek his journal. The funeral fiasco hadn't been forgotten by Drew, but he couldn't understand what Brad had to do with Addy.

"She used to fuck Brad," Derek spits out and slams his fist into the arm of the chair.

"So what?" Drew asks, drawing a look between surprise and disgust from Derek.

"So, this jackass had his hands on her!"

"And?"

"Are you mental? First, he took Kelly. And now he's been with Addy," Derek explains to his brother in frustration.

"Did Addy say she wanted to find Brad or something?"

"No. She saw the rehab picture in Dad's journal," Derek says, his voice is now calm.

"Oh. And then she told you that she knew him,"- He is unable to finish as Derek abruptly interrupts.

"Fucked him."

"Fucked him," Drew says and narrows his eyes at his brother. "And you freaked out because you have this unhealthy obsession with Brad for some reason."

"What? I don't have an obsession with him," Derek glares at his brother. Sure, he disliked the guy, but he wasn't obsessed with him.

"Yeah, you do. You think he took something that belonged to you and ever since then you've been holding on to this sick grudge. It's time to get over it, little brother."

"It's not that simple." Of course, Drew would take Brad's side, just as he had done at the funeral reception. If anyone had an obsession with Brad, it was Drew.

"Sure, it is. Do you want this Kelly girl back?"

"No. Of course not," Derek says.

"Do you love Addy?"

"You know I do."

"Then drop this stupid bullshit and let it go," Drew says. He slaps Derek on the shoulder before turning to leave the room.

"It isn't fair. He can't have Dad and Addy, too," Derek says angrily.

"Woah! What are you talking about? Dad?" Drew comes back to stand before Derek.

"He was there. Dad confided in him. He took everything I cared about. It isn't fair that he had Addy too."

Nodding in understanding, Drew sits on the edge of the desk in the study and looks upon his brother with stilted sympathy.

"You think it's easy for me that my wife was with you first? You're my brother. I love you and it killed me that I wanted her. I spent many nights hating the fact that you had her first. That I was second best. I would have given anything to erase your past with her. I thought about it so much that it started to come between me and Liv. She told me that everyone had a past, but the past could only hurt us if we let it. She told me to be present in the here and now with her or stay in the past without her. I'm telling you now brother, choose. Stay in the here and now with Addy or remain in the past without her. You can't have it both ways. Choose," Drew says and leaves Derek alone in the study with his thoughts.

Choose.

Derek had been asked to make a choice once before and that choice hadn't been Addy. He wanted to choose her now, but he didn't know how to let go of the anger he still felt towards a man that had seeped into nearly every aspect of his life. He no longer had feelings for Kelly, but the sting of her rejection hadn't lessened over the years. Perhaps that was because, always in the background, had been the rejection he had experienced from his father.

His father had been the first person he loved that had rejected his love. The allure of the bottle had been stronger than a child's love and his father had long ago disappeared from his life. Long before his death, Gary had abandoned his children. Only, he had come back. In the end it was Derek that had done the rejecting.

And then Brad showed up once again in his life, Kelly in tow. This time, though, he came with a message from his father. The journal had been created to reach out to Derek but having it delivered to him by Brad had only given it an aura of betrayal. His father had betrayed him by confiding in Brad and bringing him back into Derek's life. Every time he reached for the journal there was a brief moment where that betrayal would come rushing back.

Now, Addy reveals that she too had been touched by the man that represented everything Derek hated. How could he possibly get passed this? Once again, Brad had gotten to the woman he loved first. Derek was nothing but sloppy seconds. No, he was worse than that. He was nothing more than an afterthought. He was the last prize left at a carnival game. The one nobody wanted.

Just as Derek had done on the day of his father's funeral, he runs.

He runs from his brother's house and to his own house. He tears through his door and rushes to his bedroom. He snatches his father's journal from his dresser, grabs his keys and drives madly to the cemetery. He needs to go back to the beginning. To the man that started it all.

To his father.

29 *The Reconciliation*

It had been years since he had visited this grave. Nearly ten years to be exact. Every time he had tried to return in the past, he never made it any further than the parking lot. While he continued to re-read his father's journal, he never could bring himself to stand beside his grave. Standing beside it now Derek realizes that he has been holding on to so much anger. More than he had even thought was possible. He had told Addy that he hadn't forgiven his father. The process of forgiveness had always felt bitter to him and he had rejected it for so long that it was simply second nature for him to pass it by.

"I wish you were alive. If you were alive, I could tell you how much you messed up my life. You're dead and you are still messing it up," Derek says angrily to the cold, grey slab of stone.

Gary T. Richards. Beloved husband and father.

"Do you even care?" Derek asks this question and is answered by silence in this place of death and sorrow. It is dark now and he is alone with the ghost of his father and his own regrets.

"I read your damn words. Every last one of them. I keep reading them. I'm not sure what I'm looking for exactly, but I do know I haven't found it yet. You thought you were bringing a stranger into my life but in typical Gary Richards fashion you messed that up too. You managed to find the one person I hated more than you and you delivered him to me like he was some second coming of you.

"That hurt me you know. The fact that he reminded you of some younger version of yourself. He was a prick and an addict. I can see why you saw yourself in him, but it still stung. Like you were saying he was the son you never had. The son you actually wanted. I tried so damn hard to be the son you wanted," Derek spits out. He can feel tears forming and he tries to force them back down. He refuses to cry over the man that left his family in shambles. Despite his attempts the tears still fall.

"The funny thing is, Addy saw right through me. She knew after only knowing me a couple hours that all I ever wanted to be was you. I thought, finally, someone that sees me and only me. I thought she was mine! But, just like how you were supposed to be mine, she was his."

Derek holds up the leather journal and shakes it before his father's grave.

"Did you share these words with him first, too? While you sat next to him in group therapy did you spill your guts? Tell *him* all your regrets? Did you reach out to *him* when I wouldn't take your calls?"

Throwing the journal, it connects with the grave stone and tumbles to the ground and falls open. The tears are still falling and Derek stares down at the open journal. Laughing at the sheer agony of coming face to face with the photo that holds his father's and Brad's likeness, Derek reaches down and snatches up the offending picture.

"I hope it was worth it, Dad. In the end, you gave your best to him. And you gave me him and all the baggage that came with him. Thanks for including this in the journal, by the way. Nothing makes me feel better than seeing the two of you standing next to each other, his arm around you like you are father and son," Derek says. He goes to rip the photo in half but writing on the back catches his eyes.

Quickly, Derek flips the photo over and sees his father's familiar scrawl. He'd looked at this photo many times before but never once thought to look at the back. Usually, he would tuck the photo quickly back into the folds of the pages when he got to it. He never liked to look at it for long.

Group. Where I learned to forgive.

Derek stares down at his father's words and is reminded of another conversation he had Addy. A conversation about the power of forgiveness. She had told him that she had wanted to forgive her ex, not for him, but for her. She had said that by forgiving him she would be free of the pain.

Forgive.

Falling to his knees upon his father's grave Derek reaches one hand out and rests it on the gravestone before him. The tears fall faster now, and his shoulders shake from the sobs. For so long he had blamed others for the pain in his life. He blamed his father for drinking and leaving them all behind. He blamed his brother for following in their father's footsteps. He blamed Kelly for not loving him. He blamed his mother for going back to his father. He blamed Brad for taking Kelly from him. He blamed his father for dying. He blamed Brad for being close to his father. He blamed his father for betraying him by being close to Brad. He blamed Brad for getting to Addy first. And now, now he was blaming Addy for having a past. He blamed everyone around him but himself for holding on too long to things that no longer mattered.

"I'm sorry, Dad. I'm sorry I haven't been the man you thought I'd be. I've let you down. I guess that is the Richards' way. So quick to judge. Slow to forgive. I'm sorry I kept you away. I forgive you, Dad. I wish you were still alive so I could tell you that," Derek's shoulders sag and he pushes away from the head stone. Still kneeling, he places the photo against the stone slab.

It's time to let go.

Derek picks up the leather journal and says a final goodbye to his father. He knows where the next road will lead him. Just as his brother told him, he has a choice to make.

So, he makes his choice.

30 *The Reckoning*

Regret was not something Addy held in her heart. She didn't regret a single moment she had spent with Derek the last couple of weeks. She also didn't regret being honest with him about her past. Rachel had been right. She needed to be honest because she needed to know if their relationship was strong enough. Now, she knew it wasn't. While she was hurting from this realization, she knew the hurt was only temporary. She had pulled through the pain of loss before, and she would do so again. This time she had her family to lean on for support.

So, in the spirit of healing, she had done what she did many times before. Her ritual of cleansing the tears and pain began shortly after Derek had walked out of her home nearly a week ago. She had remained locked in her home, with her favorite being in the world and found solace in a wine glass and episodes of one of her favorite shows – *Gilmore Girls*. If Lorelei could find love, then so could she one day.

Zilla and she were sitting on the couch together, watching the Girls when the pounding started. Startled, Zilla jumped from the couch and began barking at the intrusion of their solitude. She shushed Zilla but also patted him on the head for being a good guard dog. Carrying her wine glass with her she looked out the small window on her door and sucked in a breath when she saw him. She didn't want him here.

"Addy, I know you are in there. Let me in. We need to talk," Derek calls through her door. Soon, the pounding begins again and Zilla lets loose another round of high-pitched barks.

"Go away," Addy finally says back.

"No. Addy, I'm sorry. I messed up. Please let me in," he pleads with her.

"No. Go home Derek. You said enough," Addy sniffles.

"But I didn't. I said all the wrong things. I did all the wrong things. I promised you I would fix all the broken pieces, and I ended up just breaking them more. I don't deserve it but I'm asking anyway, let me in."

By now Addy is resting her head against the door. She looks down at Zilla, who has quieted and is awaiting instructions from Addy. Quizzically, Zilla tilts his head at Addy and begins to wag his tail. With a sigh, Addy unlocks the door and steps back.

Traitor, she says silently to Zilla. He just continues to wag his tail and look innocent.

Derek wastes no time upon hearing the lock click and he twists the knob to let himself in. He is greeted by the sight of Addy, her eyes and nose red from crying. She still holds her wine glass and gives him a mock salute before downing the contents. Turning, she goes to the kitchen to refill the empty glass. Derek follows close behind her, Zilla at his side waiting for a greeting. Petting the dog, Derek finds Addy pouring herself some more wine.

"I'm sorry," he says to her.

"Yep. You've already said that," she says and tilts the bottle to him, offering him some. He shakes his head, and she shrugs.

He watches her as she walks past him to go down the steps into her sunken living room. She hits a button on a remote and the show on her television resumes playing. He doesn't say anything as he joins her on the couch. He waits patiently while she watches the women on the screen discuss their life issues. Zilla manages to wedge himself between them on the couch and the three of them sit there in silence until the episode ends and the screen goes blue, signaling the end of a DVD.

The entire scene would most likely appear comforting and familiar from an outsider's perspective. However, sitting next to Addy, in the silence, Derek is very much aware of the tension in the room.

"What do you want?" Addy finally speaks.

"You. All I've ever wanted was you," Derek responds. He is looking at Addy's profile and she continues to stare straight ahead at the blue television screen.

"You have a strange way of showing it," she says softly.

"Nothing I say can ever justify walking away from you the other day. As soon as I heard his name it was like all I saw was red. I've seen red when it came to him for so long that I ignored everything else you were telling me. All I could think about was how people I care about continue to be taken from me by him. It didn't matter that I lost what I lost because I was the one that walked away. It was just easier to blame him. But he isn't the problem. He has never been the problem. It's me. I'm the one that kept walking away. I'm the one that kept giving up.

"I gave up on my father. I gave up on all my past relationships. I gave up on my own happiness. And then, I gave up on you. Drew told me I had to choose between being present with you now or be stuck in the past, without you. I didn't hear him when he said it. It wasn't until I realized just how much I was holding on to the past that his words hit me. Then I thought about what you had told me about forgiveness. You and Drew were right. I couldn't let go of the past until I forgave. I'm sorry it took me so long to see it. I'm sorry I hurt you and I'm sorry I didn't choose you last time. But I'm choosing you now. Please choose me. Please forgive me," Derek begs her.

He sees the tear fall down her cheek when she closes her eyes.

Inhaling, she opens her eyes and turns to him. "You're running out of second chances with me," she says.

"I know. I'll take as many as your willing to give me," he says and tentatively reaches out to take her hand in his. She allows the act and intertwines her fingers with his.

"I never loved him," she says to him.

"It wouldn't matter if you did. As long as you love me *now*."

"You're beyond frustrating. Your mood swings cause whiplash, and your pancakes are just merely adequate," she states with a smirk.

"I'll work on them," he chuckles.

"Sometimes your jokes aren't funny."

"Noted," he says and smiles.

"Your lists are terrible," she says seriously, and he grins.

"My lists are awesome."

"Your obsession with *Hanson* is disturbing," she says with feign concern.

"My obsession?"

"And you snore. Like a bear."

"I do not."

"Despite all your many flaws, I do love you. I choose you," she says and smiles at him.

"Marry me," he blurts.

Astonished, she stares at him, mouth agape and eyes wide.

"You're crazy," she finally says to him.

"Maybe. But I also know I never wanted anything more than to have you in my life, now and always. We've wasted too much time already. I don't want to waste another moment. Marry me. Be mine forever. Adopt a dozen children with me. Let's get another dog. We

317

will build a million snowmen together. Anything you want, it's yours," he kisses the inside of her palm and places her other hand on his heart, his hand covering hers. She looks at their joined hands before giving him an answer.

"On one condition," she replies.

"Anything. Name it."

Addy just grins.

31 The Crescendo

"I am loving this look on you," Drew says to his brother as Derek glares into a mirror.

After he had asked Addy to marry him, she had given him a condition he had foolishly agreed to before hearing what it was. Now, he stood inside a bathroom at her sister's house, staring at his reflection, regretting his quick agreeance of her condition. Drew, on the other hand, was reveling in it.

"It's like a teenage girl's fandom threw up on you," Drew chuckles as he takes in Derek's outfit.

"Stop enjoying this," Derek says.

"Oh no. I will never stop enjoying this. Fair warning, I have Liv on stand-by out there with a camera. We are immortalizing this moment. David is going to record it too so there will forever be video evidence of this day," Drew says.

"I can't believe she invited all of you."

"I can! She knows how much we are going to enjoy this. At least you got to meet her parents before today. Before this outfit."

Derek sighs as he once again curses Addy for making him do this. Her condition for agreeing to marry him was to learn all the words to the *Hanson* song, MMMbop, sing it in front of both their families while wearing an old t-shirt of hers that had the boys' likeness on it, and a ballerina tutu over his jeans. The shirt was too small for him and his stomach was showing. The fact that she wanted him to do this in front of her parents was humiliating. Which was exactly what she had intended.

"Well, little brother. It is time. Make your choice," Drew says and claps Derek on the shoulder.

Knowing the only choice he has is to get this over with, Derek exits the bathroom with Drew behind him. Their families are gathered in the living room together and he can hear the chatter as he comes around the corner. All the noise stops as soon as he comes into view. A single laugh rings out amidst the silence and his eyes cut directly to Addy. She is holding her niece and using her free hand to hide her laughing face at his appearance. Even his own mother betrays him by releasing a small chuckle. She composes herself quicker than Addy does, however.

"Everyone, gather 'round. Derek has a special treat for you all," Addy says as she smirks at him. Zilla and Phoenix are dutifully positioned on either side of her, standing guard over their beloved human. Phoenix made it very clear that if he had to choose between Derek and Addy, it would be Addy every time. There were no doubts where Zilla's loyalties lay.

His family knew what was about to happen because he had told them. But Addy had refused to let him tell her family. She wanted it to be a surprise. So, here he was, in a *Hanson* mid-drift shirt and pink, frilly tutu before her family about to belt out one of the cheesiest songs he had ever heard. Molly, his beautiful daughter, stood ready by the stereo to hit play to start the song. Addy had recruited his own daughter in this madness. The two were thick as thieves and were constantly plotting against him.

He blinks when a flash goes off. Liv stands to the side, camera in hand, and mouths *sorry* when he glares at her. She isn't sorry if the grin on her face is any indication. She is enjoying this as much as Drew. And David is already recording the incident with his phone. Mary is happily directing her husband as he records.

Addy's mother signs and Addy quickly signs back a reply, speaking as she signs.

"He wanted to thank you all for being so nice to him, so he chose a song that is dear to me and decided to give us a concert," Addy lies through her teeth. She blows him a kiss when she catches him staring her down.

"Yeah, I don't believe that for a second but I'm still going to watch whatever this is," Julie says and gestures to Derek. Rachel and Addy's father laugh at his pained expression.

"His tummy is showing," Zachary, Addy's nephew suddenly announces. The room erupts in laughter. He just smiles tightly.

Well, the only way to do this was to own it completely.

"To display my love for Addy and appreciation to all of you for welcoming my family into your home, I give you Addy's favorite song of all time. Hit it Molly," Derek says and points to his daughter.

She takes the cue and hits play. The music of *MMMbop* flows out and Derek sings along with every word. As the song continues on, he adds a few dance moves. His family and Addy's family hoot with laughter. He moves his way over to Addy and she hands her niece to her mother, who is watching her husband as he signs the words of the song to her.

Pulling her from her chair, Derek continues to sing the words to Addy. She joins in and soon the other adults that know the words are singing along with them. In the middle of both their families, dancing and singing their hearts out, Addy and Derek join hands. Once the song ends Derek raises his eyebrows in question at Addy and she smiles.

"Dad, get ready. I'm going to need you to walk me down an aisle soon," Addy announces and the room heightens with conversation as their families take in the news.

Neither Addy nor Derek pays them any mind. For the first time in a long time, they are both finally right where they want to be and all they can hear is the cheerful barks of two dogs weaving between their legs and their whispered words of love as they get lost where they began, in one another.

The Last Journal Entry

July 29, 2007

How is a life measured when it is at the end? When judgement day comes what will tip the scales? I don't know if I've managed to tip my scales back towards the side of righteousness, but I'm not worried about that today. I've done what I could, and the rest isn't up to me. It took me many years to learn that there are just some things that are not within our control.

I believe my young life had to have all that despair because it led me straight to Carol. My guardian angel. Every good part of my life was because of that woman. She held the pain at bay for so long for me. It was through her kindness that I was able to have those early years with my children. It will be those moments I will be thinking of when the good Lord calls me back Home. The time is near now. I can feel it. Strangely, the feeling is familiar and brings me comfort.

All of my fears have fallen away, and I am overcome with peace. I don't know how I know this, but I know my family will be alright. I know they will be able to come together and be one again. I know Carol will be the rock for our children, just as she was my rock. I know Mary will raise her boys to be fine young men. I know David will always take care of my little girl, just as he promised me. I know my grandchildren will be loved. I know Drew will be there for his brother when he needs him most. And I know Derek will not only forgive me but forgive himself too. I also know he will do this because he too will find his guardian angel.

My life will be measured by the lives that continue after I am gone. It is through them that I will find my redemption and my son will finally find his peace.

I love you all and thank you for giving me even a tiny piece of heaven on earth.

Gary T. Richards

About the Author

Angeline Larson is a product of imagination and life. She is not perfect, but she tries. She is a human who loves dogs, likes watching chickens go about their daily tasks, reading, and even creating her own books. She is a mess, but she is a mess carefully crafted and that makes her unique in her own way.

More to Read by Angeline Larson

<u>Contemporary Romance</u>

Finding You – Kelly's story
Finding Hope – Jenny and Evan's story
Lost in You – Addy and Derek's story
Finding Me – Stacey and Josh's story